"The first time I heard your voice I dreamed of angels."

Winn wasn't sure why he'd said it; perhaps to warn her he wanted more than comfort.

The breeze brought the cool promise of rain. They heard the low rumble of distant thunder. After a long minute, Winn asked, "What do you look like?"

Cynthie's heart skipped a beat. She couldn't speak around the lump in her throat. She found his hands and brought them to her face. She felt a heat in her body that had more to do with desire than the warmth of his touch.

His voice dropped to just above a whisper. "I can't tell much with my fingers."

Cynthie leaned toward him, so slightly she wasn't even conscious of it. It was all the invitation Winn needed. He lowered his head and touched his lips to hers.

Dear Reader,

This month we are pleased to bring you a quartet of historical romances, all set in the Wild West.

In *Blessing* by Debbi Bedford, Uley Kirkland is caught in a lie when her relationship with an accused man forces her to come to terms with the woman she has become.

Years ago, Lucas Chandler refused Rachel Hawthorne's marriage proposal with a laugh. Now, in *Winter Fire* by Pat Tracy, he must woo the young woman he rejected in order to reclaim his family ranch.

Mary McBride's first book, *Riverbend,* was one of our 1993 March Madness titles. We are delighted to bring you her second book, *Fly Away Home,* about a sheltered Eastern girl and a half-breed Indian who find unexpected love.

Blinded during a roundup, cowboy Winn Sutton woke up to darkness. But widow Cynthie Franklin teaches him that love can find the way in *Wait for the Sunrise* by newcomer Cassandra Austin.

We hope you enjoy all four titles. And join us next month when we will be presenting Veronica Sattler's lavish historical reissue set in Regency England, *The Bargain*—as well as three other exciting books—only from Harlequin Historicals.

Sincerely,

Tracy Farrell
Senior Editor

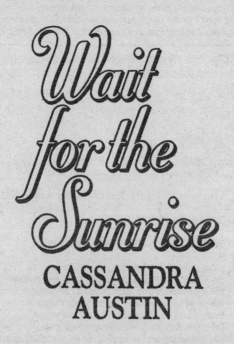

Wait for the Sunrise

CASSANDRA AUSTIN

Harlequin Books

TORONTO • NEW YORK • LONDON
AMSTERDAM • PARIS • SYDNEY • HAMBURG
STOCKHOLM • ATHENS • TOKYO • MILAN
MADRID • WARSAW • BUDAPEST • AUCKLAND

Harlequin Historicals first edition September 1993

ISBN 0-373-28790-9

WAIT FOR THE SUNRISE

CASSANDRA AUSTIN

has always lived in North Central Kansas, and was raised on museums and arrowhead hunts; when she began writing, America's Old West seemed the natural setting. Now she writes between—and sometimes during—4-H, school events and the various activities of her three children. Her husband farms, and they live in the house where he grew up.

Dedicated with thanks to the Clay Center Writers
of Kansas Author's Club

Chapter One

Kansas, June 1870

It would seem ironic later that the nightmare should begin on such a perfect morning. Winter Sutton would remember the sun spreading a red glow across the horizon as he rode toward the wagon after the last watch. A clear picture of that morning would be printed in his mind the way a lightning flash can stay in one's eyes after it's gone. A brief shower in the night had washed the air and sharpened the view. For once he could fill his lungs with sweet air instead of dust.

The cattle behind him were quiet. He watched a young rabbit bound away through the tall grass. The spirited mare he had jokingly named Lullaby had behaved herself during the night. Now she seemed to know he was distracted and stopped, practically mid-stride, and bucked, attempting to throw him over her head.

Winn laughed, patting her neck as she settled down.

"You must be tired, girl," he said. "You can do better than that."

He was used to this habit of hers and kept the reins wrapped around his hand so he wouldn't have to catch her again. He touched her with his spurs and she obediently moved forward. He would circle the herd and check on Slim before returning to camp. Slim should be somewhere on the east side of the herd, probably heading in, as well.

Slim Jackson had been hired away from his daddy's little farm in Texas for this drive, and there were many things he had yet to learn. Winn enjoyed helping him when he could; it was a way to pass the time.

It didn't seem so long ago that this had all been new to Winn. He was still grateful to the old-timers like Mike Grady, who had helped him along, and he was glad to return the favor now with Slim.

In his own case, however, he had been older and had brought with him some knowledge of the world that Slim seemed to lack. Sometimes he worried that it was becoming less a job of teaching the boy and more one of looking out for him.

As he passed near the camp, Lullaby danced a little sidestep. Winn's firm hand on the reins kept her from heading toward the remuda.

"I want rest as much as you do, girl," he said. "This won't take long." Lullaby tossed her head in disagreement.

At camp, Mike Grady rolled out of his blanket, irritated that his fifty-year-old joints complained so much. He saw Winn and the sorrel pass and chuckled. "He's got to go tell the kid it's time to come in," he said to no one in particular. At the wagon, he splashed water on his face and looked out across the prairie. All he saw was waving grass, the dark outline of the sleeping herd and Winn riding at a walk away from camp. "Like I thought. No sign of him."

"No sign of who?" The trail boss had come up behind Mike. He reached for a cup and followed Mike to the fire.

"Oh, that kid, Slim. Winn just rode by lookin' for him, I guess."

"He must have found him," Boss said.

Mike turned to look. The sorrel was running, not a recommended activity around a sleeping herd. In the distance to the east was a dark spot raising a cloud of dust. Mike had missed seeing it before.

Boss dropped his cup and hurried for the remuda. Mike followed, limping a little as he tried to keep up. The men assigned the morning watch were already saddling horses. Boss was appropriating two of these when Mike caught up with him.

As soon as Winn saw Slim in the distance, he knew the boy was in trouble; he didn't realize how much until he got closer. Slim had somehow managed to toss his rope around the horns of a big mean cow the boys called Rosie.

Rosie had caused trouble the entire drive. One of the boys had said she reminded him of a whore in San Antonio who had turned mean when he had come up a dollar short of her fee. They had named the cow after the whore and they all tried to avoid her.

Evidently Rosie had decided to leave the herd and hadn't cooperated when Slim had tried to drive her back. The cow had turned on the horse, and Slim was doing his best to keep out of the way of the horns. The horse couldn't move any farther from the cow than the length of the rope tied to the saddle horn.

"Drop the rope!" Winn called. He wasn't sure he was close enough for Slim to hear, but he was getting closer every second. "Drop the rope!" he called again.

He could see the boy fumble with the rope for a second before reining the frightened horse away from the charging cow. The horse jerked to a stop as the two animals reached the ends of the rope.

Slim fumbled with the rope again. The horse pranced and tossed his head, making it more difficult for the equally frightened boy.

With Rosie's next charge, the horse swerved and ran, nearly tossing Slim to the ground. It was only a matter of time before Rosie's horns would catch the horse, and Slim would almost certainly be killed. Slim's only chance was for Winn to distract Rosie. He pulled Lullaby to a bone-jarring stop close to the enraged animal and held her firmly as she tried to dance away.

Rosie looked at the newcomers and snorted. She only waited a second before lowering her head and lunging at Winn and Lullaby. Slim's cow pony had stayed true to training and backed away, keeping the rope tight. Rosie's charge was cut short, and the rope jerked her around.

More angry than ever, she turned back to her first enemy. Slim put spurs to his horse, attempting to dodge too early in Rosie's charge. Rosie turned, as well, to chase the frightened horse.

Winn grabbed his rope and shook out the loop as he sent Lullaby racing after them. He could see the boy's terrified face as he looked over his shoulder at the angry beast.

Winn wished he could simply shoot Rosie. That would be the only way anyone would get Slim's rope off her. But he couldn't shoot her from the back of a running horse, and she wasn't going to wait for him to stop and aim his rifle. His only hope was to get his rope around her and get her away from the other horse.

In an instant he knew he was too late. Slim's horse stumbled and screamed in pain as Rosie's right horn tore into its flank. He couldn't see Slim, but Winn knew Rosie would try to kill him if she could.

Winn sent his rope sailing through the air, and it came to rest over Rosie's horns. She let out a furious bellow and tossed her head, but her attention was still on the downed horse and boy.

Winn put spurs to Lullaby, hoping to pull Rosie away or at least restrain her lethal head. Lullaby leaped forward, bringing the rope tight, and reared. She had caught the scent of blood and fear and wanted only to be away from it. She twisted around and tried to run in the other direction.

The maneuver brought the taut rope around Winn's body, ruining his balance. He saw Rosie's maddened eyes as Lullaby leaped out from under him.

Winn lay very still. He was aware of the smell of moist earth and a strange buzzing in his ears. He opened his eyes and saw blades of fresh green grass. Something hard and cold was pressed against his face.

A rock, he realized, sticky with his blood. He tried to raise his head, but it was too heavy.

He groaned, at first in defeat and then in pain as he felt himself being rolled onto his back. His vision went hazy for a second then focused on Mike Grady.

"Slim?" he asked, remembering only that the boy was in trouble.

"Boss went to pick him up. They're on their way," Mike said.

Winn tried to sort out what must have happened but he couldn't seem to remember. The sound of running hooves came up through the ground and thundered in his head. "Rosie?"

Mike laughed. "Naw. She'll be dinner tonight."

A jolt of pain shot from his head clear through his body and left him gasping for breath. "I'm sorry, Winn." Mike's voice sounded far away. "This bleeding's got to stop."

In a moment, the pain became concentrated in his head. Mike was pressing a handkerchief against his forehead. That must have been why he couldn't see anything; he was trying to focus around the edges of a red bandanna.

"How bad is he, Mike?" Winn recognized the voice of the Double M's trail boss. Mike had lifted the handkerchief, but Winn still seemed to be looking through it. Everything was rimmed with red. There must be some blood in his eyes, Winn decided.

He didn't see Mike's shrug. Some distant sound was trying to make its way around the pain. Concentrating on it made his vision blur. "Lullaby," he heard himself whisper.

"Slim, his horse is still tied to that dead cow. Cut her loose," the boss ordered. "Take her into camp and send the cook out here with a butcherin' crew."

"Yes, sir." The boy's voice was shaky. Winn wanted to volunteer to get his own horse. He tried to rise, but Mike easily pushed him back to the ground.

"You best tie him to a horse and head for Wichita," he heard the boss say.

"You think that's wise?"

"Well, the wagon'd be as rough a ride and a lot slower. You can't just camp here."

The sun had come up and was shining behind the boss. Winn could see the silhouette of the horse and rider. Boss surveyed the area, a familiar habit when he was about to make a decision. "I'll send Slim back with provisions and an extra horse. It's a cinch Sutton's not up to handling that crazy mare. She'll cause you both no end of trouble if you try to take her along." He wheeled his mount around to head for camp then spoke over his shoulder to Mike. "You two see that Sutton's cared for, then high-tail it back to the herd. I don't have riders to spare!"

Hooves beat the ground again. They faded away into the pulse of pain in Winn's head. He had no notion of the passage of time before the pulse became the throb of the earth and the thunder of approaching horses.

Mike began lifting him to his feet. "Give us a hand, boy," he said.

"There's blood running in his beard again." Slim's voice sounded very young.

"It ain't his beard that worries me," was Mike's response.

Winn passed out while they were lifting him onto the horse. He came to on a Double M gelding known for his smooth gait. He found that he could raise his head without much pain. Strange, though, that a morning that had started out so clear had now turned hazy, he mused.

Mike noticed he was awake and pulled up to rest. "You making it all right?" he asked as he handed Winn a canteen.

"Yeah, I guess. Am I still bleeding?" Blood must be running in his eyes, he thought; the haze was tinted slightly red. He raised his hand to his forehead and felt a lump under a sticky piece of cloth.

"Not much," Mike said. "We could stop and eat if you want."

The thought of food made Winn feel sick. "How much farther?" he asked.

"Not more than ten miles. I was thinking you might sleep the whole trip."

"I wish I had." Winn's head was throbbing and the haze seemed to be getting deeper. Slim rode up beside him and straightened him in the saddle before he realized that he had started to lean. Slim looked very pale. It seemed odd, since everything else was turning red. Maybe it was sunset, but he could feel the warmth of the sun on his shoulders. Winn closed his eyes, hoping to lessen the pain.

He was aware of the horse moving, aware of the sounds of horses breathing, creaking leather and

sometimes startled birds. Time didn't seem to pass like
it normally did. Surely they were near Wichita by now.

He thought he could hear a strange sort of dis-
torted music. He opened his eyes to look around and
knew he had been dreaming. He was on a dimly lit
street. There seemed to be a lot of activity for this time
of night. Mike was getting directions to the doctor's.

Suddenly he felt foolish for being tied to his horse.
He remembered the wound on his forehead; he had
forgotten it for a moment. Anyone who saw that he
was tied to the horse could also see that he was hurt.

Slim didn't seem to be having trouble seeing in the
dark. He flicked a fly away from Winn's face. "It's
those buffalo hides that attract the flies," Slim said.
"Saw a bunch of them stretched to dry just outside of
town."

"Bet that's what I smell." Winn had been busy trying to sort out sounds in the dark, and only now became aware of the pungent smell of drying meat and
leather.

As Mike led the way to the doctor, a strange orange
blaze became visible between the buildings. Winn
stared at it for a moment, though it made his eyes
ache. What kind of fire would make a light like that in
the distance?

"Don't stare at the sun, boy," Mike said, urging the
gelding to move faster. The blaze disappeared behind
another building.

Sun! Winn felt panic rise inside him. What kind of
a day was this, bright morning, hazy afternoon and
then nearly dark with the sun still up? A dust storm

with no wind? How could that have been the sun? Was
he dreaming again?

They reached the doctor's office. Mike and Slim
untied him and helped him down from his horse. Inside, the office was dark, yet the doctor made no move
to light a lamp. He was talking to Mike but Winn
wasn't listening. There was something in the back of
his mind trying to make itself heard while something
else was trying to keep him from hearing. Confusion.
There was no pain, only confusion. Something was
wrong and it had to do with the haze and the sun.

Cynthie Franklin rode across the prairie, oblivious
to everything but the feel of the wind in her face. The
sleek black horse stretched out beneath her, his tail
streaming behind her own glossier black locks. This
was freedom! This was a kind of exhilaration she had
never known back in New York.

When she neared the ranch yard, she slowed Obsidian to a walk. Her foreman, Louie LeBlanc, would
scold her if he caught her coming in at a dead run. It
wasn't Louie who waited for her, however. Standing
in the shade of her front porch, his horse's reins still
in his hand, was Kyle Dempsey.

She studied him as she rode forward. He was tall
and trim and, as always, carefully dressed and
groomed. She could see the play of shadows on his
face when he tipped his hat back to watch her. He was
clean-shaven except for the dark blond mustache. A
handsome man, really, she decided. He dropped his
cigar and ground it with his toe before walking to the
barn to meet her.

"Do you know how beautiful you look?" he asked, his own opinion clear in his eyes.

Cynthie laughed. "How long have you been waiting? Let me take care of Obsidian and I'll . . ."

"You have men to do that," he interrupted, taking the reins from her. Peter Merlin was coming toward them from the bunkhouse as they spoke. He was bareheaded, and the wind ruffled his light yellow hair. Cynthie always had an urge to do the same. Tall as he was, he still looked like a child. Kyle shifted his weight to the other foot, betraying his impatience as the boy sauntered forward.

"Where's Greg?" Cynthie asked. Her young son had been tagging after Peter when she had gone for her ride.

"Sleepin'." The youth tipped his head toward the bunkhouse, a shy smile appearing on the serene face for a moment. He took the reins from Kyle and led both horses to the barn.

"I don't think it's in that boy to hurry," Kyle whispered as he put an arm around Cynthie's waist and led her toward the house.

"I don't mind," she said. "He won't hurry when he takes care of Obsidian, either."

In the kitchen, Kyle took a chair at the table and stretched his long legs out in front of him. As Cynthie put coffee on she asked over her shoulder, "What are you doing here, Kyle?"

"Does a man need an excuse to come see you?"

"No." She laughed. "But you usually have one."

Kyle leaned back in the chair, taking great pleasure in watching Cynthie move about her kitchen and feeling very much at home there. Her straight black hair, loose and windblown from her ride, hung to the middle of her back. As he watched, she took a ribbon from her pocket and absently tied it at the nape of her neck to get the shiny tresses out of her way.

He liked the way the movement strained the bodice of her riding habit. The clothes she wore always spoke of good breeding and money. She was a lovely woman but she never seemed aware of it.

She caught him watching her as she turned toward the table with the cups. He smiled and asked, "If I'm ever unable to think of an excuse, can I come anyway?"

Cynthie set the cups on the table and took a seat across from him. "But I look forward to your excuses," she teased.

Kyle reached into his shirt pocket. "Well, this is a new one," he said. "I was in town this morning and a couple of fellas were asking around, trying to find out if any of your men were in town. It seems the doctor wants to talk to you."

Cynthie took the note, mystified. "Dr. Gordon? Do you know what this is about?"

Kyle leaned back in the chair again. "Well, I know these men came in last night with a third man who was hurt. That's all anybody seemed to know. Looked like drovers to me."

Cynthie read the note through carefully then read it again. "Did you read this?" she asked, holding the note toward him.

"I am insulted, ma'am!" He put his hand on his heart in counterfeit shock.

Cynthie didn't smile. "Read it now," she said.

Kyle read it quickly and tossed it to the center of the table. "Ignore it," he advised.

"I don't think I can."

Kyle shook his head. "You don't owe this man anything." Cynthie tried to interrupt but Kyle wouldn't let her. "It says he needs someone to look after him until his friends can come back for him. If you have to play Good Samaritan, lend him money for the hotel and hire someone in town to nurse him."

Cynthie got up to get the coffeepot. "It says he's blind, Kyle. I might be able to help him."

"You don't have to remind me that your father was blind. I was always impressed by what he could do, but he was your father. This is, well, God knows who." Kyle saw the resistance on her face and sighed. "Doc's note also says it's probably temporary, just a reaction to the swelling. It seems to me you have enough to worry about, with little Greg and the ranch, without giving yourself more to do. Which reminds me, do you know any more about the stolen cattle?"

Cynthie poured the coffee and sat down. "I haven't had a chance to study the books yet to make sure it isn't all just a bookkeeping error. I probably shouldn't have mentioned it."

The clock in the next room chimed three times while Kyle toyed with the gilt handle of the china cup. "I want you to feel like you can come to me with any problems you have. I want to take care of you."

"Kyle," Cynthie began, but he raised a hand to stop her. He knew what was coming.

Cynthie laughed and relaxed. "Sorry," she whispered.

"It's all right, but listen to one word of advice. Go into town and meet this man before you invite him into your home. And remember, you're not a nurse. He may need more help than you know how to give."

Cynthie took his advice the next morning and rode into Wichita, putting her horse up in the livery. She didn't plan to stay in town long, but Obsidian made too tempting a target for horse thieves. She walked the few blocks to the doctor's office, ignoring the heads that turned in her direction. Lifting the hem of her maroon riding habit, she crossed the rough, muddy street and turned up the walk by a sign that read Dr. Kenneth Gordon. More than one man watched her until she disappeared inside.

Dr. Gordon was sitting at his desk going through his books. He had just marked another entry uncollectible when he heard the door open. "Mrs. Franklin!" he said with obvious pleasure. He put the pen in its holder and capped the bottle of ink. "Dempsey must have delivered my letter."

Cynthie sat down in a chair beside the desk before he had a chance to rise. "Tell me about this man," she said.

Doc took a deep breath. "Two days ago he fell from his horse. The center of his forehead hit a rock. The wound's swollen but looks like it'll heal fine. His sight has gradually faded, and by last night all he could make out were shapes. I don't know, even that may be gone now."

"What else do you know about him?"

"His name's Winn Sutton. He's with a herd of cattle headed for Abilene. He's a decent enough fella, I'd guess. His friends are plenty loyal. They won't leave town until they know he's being cared for."

"I'd like to talk to his friends," she said.

"That won't be hard. They stop by about every ten minutes." The irritation in his voice told her he was not exaggerating.

She smiled. "Can I see him?"

Doc pushed his chair back from the desk and turned to face Cynthie. "I gave him a dose of laudanum. The pain is pretty severe. He should sleep for another hour." He sighed and shook his head. "It seems like such a waste," he muttered.

"You think his blindness is permanent, then?"

"No, probably not," he said quickly. "I've seen blindness as a result of swelling, but the longer I practice medicine, the less I'm sure about."

Cynthie watched the doctor's face closely. She couldn't remember seeing him so uncertain. Perhaps he didn't normally allow himself to show it. "Yet you sent for me," she prompted.

The doctor straightened in his chair and seemed more his old self again. "You're the only one I know who has had any experience with a blind person. There might be folks here who would be willing to board him. But if I'm wrong, and he never sees again, you could give him a better start. Do you have the address of that doctor your father knew in New York?"

Cynthie nodded. "I'll write to him," she promised.

As they spoke, two men came in the front door. The younger man stopped with a start when he saw Cynthie.

"Oh, good. You're back." Doc stood up and waved them toward some chairs. "This is the young lady I told you about."

The men walked toward Cynthie, but neither of them sat down. "Mrs. Franklin," the older one began, turning his hat in his hands. "I'm Mike Grady and this here is Slim Jackson. The fella in there—" he waved his hat toward the patient's room "—is a good boy. We'd be much obliged if you'd see to him until we can collect our pay and get back here."

"Boss don't pay none of us till we get to Abilene," Slim blurted and fell into an embarrassed silence.

The doctor sat down at his desk again and Cynthie hoped the men would be seated, as well. "Tell me about Mr. Sutton," she requested.

In the next room Winn awoke to total darkness. The feel of a bed under him made him start before he remembered the accident. He was in Wichita at the doctor's home. He rubbed his eyes and tried to look around him, tried to see his hand. *Was he truly blind?* He felt his hand shake and settled it onto the bed. He closed his eyes, not wanting to test them any more. Surely it was night this time, and he would wake up in the morning to sunshine again.

There was a funny taste in his mouth and his head felt heavy, the results of the painkiller, he assumed. There were noises in the other room, voices; one of them was a woman's. He had a vague feeling that he had been dreaming of angels. He hoped that he was still dreaming, that the accident was a dream, as well, but the pain in his head was just too real.

He tried to listen to the conversation on the other side of the door. The voices were too faint, and there was some buzzing in his ears. He gave up with a sigh. He didn't care what they were saying anyway.

He raised a hand and gingerly felt the lump in his forehead. It seemed huge, and he remembered the size of the rock that had made such a lump. He shouldn't be surprised that he was blind. He was surprised he was even alive.

He might have lost track of a little bit of time but he was sure it couldn't be more than a day after his fall. If he could rest here a day or two more, he and the boys would still be able to catch up with the herd. It was just an unlucky break.

It made him wonder about Lullaby. He knew none of the other boys were going to ride her. She would be worse than ever when he finally caught up with her again. "You really did it this time, girl," he said under his breath.

The need to see, to convince himself that he could see, came back to him. He blinked his eyes and tried to find the window. He had seen the lighted square earlier, but now it was too dark outside to see it. That had to be the reason it wasn't there—it was a dark, moonless night.

He listened for night sounds but all he heard were the voices from the other room. It was night, he repeated to himself, it had to be.

He closed his eyes and took a deep breath. He was feeling very drowsy. It was getting hard to think. He had been trying to figure something out, but he couldn't remember what. Night and stars and sounds and angels flitted through his mind. Something. An angel's voice. He had been trying to hear an angel's voice. As he tried to separate it from the other voices he drifted back to sleep.

Chapter Two

Dr. Gordon wrapped the bandage around the little girl's arm and calculated her age to be about six. He looked at her freckled face and winked, receiving a grin in return.

They both turned as the front door opened. Cynthie stepped into the room, giving them a nod in greeting.

"Now, tell your mama not to worry," he told the child as he tied the bandage in place. She hopped down from the table without waiting for the doctor's help and proudly held the bandaged arm up for Cynthie to admire.

"Be more careful where you play," the doctor reminded her. He shook his head in amused resignation as the little girl left his office.

"Did you find a wagon?" he asked over his shoulder as he put his supplies away.

Cynthie allowed herself a frown before answering. "All set," she said as Doc Gordon turned to face her. "Are you sure it isn't too early to move him?"

"I don't think so. There's no sense in him getting used to this place then starting all over at yours."

Cynthie nodded and followed the doctor toward the closed door. With his hand on the knob, he turned and whispered, "I warn you, my dear. He's a handsome devil."

Cynthie grinned as she followed him into the room. Her first look at the man came as somewhat of a shock. Handsome devil, indeed, she thought.

Winn Sutton sat on the side of the bed, his hands braced against the mattress on either side of his body. The muscles in his upper arms and broad shoulders were taut under the blue shirt. Dark brown hair curled over the bandage around his forehead. The lower half of his face was covered with a neatly trimmed beard a shade lighter than his hair. Under it she could see the outline of a square jaw and depressions on his cheeks that promised dimples.

She felt her mouth go dry. She had been imagining someone like her father, or maybe Louie. She hadn't expected a man in his prime or a man who was so...

She heard the doctor speak her name and decided it was best her thoughts were interrupted.

"How do you do?" She stepped forward, thinking belatedly what a foolish thing that was to ask.

"It's good to meet you, ma'am." He reached a hand toward the voice that sounded somehow familiar. He tried to remember if he might have met her earlier but was sure he had not. The hand she placed in his was soft and warm and seemed very small.

"Mrs. Franklin has a wagon outside," the doctor said, taking Winn's arm and helping him to his feet.

"She's going to take you to her ranch until you're better."

Winn started to ask why but being on his feet made him feel dizzy. It took all his concentration to keep from leaning on the doctor as he guided him out the door.

The air outside was warm and filled with sounds. He knew it was daytime but he couldn't help thinking it was night. The woman with the sweet voice and soft hands was walking beside him. She occasionally brushed his arm, and the wind blew the flowered scent of her hair toward him.

"This is my neighbor, Reuben Ott," she told him. The man shook his hand and, along with the doctor, helped him into the back of the wagon. Winn had a bed of sorts amid the sacks there.

A horse had been tied on behind and it leaned forward now to nudge his shoulder. It made him think of Lullaby, and he reached up cautiously to stroke a silky jaw.

"I appreciate the ride, Mr. Ott," Mrs. Franklin was saying. Something in her voice sounded less than appreciative.

"Glad for the chance to be neighborly," the man answered.

Winn wasn't sure what was going on but he would go along with it. The boys would be around later to explain. He supposed the doctor needed him out of his house, but he wasn't sure why he was moving to this woman's ranch. Maybe she was a nurse. He decided it was the drug that kept him from objecting. It took too much effort to try to understand.

All he was sure about was that a short time ago, the doctor had assured him that his sight would probably return once the swelling was gone. He remembered the doctor's words, almost chanting them in his head, as the panic started to rise.

"I'll look in on you soon," the doctor said. Winn heard his steps as he walked away.

"Are you comfortable, Mr. Sutton?" the woman asked.

"Yes, ma'am," he said, laying his head back against a sack. He felt the wagon rock as the man climbed aboard. Ott spoke to the team and the wagon lurched forward.

Cynthie turned to watch Winn as they moved slowly along the rutted street. With every bump he was jostled about. More than once she saw him grab for something to steady himself. She was as grateful as he was when they reached the river at the edge of town and stopped. "We have to wait for the ferry," she told him.

Winn's only reply was a deep sigh.

"It'll be a smoother ride for him on the prairie, Mrs. Franklin," Ott assured her, jumping down to unhitch the team. Cynthie didn't answer. The prairie was full of gopher holes. The road was merely earth packed down by the weight of wagon wheels. She doubted that it would be much better than the streets in town.

Cynthie was feeling doubtful about several things right now. It was probably too soon to move Mr. Sutton. The ride was bound to be very uncomfortable for him, and maybe even dangerous. It might all be a mistake anyway. Taking him in had seemed like the right thing to do, but now she wondered if she shouldn't have listened to Kyle instead of letting Dr. Gordon talk her into this. She certainly didn't need one more problem to worry about.

She looked at Mr. Sutton and felt reassured. She didn't quite admit to herself that she found him intriguing. He needed her help and she couldn't refuse, she told herself.

The ferry arrived. Cynthie climbed down and untied Obsidian, leading him onto the ferry as Ott and the ferryman rolled the wagon on board. She went to stand behind the wagon holding the stallion's bridle, watching her passenger.

"Did you use the ferry when you came in yesterday, Mr. Sutton?" Cynthie asked.

Winn frowned. "If we did I slept through it."

"There's talk of a bridge," she continued. "Actually there's talk of two bridges, but I imagine only one will be built."

Winn nodded. He didn't want to be rude but he didn't feel like talking, either. The plans this little town might have didn't interest him at the moment. He tried to relax and ignore the rocking motion of the ferry. He had driven herds of cattle across enough rivers to know the dangers and he hated boats. Crossing water on the back of a good horse was one thing; sitting helplessly in a wagon on a ferry was quite another, especially in the dark.

Cynthie gave up any hope of conversation. She turned to face the wind, bending her knees in time with the rocking motion as the current tugged at the ferry. What she really wanted was an excuse not to ride with

Reuben Ott. She glanced at him, helping to guide the ferry across. He was past middle age, long and skinny. Nothing about him gave a hint of the scoundrel she believed him to be. It was just bad luck that he had been in the store when she had gone in to ask about renting a wagon. Why had he volunteered to give them a ride? He probably wanted to know what she was up to. He hadn't asked many questions yet, but Cynthie was sure he would.

The ferry reached the opposite bank and when it was secured, Ott led the horses off, then helped the ferryman push the wagon. Winn felt the wagon jerk as the wheels rolled from the planks onto the softer ground.

When the team was hitched, Ott went to the back of the wagon and tied the stallion securely. "How's our passenger, Mrs. Franklin?" He gave Winn a pat on the shoulder. "Hang on, friend. I think the worse is over." He took Cynthie's elbow to lead her forward and helped her aboard.

Cynthie tried not to show her irritation. It was as if he knew she would rather ride Obsidian and had come back to make sure she didn't. When he was seated next to her, he flicked the reins and the team started forward.

Ott cleared his throat and gave his companion a sidelong glance. "Tell me, Mrs. Franklin, is everything going all right for you at the ranch?"

"Fine, Mr. Ott," she replied tightly.

Ott nodded, making little approving sounds. "Your herd got off late, I understand. Word is you were missing several head."

Cynthie gritted her teeth. "I don't see that that's any of your business, Mr. Ott."

"No, ma'am, maybe not. But if there's trouble affecting one settler, it soon affects the rest." He nodded for emphasis. "I like to keep up on things in my neighborhood."

Cynthie didn't answer. She suspected Ott knew as much or more about her missing cattle than she did.

"Who knows," Ott added. "Someday I might be able to help you."

"That's very kind of you, Mr. Ott. I'll be sure to call on you should I need help." Cynthie hoped he would get the message and keep quiet. If not, it was going to be an awfully long trip.

Cynthie turned to watch Winn. He seemed to be sleeping. The wagon was shaking him but not tossing him about as it had before.

She hoped she wasn't making a big mistake. Care of an invalid was considerable work. She wasn't at all sure she could handle it. Teaching him to live without his sight might turn out to be impossible.

"Where do you know him from?"

Cynthie looked at Ott sharply. Explaining that she was taking a complete stranger into her home would sound crazy. It was a certainty that whatever she told Ott would be all over the country in no time. "He's my cousin," she said firmly. "On my mother's side."

"I see," Ott said mildly.

Across the waving prairie, Cynthie could just make out the shape of the cottonwoods that lined the little creek near her home. She hoped they could travel the distance without Ott saying another word. She stared at the trees, willing them to grow closer.

"How's that little boy of yours?"

Cynthie let out a slow breath. "Fine. Fine." She tried to smile.

"Hard on a boy growing up with no father," he said. "I'd be proud to help if I could. You know, I could take him riding or fishing or something. How old is he now, about five?"

"Four," she corrected. "Louie and Peter spend a lot of time with him."

"That's good," he said and fell silent again.

Cynthie went back to watching the trees. She could make out the trace of green leaves like a light wash of color on the sketchy branches. The ranch buildings were dark shapes in the foreground. They were almost there.

"Mrs. Franklin," Ott began. Cynthie actually jumped. He hesitated as if uncertain exactly what to say. Finally he cleared his throat and spoke. "I'll be over in a week or two with the last payment I owe you."

"Thank you, Mr. Ott." That last payment would be reason to celebrate. There would be no more need to deal with Reuben Ott. Oh, how Cynthie wished her late husband had never loaned him that money.

When Ott pulled the wagon to a stop in the ranch yard, Louie was there to meet them. He had worried about Mrs. Franklin, leaving as she had without explanation. He knew something unusual had happened in town or she wouldn't be riding home with her least favorite neighbor. He greeted Ott and gave her a quizzical look as he helped her down from the wagon.

"Mr. Ott was kind enough to give us a ride," Cynthie explained.

"I'm glad to be of help to you and your cousin," Ott said.

Louie took in the large man struggling to sit up in the back of the wagon. He cast his boss another questioning look.

Cynthie wanted to get rid of Ott before she explained anything to Louie. "Please help Mr. Sutton inside." More softly she added, "He can't see."

Winn had barely managed to sit up in the wagon. His head ached so bad it was hard to hold it up. He was sure the world would be swimming in front of him if he could see it. Right now, he was not exactly certain which way was up.

Strong arms caught him before he hit the wagon box, and with their support, he managed to get his feet on solid ground. He was surprised to discover that such strength belonged to so short a man, a good ten inches shorter than his own six foot four.

"Do you need a hand?" he heard Ott ask.

"Louie can manage, I'm sure," replied Mrs. Franklin.

Winn tried to straighten and take more of his weight himself, not wanting to prove the lady wrong. He heard her dismiss the neighbor and call for someone named Peter as Louie slowly guided him away.

"Rough ride?" Louie asked.

"Not too bad, just long." Winn resisted the urge to hold his hand out in front of him.

"Three steps up and there's a porch post by your right shoulder." They went up the steps slowly and Winn found the post. He leaned on it a moment, resting his head. Smaller feet tapped quickly up the same steps and Louie moved out of the way, keeping a supporting hand on Winn's arm. He heard a door open.

"Bring him into my father's room, Louie. We can worry about sheets and things later."

Louie was already leading him forward. Winn followed cautiously, expecting to hit a wall or knock over some piece of furniture with each step. Finally his knees bumped the side of a bed. He lay down gratefully and felt the strong hands lift his legs onto the bed.

"The lady won't want boots in her father's bed." It was Winn's last conscious thought before passing out. He didn't realize he spoke it aloud.

"Way ahead of you, son," Louie said, pulling off one boot and then the other, letting them drop to the floor. He helped Cynthie cover him with a blanket then walked behind her out of the room.

Now that his hands were free, Louie removed his hat and smoothed back his thin gray hair. "Do you want to tell me who he is?" he asked his boss.

Cynthie looked at her foreman. He was only slightly taller than she but he had a way of making people forget that. Even approaching sixty he was powerfully built. The look he gave her said, "You're the boss, but..." It was obvious he hadn't bought the cousin story.

Cynthie sighed. "He's injured and needs someplace to stay for a while."

"And you happened into him on the street?"

Cynthie laughed. "No. If you must have the whole story, Dr. Gordon sent for me. He asked me to look after him."

"And Doc decided you'd be an expert," Louie added.

Cynthie's chin came up and Louie recognized the stubborn light in her eyes. "That's right," she said.

Louie knew when to quit. "Don't try to do everything yourself. Call on me and Peter. That boy has more patience than anyone I ever knew."

Cynthie smiled. "Thanks. For now, send Greg up to the house. He can help me get some things ready for Mr. Sutton."

"Yes, ma'am." He started to leave but turned back. "The cousin bit was a good idea."

She smiled as she watched him close the door.

Hours later, Cynthie sat down at the small writing desk and turned up the lamp. The house was quiet. Greg was tucked into his bed upstairs. He hadn't been happy about being called away from Peter and the horses but had helped her eagerly when she had explained about the new houseguest. In his excitement, he had had trouble keeping his voice at what his mother considered an acceptable level.

She needn't have worried. Winn hadn't stirred since he arrived, but he might awaken in the night and need something. Fearful that she wouldn't hear him from her room upstairs, she had brought down a blanket and planned to spend the night in a chair in the front room.

Now she took white paper from a drawer and dipped the pen in the ink. She wrote the doctor in New York who had tried to save her father's sight, hoping with each stroke of the pen that he would know what might save Mr. Sutton's.

Winn awoke with the uncomfortable feeling that he wasn't alone. Had he heard some small sound, or was it his imagination? He blinked, trying to adjust to the darkness, and remembered that the darkness didn't go away. Damn, he would be glad when this passed!

He heard something again, a small sigh, he thought. "Is someone there?" he asked. There was a shuffling noise, and a floorboard creaked. It seemed odd that his visitor didn't identify himself. He felt a prickle of alarm. He felt more helpless right now than he could remember ever feeling. "Who's there?" he asked again.

"Greg," a small voice answered.

Winn smiled. The tiny sound, the hesitancy to answer and the shuffling feet all fit together to form a picture of a little boy. He thought he could remember Mrs. Franklin mentioning a son, but he wasn't sure. So much of his memory seemed to be hazy. "I'm Winn," he said, reaching his right hand toward the sound. "It's nice to meet you, sir." A very tiny hand tried to shake his large one.

"How do you do?" The child giggled.

"Are you Mrs. Franklin's son?" Winn asked, swinging his legs over the side of the bed and coming cautiously to a sitting position. His head hurt but it was a clear sharp pain with little of the groggy feeling. The effects of the laudanum were wearing off.

He hadn't heard an answer to his question but he felt the boy climb up beside him on the bed. He guessed that Greg had either nodded or shaken his head. "Is your father around?"

"No," came the reply. "He's dead."

Winn was startled by the matter-of-fact tone and wished he could see the child's face. "I'm sorry," he said.

"Do you have a daddy?" Greg asked.

"No, I'm afraid mine's gone, too."

"Yeah," the child said as if that was to be expected. "This is my granddaddy's room but I'm afraid he's gone, too." The child wiggled around on the bed until his legs were free to swing against the side. He set up a rocking motion that threatened Winn's sense of balance.

"Maybe you can help me with something," Winn began. He was suddenly uncertain how to ask this. He brought a hand down instinctively to still one small knee. He cleared his throat. "I need to relieve myself but I can't see. Can you help me?"

Greg was silent for a moment. "You need to go to the outhouse," he said, delighted that he had figured it out. "Mama gets mad 'less I use the outhouse."

Winn suppressed a smile. "Women sometimes have foolish notions but it's best to accommodate them."

"Yeah," agreed the child knowingly.

"Can you lead me to the outhouse, sir?"

Greg giggled again. He had never been called sir before. "Me and Mama put a rope from the back door. Mama's in the kitchen fixing breakfast. That's where the back door is.''

"Is there another way around? It's embarrassing to need help with something like this, you understand?''

"I don't need help with nothin' much,'' Greg assured him, leaping from the bed.

Winn pulled on his boots, which Greg had found and handed to him. He stood up and felt the boy's small hand wrap around his finger. Winn began to wonder if this had been a good idea after all. "You'll have to tell me what's in front of me so I don't bump into things,'' he reminded him.

"Nothin's in front of you for four steps.''

"Your steps or mine?'' Winn questioned.

"Your steps.'' Greg responded quickly to the odd question. "I can't walk for you.'' As Winn started forward he added, "But take little steps.''

They made it out of the bedroom and into the front room with little difficulty. Cynthie heard her son's voice and stepped to the kitchen door to investigate. Greg had evidently gone straight to Mr. Sutton's room this morning. He had put on a shirt, which he had misbuttoned, and half tucked it into a pair of short pants. His feet were bare, as usual, and his straight black hair was sleep-ruffled. He looked so tiny next to the big man but was very intent on directing him step-by-step toward the front door. She put her hand to her lips and watched them.

"There's a table right there,'' Greg said, pointing.

"Remember, I can't see where 'there' is.'' Winn's voice was patient.

"Here." Greg smacked a little hand on the table-top, rattling the glass bowl that sat there.

Winn moved slightly to the left. "Will I miss it?"

"Yeah." Greg tugged on his hand again. "Now you can go a long ways."

"How big is this room?"

"I guess it's huge," Greg sympathized.

"We can go faster outside."

"How come you can't see?" Greg asked. He had stopped Winn and was opening the front door.

"My horse threw me and my head hit a rock." He moved forward as Greg tugged his hand.

"Your eyes don't look broke. The bandage is up above them."

Cynthie watched them step out onto the porch. When she heard Winn send Greg to close the door, she ducked into the kitchen so he wouldn't know she had been watching.

She went back to work, glancing out a window from time to time. She saw them on the way to the out-house, and deep in conversation later. It seemed like a long time before the two of them appeared at the back door. When Greg led his charge inside, she saw why. They had made a trip to the well. Greg's shirt-front was damp, and drops of water glistened on Winn's beard.

"Good morning, ma'am," Winn said, standing stock-still where Greg had put him, fearful that any movement could knock something over.

"Good morning, Mr. Sutton," Cynthie answered, winking at Greg. The big man couldn't know that the little boy had planted his feet wide apart and clasped his hands behind his back, mimicking his new friend.

"We washed," said Greg, wanting to be sure he received proper credit for this extraordinary deed.

Cynthie smiled. "You both look very nice. Show Mr. Sutton to his seat, Greg."

"I'm supposed to take Winn..."

"Mr. Sutton," Cynthie corrected.

"He said he was Winn," Greg responded stubbornly.

"It's true, ma'am," Winn said. "Under the circumstances I didn't see the need to be so formal." The dimples deepened beneath the beard.

"I see." Cynthie watched the pale blue eyes that seemed to watch something far away. At least he wouldn't see how flustered she was by his charming smile. She was grateful the little boy provided her with a distraction.

"He calls me sir," Greg announced.

"So much for informality." Cynthie laughed and Winn shrugged, his dimples deepening again. "Please sit down."

"I'm supposed to take him back to bed," Greg insisted.

Winn hastened to explain. "If it wouldn't be too much bother, could you bring something to your father's room for me? I'd be more comfortable eating in private." He unclasped his hands, dropping them slowly to his sides, hoping to come in contact with Greg before he had to grope around for him. Fortunately, Greg grabbed his hand eagerly and began to lead him forward.

"Mr. Sutton," Cynthie said, "I eat with a four-year-old."

"I understand, Mrs. Franklin, but I'm not four."
Winn hoped she wasn't offended but he had no way of gauging her reaction. As Greg led him slowly from the kitchen and through the front room, he tried to remember how her voice had sounded. She had laughed at him for calling the boy sir. Otherwise, she hadn't sounded especially warm or friendly. He remembered how she had treated the neighbor they had ridden with the previous day and felt mildly apprehensive.

"Do you think we hurt your mother's feelings?" he asked when Greg had deposited him safely beside the bed again.

"Naw," said Greg, dismissing the notion.

"You better hurry back and have your breakfast."
Winn was sitting on the bed, although he felt tired enough to go back to sleep. He heard purposeful footsteps coming through the front room and stood up.

Cynthie carried the tray to a small table and set it down. "Here's your breakfast, Mr. Sutton. There's a knife and spoon to the right, fork to the left, napkin in front. On the plate are scrambled eggs at two o'clock, ham at six and biscuits at ten. Your coffee cup's above the knife. Do you take sugar or cream?"

"No, ma'am," he answered, surprised by her efficiency. It was odd listening to a voice that he could put no form to. How big was she? What did her face look like? What color was her hair? Greg, with all his open chatter, was easier to picture.

Cynthie took his hand and led him to the table, counting the steps aloud as he walked. She turned him so he was between the table and a chair. "The bed is four steps to your right, Mr. Sutton." She made sure he had located both the chair and the table. He stood hesitantly, fingertips lightly touching the tabletop next to the tray.

Cynthie waited a moment and realized he wasn't going to sit down until she either left the room or sat down herself. "Where are you from, Mr. Sutton?" The question was out before she thought. He would think her as ill-mannered as her curious little boy, but he neither talked nor acted the way she expected. Nor did he look like she had expected, but she dismissed that thought as foolishness.

"Virginia, ma'am," he replied. She had a feeling he would have tipped his hat and bowed if he had had his hat and could have bowed without endangering the tray.

"Enjoy your breakfast," she said, taking Greg's hand and leaving Winn alone.

Winn sank carefully into the chair. Maybe he shouldn't have told her, but she had asked. She might easily hold it against him, though. A lot of people he knew were still fighting the War in their hearts, and she sounded Northern to him. The doctor had said something about New York but he couldn't remember just what.

He felt the tray lightly, finding everything she had mentioned except the coffee. He was afraid to reach for it. If he spilled the coffee on the plate he would lose his whole breakfast. He would save the coffee for last.

What was he doing in this place? He felt like a prisoner. "Don't leave me here too long, Mike," he muttered, lifting the fork.

North of Cynthie's ranch and slightly east, two riders leading a third horse topped a rise and pulled up to rest their mounts, loosening the reins to let them graze. Mike removed his hat and wiped the inside band with his handkerchief, shook the damp cloth to cool it and wiped it across his brow. The prairie stretched as far as they could see—low rolling hills and endless grass. A distant cloud of churned-up dust pinpointed the moving herd.

"Boss'll water 'em at the Little Arkansas. Probably plans to cross it and push them a few miles farther a'fore beddin' 'em down," Mike drawled, raising his canteen to his lips.

The younger man replied with an inattentive grunt.

Mike swung a leg over the saddle horn in an effort to ease a sore hip. From his pocket he took out the makings and began to roll a cigarette. "Ya want to tell me what's botherin' ya?" he asked quietly.

"We shouldn't'a left him," Slim said flatly. "One'a us should'a stayed or we should'a brung him with us. We shouldn't'a just left him."

"Brung him with us?" Mike repeated with a chuckle, eyeing the young man over the match as he lit it with a thumbnail. Slim fit his nickname, long and awkward except in the saddle. If he had yet reached his seventeenth birthday it couldn't have been long ago. And unless the boy could develop some sense, he wouldn't make it to many more.

"Well, leavin' him there's about like leavin' him out in a desert or somethin'! We just up and left him when he needed his friends the most." Slim jerked off his hat and wiped his brow with a dusty sleeve.

Mike grinned. "That little lady we left him with didn't exactly look like the desert to me." He puffed on the cigarette, shifting slightly in the saddle.

Slim gave his hat a vicious slap against his leg, sending dust into the air and a comforting pain into his leg. "He can't *see* her, Mike. He can't even *see* her! What good's a pretty woman you can't see?" He ignored Mike's chuckle. "Besides, that ain't the point."

"The point," Mike said quietly through the thin veil of smoke, "is we done all we could for Winn. We got him to a doctor. He's in good hands. Now we gotta get on with our lives."

"Get on with your lives? I wouldn't even have no life if it wasn't for Winn!" Slim was staring at his friend in disbelief. "You don't plan to go back."

Mike dropped his leg over the saddle and slid his toe into the stirrup. Catching up the reins again, he started down the hill. Slim caught up with him quickly and grabbed the halter to stop the other horse. He looked into the older man's face, demanding an answer.

Mike carefully stubbed out the cigarette on the saddle horn, leaving a new burn on the scarred wood. "If Boss'll pay us what's due Winn, we'll bring it back to him. That, along with that crazy mare. Will that satisfy you?"

"No!"

"Look, son. I fought in the War and watched people die. Some things is worse. Men came back from the War missing arms or legs or blind from some exploding shell." Mike leaned forward for emphasis. "They come home to sit on their porches, Slim. Think, boy, you've seen 'em, too, these past few years. Like old men, but they ain't old. They can't *do* like they used to so they can't *be* who they used to be."

Mike swung his horse's head away from Slim and started on. "The Winn we knew is dead," he said. "It might'a been better if we hadn't tried so hard to help him."

Slim looked after him in shock. He had grown up believing life was always preferable to death. He quickly caught up with Mike and rode beside him. "The doctor said he might not stay blind."

Mike glanced at the young man's defiant face and said gently, "You ever know a blind man what could see again besides in the Bible?"

They were silent as the horses walked slowly on. A killdeer burst noisily into the air and flew low in front of the horses, trying to lead them away from her nest. Mike made a wide detour around the spot where she had risen.

Finally Slim cleared his throat. "Doc said somethin' about swellin' on some nerve." His voice trailed away at the end. What had seemed like reason to hope back in Wichita sounded foolish now.

"We better catch up with the herd," Mike said, and they kicked their mounts into a faster pace.

Winn wasn't sure how big a mess he might have made. Mrs. Franklin seemed to have thought of everything. The meat had been cut, the biscuits buttered, everything planned except the coffee. The cup had felt too fragile in his hands. He imagined himself setting it down in midair. He wished she had served his coffee in a tin cup. His luck might not hold.

He had a tin cup with his gear if she didn't own one. Winn frowned and rubbed his forehead. He wasn't sure where his gear was. It might still be with the herd. Yes, of course. His knapsack had been in the wagon. He didn't think anyone had thought to get it before Mike and Slim hurried him off to Wichita. His saddlebags had been on Lullaby's back. He could remember the boss saying Lullaby would slow them down.

It hurt to think. He was suddenly very tired. His head ached more the longer he was upright.

He counted his steps to the bed and was surprised to find that it had been made with sheets and turned down for him. Mrs. Franklin must have done it while he was out with Greg. He sat on the edge of the bed and removed his boots. He would have liked to remove his trousers, too, but he never knew when the lady might come in.

A few minutes later he heard the sound of footsteps outside the door and a light rap. Winn felt too tired to answer. The door opened with only a whisper of sound and the footsteps were inside the room.

"Mr. Sutton?" The soft voice made him think of angel voices urging him toward sleep.

Not so much as a twitch betrayed the fact that he had heard her. Her shoes made light taps on the floor as she came closer to the bed. He ought to let her know he was awake. Somehow, it would have taken more energy than he could muster.

She pulled the blanket more snugly over his chest. The part of his mind that was still conscious was praying she would go, but she seemed to hover over him. Cautiously, gentle fingers touched his beard with one slow movement from his cheekbone to his chin. It brought him fully awake, but he didn't move. Her skirts rustled as she turned quickly away. She took the tray and left the room in a matter of seconds.

As Winn fully gave in to sleep, he was trying to decide what meaning to attribute to the gentle touch.

Chapter Three

Cynthie was in the garden carefully pulling the grass that had come up along with the carrots. It would have been smarter to have done this earlier in the morning while it was cooler, but she had needed to take a look at the books. In less than an hour she had realized she was wasting her time.

She gave a young weed a vicious shake before tossing it away, as if pulling it up might not be enough. Why hadn't Victor let her help with anything? Why hadn't he at least talked to her about his businesses? She knew the answer; it wasn't "her place." Well, now it was her place, and she was lost.

The freight company she thought Victor had created to give her father something to do had expanded into something more, much more than she had realized. The books were filled with records of loans and foreclosures on half a dozen farms. Ott's loan was the only one Victor had ever mentioned.

Cynthie had found the ledger where he kept the cattle records, but by that time her mind had been so full of figures warring with one another that she had set it aside for another day. She had come out to the garden to try to clear her mind, but it hadn't worked.

She stood up, brushed the dirt off her apron and stretched to ease the ache in her back. She had weeded nearly half the garden. The rest would have to wait until tomorrow. Her back had taken about as much as it could, and she had a son and a patient to check on.

Inside the kitchen she found Greg on a chair trying to reach the cookie jar. "I'm packing a lunch," he said quickly. "Winn and me's going to eat on the porch. Can you slice us some bread and cheese?"

"It won't be shady on the porch until almost noon." Cynthie lifted Greg off the chair and moved the cookie jar to the table where he could reach it.

"The clock already chimed twelve times."

Cynthie laughed. "You can't count past seven." She lifted a basket from a hook in the ceiling and set it on the table.

"Winn told me." Greg ate a cookie from one hand as he set more aside with the other.

Cynthie hadn't realized it was so late. She cut thick slices of bread and cheese and wrapped them in pieces of cloth. "Can I come to this picnic?"

They heard a door open and close and looked at each other in surprise. Greg ran to the doorway. "We're in here, Winn," he shouted.

"My hearing's fine. Just tell me if there's anything between us. I'll head for your voice."

"Naw, you're all right. You just come on. Mama wants to know if she can come to the picnic." Greg's tone made it clear that he had not invited her.

"Of course she can," Winn said. He had reached Greg and stood with one hand on the door frame. "A gentleman's always glad for a lady's company."

Greg didn't look like he agreed but his face quickly brightened. "Will you make lemonade?"

Cynthie smiled. "Fetch some cold water from the well," she told him and he ran to comply.

"Would you care to sit down, Mr. Sutton?" Cynthie offered as she went to the cupboard for the pitcher and glasses.

"No, ma'am," he said. "I would like to ask you if you know where my friends are."

"Mr. Grady and Mr. Jackson? I understand they returned to the herd." She sliced a lemon in half and the tangy fresh scent made her breathe deeply. "I love the smell of lemons."

"Do you know when they left?"

Cynthie stopped squeezing the lemon and regarded him thoughtfully. "I'm sorry, Mr. Sutton, I thought they would have told you. They left yesterday, about the same time you came here." Cynthie watched both disbelief and anger flash across Winn's face. She spoke softly, hoping to reassure him. "They promised to return for you after they got the herd to Abilene."

"Why would they leave unless..." He seemed to be talking to himself. Cynthie came around the table toward him. She stopped short of touching him as he spoke again. "Did the doctor say how long before I can see again?"

"When the swelling goes down you'll probably get your sight back," she said kindly. "But that could take several days."

He seemed to brace himself against the door frame. She reached toward him, wanting to comfort him, to let him know he wasn't alone, but she heard Greg struggling with the back door and turned toward him.

While Cynthie held the door, Greg came in and set the half-filled bucket on the floor. "That's heavy!" He scrambled onto a chair and reached for the cookie jar again, only to have Cynthie snatch it away and put it back on the shelf. She returned with the sugar canister.

"Help Mr. Sutton to the front porch, young man," she half scolded. "I'll be along with the lemonade in a few minutes."

Winn turned when the child took his hand. He hadn't seen the attempted cookie theft, but he had heard the mother's tone. When Greg whispered, "She's mean," on their way to the front door, he didn't know what to think. She seemed to change too quickly.

Several things didn't make sense. This was obviously a large two-storied house; he had heard footsteps overhead during the night. He remembered how Mrs. Franklin's skirts had rustled. The calico dresses he had seen most women wear in these prairie towns did not rustle. The sound had made him think of his sister. Even her skirts probably didn't rustle now. It all made him wonder why he had been brought here. Surely his friends wouldn't have left without telling him.

Was there something he wasn't remembering, something the doctor had told him? He rubbed his bandaged forehead. So much of his recent memory was cloudy. A faintly familiar clattering seemed a part of his confused brain.

"You all right?" There was an insistent tug on his elbow. He realized he was sitting in a porch swing and Greg was climbing on his leg.

He lifted the boy and settled him onto his lap. It seemed the natural thing to do. Greg was probably the age his nephew had been the last time Winn had seen him. That would be nearly three years ago. He had a niece now, too, a niece he had never seen.

Greg leaned against his chest. "You scare me when you look so sad."

Winn wrapped the boy in his arms. "It's just a headache," he whispered.

The clattering continued. He could place its location now, above him and to the right. The rise and fall of the sound told him it was influenced by the wind. He realized he had heard it the other times he had been on this porch.

Cynthie came through the door and set a tray on a table at his left. His arms tightened automatically around the child, prepared for her objection.

Cynthie stood still, the basket over one arm, watching Winn rock her son. In less than twenty-four hours Greg had accepted Winn so completely he could curl up on the man's lap. They made quite a picture. Her baby, who was growing up so quickly, looked very tiny again. Yet Greg's friendship with this stranger was based in part on the fact that he could help someone else for the first time in his life.

She began to feel awkward and broke the spell. In a conspiratorial whisper she said, "If you rock him to sleep we can have all the lemonade."

Greg sat up so quickly he nearly slid off Winn's lap. He scrambled onto the porch railing and straddled it. "Put my lunch here," he said, patting the flat board between his legs.

Cynthie handed him the cloth that contained his portion of bread and cheese. "I guess if you fall it won't be the first time," she said.

Winn wondered where the boy was and if the boy was really in danger of falling. The mother didn't sound truly concerned. He took the cloth-wrapped portion she gave him, and when she asked where he would like her to set his lemonade, he answered, "Perhaps I should wait until I've finished this, ma'am. I also wanted to suggest a tin cup. I'm afraid I'll break something."

"I want a tin cup, too," announced Greg through a mouthful of bread.

Winn heard the musical sound of a spoon being turned in a liquid-filled glass. "Lemonade, gentlemen, is always served in glass." He heard a glass being filled and set down on wood. This was followed by a definite slurping sound, and Winn had to smile. "Coffee and milk," Cynthie added, "can be served in tin cups."

"Goody," slurred the boy around the glass.

Cynthie took her lemonade and sat on the top step. Her face was in the shade of the overhang but her legs were in the warm sunlight. She was briefly tempted to pull her heavy skirts up and let the sun beat directly on her stockinged calves. She wondered what this Virginia gentleman would think of that. But she couldn't do it even though she knew he wouldn't see her.

The warm weather made her think of wading in streams and running barefoot in the fresh grass, things Victor had frowned on but she and Greg had done anyway. This spring she had been too busy to think of games.

"Let's go fishin'," Greg suggested.

Cynthie was pleased that his thoughts had been so close to her own. She was sorry to have to discourage him. "There are clouds building up in the west. We might get caught in a rainstorm."

"I don't see no clouds."

"That's because we're facing east," Winn said. Into the silence that followed, he asked, "Am I right?"

"Yes, you are," Cynthie said. "How did you know?"

Winn was trying to figure that out himself. "Maybe I felt the sun this morning," he said.

Cynthie noticed that Winn had finished eating and brought him his glass of lemonade. She watched him take it carefully in his hands, taste a tiny sip and lower the glass to his lap. "My guess, Mr. Sutton, is that your sense of direction has always been good," Cynthie said.

Winn decided there were times when he liked this woman's voice. "Maybe," he said. Maybe the compass in his head had a needle that pointed straight to Virginia. It was funny how suddenly, after three years, he was homesick. Maybe it was the lemonade. He took another sip; it tasted right, but there was no mistaking this porch in Kansas for his veranda at home. That was a curious thought. Why was it different? Why couldn't he imagine whatever he wanted around him?

The prairie smells were different from the flower scents of home. The air felt different, warm but not as soft. And there were none of the sounds of home.

He pulled himself out of his thoughts. It wasn't good to dwell on memories. "What's the rattle I hear?" He pointed in the direction of the sound.

"Mama's wind chimes," Greg said. Winn heard bare feet slap the porch floor. "You want a cookie? They make the lemonade taste sour."

Cynthie laughed. "He's not trying to talk you out of your dessert. He likes it that way."

"You may have my cookie, Greg, but you'll have to do me a favor in return. Tell me about the wind chimes. I've never heard any that sound like these."

"It's made of shells," Greg said, biting into a cookie. "Mama tied them to a ring with fishin' line. Couldn't we go fishin' in a hurry, Mama?" Greg persisted.

"I'm afraid not, baby," Cynthie answered. "My family made a trip to the beach once when I was a child," she said to Winn.

He smiled. Everyone out here brought memories of distant places. It made him feel less alone.

"Somebody's comin'," announced Greg.

Winn strained to hear some sound in the distance. Maybe Mrs. Franklin had been wrong about his friends; maybe it was Mike and Slim come to get him. "Can you tell who it is?" he asked.

"I think it's Kyle," said Cynthie.

Greg handed his empty glass to his mother. "I'm gonna see Sorry," he said.

"Sorry's a stray dog Peter found," Cynthie explained. "He calls her that because she's such a sorry-looking thing."

"Wanna come?" Greg put his hand on Winn's knee.

Winn shook his head. "Maybe another time."

Cynthie watched her child run toward the barn and wished Greg liked Kyle better.

The rider was still a long way off. Winn seemed almost as distant. "Can I get you anything else, Mr. Sutton?" she asked.

"No, thank you, ma'am. If you could help me back to your father's room, I believe I'd like to lie down again. I'm afraid I give out pretty fast."

"That's to be expected," she said, taking the glass from his hand and setting it on the tray. She took his arm and directed him to the door. "You should count the steps from one place to another. You can get around without a guide that way."

"I think I can stand being led around for a few days, ma'am. Besides, how often does a cowboy like me get to have a young lady on his arm?"

They had reached the door to her father's room. She guided his hand to the knob and stepped away. "As easily as you can turn on the charm, Mr. Sutton, I'd guess about as often as you like."

The dimples under his beard deepened. "Sorry, ma'am. I do appreciate the advice, but I'm not going to need it."

"I hope not, Mr. Sutton."

She watched him disappear behind the door and, with a sigh, walked to the porch. She gathered up the remains of the picnic and set the tray and basket inside the house while she waited for Kyle. She wasn't sure why, but she suddenly felt disappointed.

Cynthie lay awake listening to the approaching storm. The house was warm and she had left the windows open, hoping for a breeze before the rain. Thunder rumbled in the distance and an irregular pulse of lightning played outside her window. She told herself she was staying awake to close the windows at the last possible moment, but she knew she wouldn't have been able to sleep anyway.

Somehow Kyle's visit had upset her. He had come primarily to find out if she had taken in the stranger. Surely, he had only her best interests in mind. Yet she hated to have him checking up on her or questioning her decisions. She hadn't invited him in or offered him the last of the lemonade. They had talked briefly on the porch, and she had all but sent him away.

She tossed away the sheet that covered her and scooted over, trying to find a cooler place in the warm bed. She knew what she was feeling—guilt, and it was becoming familiar. Recently, after Kyle's visits, she was left feeling vaguely guilty, as if she had not been fair to him.

Today had been the worst. She had treated him as if he was the outsider. He had broken up Greg's picnic, driven the boy to the barn and Winn to his room. He had put an end to a very pleasant lunch. Even as she thought it, she knew she was being unfair.

Why were there times when she did not want to see Kyle Dempsey? He had asked her to consider marrying him. God knew he was better than the other men who had asked, some of them before the dirt had settled on Victor's grave. Something made her cringe at the thought of marrying Kyle. He was too much like Victor.

A sudden clamp of thunder made Cynthie jump. It was as if God took exception to her thoughts. She had loved Victor. She should be happy to marry someone like him. It was a dishonor to Victor's memory to think of herself as better off without him.

But she couldn't help the way she felt. She had been so young when she had married Victor that until his death, she hadn't known what it was like to go through an entire day without being told either what to do or what she had done wrong. He hadn't been mean to her, exactly. He had been like most husbands, she supposed. If her mother were alive she would probably tell her she was getting too independent, a terrible sin in that woman's book.

She heard the patter of the first few drops of rain and got up to close the windows, grateful for the activity. Maybe then she would be tired enough to sleep and the strange thoughts that were playing in her head would stop troubling her.

In Greg's room, she closed the window and kissed his cheek as he lay sleeping peacefully.

She systematically closed the other windows until she came to the room where Winn Sutton slept. She had put that window off until last, feeling uncomfortable about entering his room. She turned the knob as gently as possible and left the door open as she crept to the window. It creaked in protest as she lowered it, in spite of her efforts.

She turned toward the bed to see if she had disturbed the man sleeping there. She could discern no movement, but it was too dark to see. She stepped closer to the bed as a lightning flash lit the room.

Winn slept sprawled across the bed, the covers thrown off much as her own had been. He was barechested, his shirt lying in a tangle with the sheets on the floor. The light lasted only a moment and left Cynthie with an image of a broad chest and a bearded face as pale as the bandage above it. His was not a peaceful sleep.

Not two seconds after the flash came the thunder, an explosive sound that shook the house. Cynthie jumped and gasped, putting her fingers to her mouth. The cry she had heard had not been her own. "Mr. Sutton? Are you all right?" Without thinking she stepped next to the bed. He was mumbling something in his sleep. "Rosie," she thought he said.

Another flash of light revealed Winn's face, still lost in troubled sleep. With the answering clap of thunder, Winn sat up abruptly. "Mr. Sutton." She was close enough to lay a hand on his bare shoulder.

With a groan he pulled her to him, bringing her down beside him on the bed. She found herself nearly sitting on his lap, her face pressed against his warm chest. He seemed to gulp his lungs full of air, then, with another groan, he buried his face in her hair, which hung loosely over her shoulder, and held her more tightly against his chest.

Cynthie could feel the warmth of his body through the thin fabric of her gown. His face felt feverish against her neck. Her whole body seemed to feel his racing heartbeat. Somehow her fingers had lost themselves in the soft hairs that curled at the back of his neck. She was aware of a warm tingle in her breasts that made her want to press more tightly against him even as her mind told her it was time to pull away.

Another clap of thunder rumbled and Winn raised his head and loosened his grip. As the sleep gradually left his brain, he remembered where he was and who he was holding so tightly. He became aware of lilac-scented hair that had caught in his beard and a small soft body that fit easily in his arms.

He was half naked and she was wearing something so thin he could feel the hard points of her nipples through it. In his confusion, he had taken liberties she might make him regret. He gently pushed her away but kept his hands on her shoulders, afraid she would run away before he had a chance to explain.

"I'm sorry," he began.

"Shh, you had a bad dream." He felt her hand caress the side of his face. It reminded him of another touch, one he had decided was only imagined.

"Did I wake you?" he asked.

"I was up to close the windows."

"It's strange to hear thunder and not see the lightning." He had tried for a casual tone, but a conversation with her in this position seemed even stranger. Though he had pulled away, he was sure he could still feel her body heating his.

"Does your head hurt?" She could see his face only because of the sporadic lightning. She kept her hand against his bearded cheek to know where he was, she told herself, not because the touch was so exciting.

"My head always hurts, but the dream's over." He dropped his hands from her shoulders and eased back against the pillow, pulling away from her touch. Another clap of thunder seemed to come from inside his head.

"The doctor left medicine for pain."

"No. It makes me feel groggy and stupid. The pain's better."

To his amazement, she leaned forward and caressed his temples. "I'm sorry," she whispered.

He caught her hands quickly, holding them tightly in the space between their bodies. "It's not bad. Really. Thanks for trying to help, but I'm all right now." He let her hands go.

She took the hint. "Good night, then, Mr. Sutton." She rose and quickly left the room, closing the door gently behind her.

Winn groaned softly and tucked his hands behind his head. All he needed now was to get entangled with this woman. He wasn't even sure why he was here or what she expected from him.

He couldn't have held Cynthie Franklin the way he had and not felt desire for her. But a woman like her wouldn't feel those same things for a man unless she had some long-range ideas. What kinds of plans could a woman like Cynthie Franklin have for a man like him—even after his sight returned? Surely she had no shortage of suitors. Winn knew for a fact that she was neither fat nor skinny, and her hair was soft as silk, and bound to be shiny and beautiful no matter what the color.

He could feel his blood pump faster in his veins as he remembered her scent and her touch. He tried to shake off the feeling. No, if she was desperate enough to want a blind, broke cowboy, she must be just plain ugly. And if he was blind, what difference would that make?

The thought made him smile. He could ask Greg, but all little boys thought their mamas were pretty.

That led to another idea. She had probably comforted her child after nightmares. That was all she had done tonight. He had mistaken a comforting touch for something more, expecting her to be feeling the same things he was. He frowned and wondered why this disappointed him.

The rain was coming down steadily now. It reminded him of a night when he had been on watch during a storm. He remembered the sound of the driving rain as it hit his slicker and hat, pouring off the brim to make a curtain he couldn't see through. It hadn't lasted long, but the beauty of the morning had seemed to make the discomfort of the night worthwhile. He remembered the clear bright sky and the soft springy earth.

He shuddered as he remembered what else had happened that morning, and his nightmare came back to him. Suddenly the room was far too warm. The window was closed and the rain tapped against the glass. If he could open the window and let the air in, he could breathe easier. He wasn't sure he could find the window.

He wanted to go outside and stand on the porch. It would be cooler out there, but he couldn't do it. He was trapped, a prisoner in this bed as if there were chains holding him. This was every bit as bad as the nightmare. He stared at the blackness around him. "Oh, God!" he whispered. "What if this nightmare doesn't end?"

Upstairs Cynthie stared into her own darkness. Her cheeks burned when she remembered how it had felt to be in Winn's arms. What kind of a woman was she turning into? She was lusting for a stranger! She hadn't felt desire since her courtship with Victor. Theirs had been a kind of wonderful anticipation that gradually passed during the early days of their marriage. Surely she wasn't such a fool to believe in girlish fantasies again!

Maybe she should consider Kyle's proposal more seriously. He was at least someone she knew and he had been calling on her for months. Besides, he was very handsome and always clean and neat. She could at least let him kiss her, really kiss her, not just the brief touch she had allowed him.

She closed her eyes and tried to imagine what it would be like. He was much taller than she. He would smell like the tobacco he smoked. He would hold her gently in his arms, her breasts pressed against his hard chest. His beard would brush against her face as their lips touched—

She sat up with a gasp. Kyle didn't have a beard. The man she was imagining was Winn Sutton! It was Winn's touch that had brought on all these feelings.

Winn Sutton. She wanted to cry. He hadn't even wanted her to hold him. He had been dreaming of someone named Rosie. As soon as he had realized who was in his arms, he had pulled away. He had politely apologized for touching her and had pushed her away!

She sank back against the bed with a groan. What was she doing, daydreaming like a schoolgirl? She was twenty-four years old, a widow with a child. She told herself firmly that she needed some sleep. She tried to brush everything from her mind except the sound of the rain. Unfortunately she had no control over her dreams once she was asleep.

Chapter Four

Winn sat on the porch swing listening to the shells rattle in the wind. It was Sunday morning, and Greg and his mother had gone into town for services. The house was empty without the little boy, and Winn realized how much he counted on Greg's chatter to pass the time.

He had been staying here just over a week. The Double M herd should have gotten to Abilene, and in a few days his friends would be back to get him. He would be more than ready to go. The possibility that he might not have regained his sight by then entered his head and he shied away from it. Of course he would be well. The headaches had decreased, and he knew he was doing much better.

Dr. Gordon had been out on Friday and he had confirmed Winn's opinion. The swelling had not completely subsided, but Winn was certain he would see again once it had. He touched his forehead gingerly; it was still tender. At least he was through with the bandages.

Winn allowed the swing to rock gently. He felt more comfortable out here at night. He didn't know how many people might still be around the ranch or what they would think of him sitting here. He had learned to get around the house a little and even around a small part of the yard. He could find the well to get a drink and, thanks to Mrs. Franklin's rope, find the outhouse without help. He smiled. He remembered Greg counting off all the things he had learned to do.

During the past week, he had spent a lot of time with the boy. Mrs. Franklin brought him his food, offered instructions, but it was Greg who spent the day with him. In fact, now that he thought about it, Mrs. Franklin had seemed very cool toward him since the night of the storm.

Through the open window he heard the clock chime once. It was half past something. He would have to wait thirty minutes to find out what. Ten, he guessed, because it was already getting warm.

He rolled up the sleeves of his blue shirt. He knew it was blue because it was his own for a change, not one that had belonged to Mrs. Franklin's husband. He hadn't noticed the others being uncomfortably tight, but he could move more freely in this one.

Maybe he should have gone to town with the others. The offer had seemed sincere. But the thought of a church full of people to bump into hadn't been appealing, and the picnic dinner that was to follow had been terrifying.

What was she planning to tell all those people, anyway? "This is a blind man I'm looking after out of Christian charity"? Winn knew some people did things to help others without expecting anything in return. He tried to himself, sometimes. Mostly, though, folks contented themselves with small acts of kindness. Taking in a stranger with only the clothes on his back was more than most people were willing to do.

Maybe she took him in so she could show everyone how good she was. He knew people like that, too, but she didn't seem to act the way they did. Anyway, if that was the case she would have insisted he go to church with them.

He couldn't figure her out, and something about her made him hesitate to ask questions. He couldn't watch her face to know what she was thinking. He almost chuckled out loud. Being blind was turning him into a coward, at least where this woman was concerned.

He heard a faint whistling in the direction of the barn and corral. Smell alone had determined their whereabouts when he had gone to the well with Greg. The whistle was a nearly tuneless strain that ended briefly and started up again. As often as he had been outside he could not remember having heard whistling before. The sound grew louder, and Winn put the pieces together. Someone unused to whistling wanted Winn to know he was coming.

Winn heard the visitor's feet crunch on the gravel in the yard. The whistle was weakening. "Good morning," Winn called.

"Good morning, yourself," came a warm, deep voice. The steps continued toward the porch with a quicker stride. Spurless boots came up the three steps, and the porch post creaked slightly when a heavy frame leaned against it. "Louie LeBlanc," the voice said. "I met you when you first came."

"Winn Sutton," he said. He reached a hand toward the voice and felt it gripped firmly by a hard, callused hand.

"Mrs. Franklin asked me to check on you while she and the boys are gone," he explained. "Can I do anything for you?"

"No, I'm fine," Winn answered.

"Wanted to invite you down to the bunkhouse come noon. I don't cook as good as Mrs. Franklin but it'll fill your stomach."

And pass the time, Winn thought. "I'd be obliged. The other hands all went to church?"

"Peter did," Louie said. "He and I are all that's left around here till the others get back from the drive. You met Peter?"

Winn grinned. "Not yet, but I hear a lot about him. Greg thinks he's quite a hero."

Louie laughed, a relaxed, easy sound. "Well, the boy does have a way with horses, and that's about tops in little Greg's book." Louie paused and studied the big man. He seemed curiously out of place on the docile swing. Strong forearms showed beneath the rolled-up sleeves, and the loose shirt couldn't hide the broad shoulders and hard muscles from Louie's practiced eye. His job called for him to pick men the way Peter could pick horses.

He watched Winn's face for signs of shame or pride as he continued. "He talks about you a lot when he's down with Peter." Winn didn't respond and Louie grinned. "Yeah, seems like you're a real cowboy and all of a sudden Peter and I no longer qualify. Sleeping in a bunkhouse is our main failing, I think."

Winn laughed. "He does ask a lot of questions about the drive."

"Questions he's good at. Well, enjoy the quiet while you've got it." The post creaked again as Louie pushed away from it. He clapped a hand firmly on Winn's shoulder. "Give a holler if you need anything."

Winn nodded his thanks and Louie walked down the steps. Halfway across the yard he turned to look at the man on the swing. If he stayed blind, those hard muscles would soften and he wouldn't look out of place on the swing anymore. It was a shame, too, Louie decided. Sutton looked to be the kind of man he would have liked to work with.

The same Sunday morning, Mike Grady and Slim Jackson rode south out of Abilene. Winter Sutton's mare, with his saddle and gear strapped to her back, was secured to Slim's saddle horn by a lead rope. The boy occasionally turned to regard the animal with distrust.

Mike noticed the action with some sympathy. The boy had developed a fear of the horse that wasn't altogether uncalled for. She did seem to enjoy trouble, though she wasn't quite the witch Slim seemed to think she was. He would take over the responsibility of leading her as soon as this headache went away. He looked up at the cloudless sky and realized that instead of improving, the day would probably get worse as the sun grew stronger.

Last night had been a disappointment. Saturday night in Abilene with money in his pocket and all he could think of was Winn Sutton. He kept imagining the fun he would have been having if Winn had been around, and every time he thought of Winn he had ordered another drink. To make it worse, he had been saddled with the care of this youngster who planned to take all his money home to Papa. Slim hadn't turned out to be any fun at all.

He eyed his companion again. The boy disapproved of him. That was easy to see. Mike wanted to groan in frustration but resisted the urge. Why did he have to inherit the kid from Winn anyway? It was Winn who liked to take the babies under his wing, not him!

Now he had to play nursemaid all the way to Texas. Boss had figured the two of them should be the ones to go to Wichita with Winn's horse and gear, so he was even denied the company of the other men on the way home.

The kid was bound to cause trouble when they got to Wichita, too. He had his mind set on taking Winn home with him. Did he think Winn would still have a job even though he was blind? Was he going to take him home to Papa's little dirt farm and say here's another mouth to feed? There was just no explaining anything to the boy.

Mike watched Lullaby prance up beside Slim and saw the boy urge his horse away from her. He dropped back a little and began fishing in a saddlebag for a bottle. A little drink would ease the headache. Maybe he would let Slim lead that crazy mare all day. It would keep him too busy to talk, and Mike had heard enough of what the kid had to say.

The clock slowly chimed out the hour. Winn lay still and counted twelve chimes. Louie would come for him soon. He had gone back to bed an hour before, his head feeling tired while the rest of his body seemed to resent the inactivity. Maybe it was just boredom.

He sat up and found his boots where he had left them. Running his fingers through his hair, he wondered what he looked like. He had always taken a certain amount of pride in his appearance, and it bothered him that he couldn't trim his beard. His habits had afforded him considerable teasing since he had come west.

He realized with some amusement that he was nervous. This would be the first time he had eaten with anyone besides the bread and cheese picnic Greg had arranged nearly a week ago. He didn't really think an old-timer like Louie would be too upset by his manners, but he was nervous just the same.

Sitting here waiting for Louie to come wasn't going to help. He had a fair idea of the direction he needed to go to get to the bunkhouse. He would probably hear Louie when he got close anyway, or Louie would be on his way to get him. At the very worst, he could get lost and have to holler for Louie to find him. Even that would be better than waiting.

Winn got up quickly before he had time to reconsider and counted the steps to the bedroom door. He started across the front room determined to ignore the persistent thoughts of tripping over things and walking into buildings.

He felt the tabletop bump against his thigh an instant before he heard the crash of breaking glass. He had somehow veered too far to the right or taken longer steps than usual. This was the table Greg had warned him about the first time through this room. He had always remembered it until now.

The table still rested against his legs. He had very nearly knocked it over. He stepped back and righted it, pressing his hands on the top to make sure it was stable. Its legs didn't seem to be damaged, but his own were shaking. What had he knocked off the top?

Whatever it was, it sounded like it had shattered. He eased around the table. Stepping on a piece of glass would scratch a polished floor, and for some reason that was how he pictured Mrs. Franklin's floors—polished and hard and cold. He shuddered.

Bending, he felt gingerly along the floor. His callused fingertip nudged a piece of glass and he carefully picked it up. It was thin, but not as thin as his mother's crystal. He didn't know enough about such things to tell by its feel if it had been valuable.

He pictured his mother's crystal goblets in shattered pieces on the dining room floor the way his sister had described them. He felt a surge of resentment and knew it was irrational. That was a long time ago and had nothing to do with this.

This was something he had broken. He was the outsider here.

With a flick of his wrist he cast the piece aside. The quick movement brought his hand in contact with a larger piece, its jagged edges several inches from the floor. He felt the sting and knew he had been cut. It seemed odd that he couldn't tell how badly when he couldn't see it. He clapped his other hand hard against the cut. It was slick with blood.

He heard the sound of boots on the porch and Louie calling his name as he opened the door. Winn rose slowly to his feet. "I think I cut myself," he said.

"I think so, too," Louie answered. The older man was soon beside him, moving his hands so he could see the cut. "What were you doing down there?"

"I wanted to see what I had broken," Winn said, embarrassed by his own choice of words.

"Did you learn much?"

Winn smiled. "I think whatever it was got revenge."

"Small revenge, I'd say. You'll heal sooner than it will."

Winn tried to laugh. "What was it anyway?"

"A bowl Mrs. Franklin kept on the table. She put flowers in it sometimes. Don't know if she set store by it." Louie could tell the incident had left the younger man shaken. He tried to imagine how helpless he must feel. "Do you want to lie down while I clean this up?"

"No," Winn answered quickly. "I'm fine."

Louie led him to a chair where he sat and listened as the broken pieces were dropped into some kind of metal bin. Winn was afraid to touch anything because both his hands were bloody. He wondered if blood had dripped on the floor and if Louie would be able to remove the stains if it had. He didn't ask.

Winn no longer felt hungry and considered skipping dinner with Louie, but what would he do? He was tired of doing nothing.

He felt Louie's hand on his shoulder. "Let's go eat," the older man said. Winn let himself be lead out the door, down the steps and across the yard. Inside the bunkhouse, Louie helped him wash in a basin by the door. It made him feel like a child.

He sat where he was directed and listened to the sounds Louie made with lids and spoons and tin plates. The handkerchief around his hand was wet, but he didn't want to ask for another.

"Those headaches any better?" Louie asked.

"They come and go," Winn replied.

Louie set a plate in front of Winn. "Saw Doc was out the other day. He have anything good to say?"

Winn inhaled the warm spicy smell and tried to decide what he was being served. "I'm healing all right, I guess."

Louie dipped up a plate for himself and took it to the table. He helped Winn find his spoon and watched as he hesitantly dipped it into the food on the plate. "This is my specialty," Louie said. "It's kind'a like hash, I guess. I like it best with antelope but this is plain old beef." He noticed Winn had yet to taste it and grinned. "Yes, sir! When I first found Peter he was fixin' to starve. He claims it was my hash what nearly finished him off."

Winn chuckled. "Now you've got me wondering if there's some reason you want to get rid of me." He raised the spoon to his lips, hoping there was something on it. There was, and it was good. He knew his face must have registered his surprise when he heard Louie laugh.

Winn decided it would be best to keep the other man talking. He would be less likely to notice how he ate. "What did you mean when you said you found Peter?"

"Well, I didn't exactly find Peter. He found me, you might say. I was in town, see, and there was this kid, only about twelve, you understand, and he was asking everybody about a job. He was trying to tell people what he could do and they were asking him where his folks were. I watched him a while. No one was taking him serious but he just acted polite, you know, and went on to the next person or business or whatever.

"Finally he got to me. He asked if I worked on a farm or ranch and if I knew of anyone hirin'. By then, I couldn't resist. I just said, 'Why, shore,' and brung him on home with me."

"You brought him here without finding out where he belonged?"

Louie laughed. "Well, I always figure it's first things first in this world. I meant to feed him, give him a place to sleep and then go about trying to figure why he was out on his own."

Louie shoveled a forkful of hash into his mouth and Winn waited for him to finish the story. After a few minutes of silence he asked, "Did you find out?"

"Yep."

Winn waited again. In spite of his determination to mind his own business, he was interested in this young boy's story. It gave him a chance to forget his own problems. At the same time, it didn't seem right to ask questions. Louie would finish the story sooner or later. When Louie finally spoke it was to offer him more hash, which he spooned onto Winn's plate without waiting for an answer.

Louie spoke again as he set the pot on the stove and returned to the table. "I used to do some trail driving, myself. Fact is, last couple of years I led Franklin's herd to Abilene. 'Course this ain't nothing like bringing a herd all the way up from Texas. I done that a few times, too. Always got tired of the food. I expect we could have hired the best cowboys if we'd had an inventive cook."

Winn grinned but offered no comment. He found himself relaxing. The food was good. The coffee was good. The big tin cup was easy to find and didn't clatter dangerously like Mrs. Franklin's china. He mentioned it to Louie.

"She came and got a couple of tin cups from me. I figured she was usin' 'em."

"Well, sometimes, but it's not something I can count on. It's almost like she's trying to wean me away from them."

Louie laughed and Winn spoke again. "Can I ask you a question, Louie?"

"Fire away."

"Since your cooking didn't kill me, are you waiting for me to die of curiosity?"

Louie pretended surprise. "You're wondering about Peter? Well, there's not that much to tell, after all. His folks had come out from Kentucky. Didn't have much. His ma died of a fever and then his pa was killed, some kind of hunting accident, I guess. Peter was kind of vague on that.

"Anyway, he figured there wasn't nothing to keep him there so he buried his pa, packed up what was useful and rode the old mule to town. He'd been working since he could walk so he figured he could look after himself. Funny thing. People got upset with us givin' him a job here even though kids his age would be doin' the same work on their pa's place."

"Did you try to find any family back in Kentucky?" Winn asked. He admired Louie for taking in the child but it seemed like Peter should have been with his own kin. Twelve was too young to be alone.

"Seems his pa left because of family and didn't none of them want the boy. We're his family now. Franklin wasn't too happy with the boy but he died before he got around to doing anything about it."

Winn noticed a certain lack of sorrow at the mention of his late employer's death. He caught himself getting curious again. He had already pried into other people's lives more than he intended.

Louie watched Winn as he finished his dinner. He did surprisingly well for a blind man, but he was painfully careful about every move he made.

After he led Winn to the house, Louie continued to think about him. What would the man do if his sight didn't return? Did he even think about it? If he did see again, Louie decided, he would sure like to hire him. If Mrs. Franklin was serious about staying out here, they could use another hand.

Of course, this had been a tough year and she might decide to give it up. She could go back to New York to her pa's shipping business and live like she was meant to.

Louie chuckled to himself. That was a possibility he didn't much like to think about. He was too old to go looking for another job. He decided he couldn't blame Winn if he didn't spend much time thinking about the future.

He went to the bunkhouse to clean up the dishes. As he went about his afternoon chores, he kept an eye out for Mrs. Franklin's wagon. When it pulled into the yard in the middle of the afternoon, he went to meet it in front of the barn. He helped Cynthie down from the wagon seat as Peter jumped from the other side. Greg was slowly pulling himself out of a doze in the back.

"Your Mr. Sutton had a little accident," Louie told her. "Nothing serious. Just a broken dish and a cut hand."

"Things like that are to be expected," Cynthie said with a sigh. "How badly was he cut?"

Greg had shaken off his sleepiness to hear part of the adults' conversation. "Is Winn hurt?"

"Just a scratch," Louie assured them both.

Greg jumped from the wagon. "I told you not to leave him alone! Now he's hurt and it's your fault!"

Cynthie reached out a hand to stop the child as he made a dash for the house but she was too late. She let her hand drop slowly to her side.

"This isn't anything to worry about, ma'am," Louie told her. "I just wanted you to know before you went inside."

"It's nothing to worry about unless he agrees with Greg." Cynthie turned and walked away, leaving Louie to wonder if he had missed something. He sent a questioning look at Peter, who shrugged and continued to unhitch the horses as if the ways of adults were always somewhat mystifying.

As Cynthie walked toward the house, she tried to think of what to say to Winn. He needed encouragement. The worst thing for him right now would be to start to think, like Greg, that he should never be alone. Greg, however, had taught her that there were also dangers in pushing too hard.

She was dealing with an adult, an adult she hardly knew. How honest could she be with him? He had openly rejected her advice already, even though she suspected he was applying some of it anyway.

And what if he blamed her the way Greg did? She tried to tell herself that it only worried her because it would effect how he listened to her advice. What he thought of her personally made no difference otherwise.

She stepped resolutely into the house and entered Winn's room. One look at the handsome face told her she was lying to herself. She cared very much what he thought of her.

He was seated in the chair, listening intently as Greg recounted the trip to town. The boy was swinging his legs over the side of Winn's bed but stopped abruptly when his mother came in.

She smiled at the little boy to cover her agitation. "Go change out of your good clothes."

"I'll be right back," he said to Winn and ran out of the room.

Winn waited for Cynthie to break the uncomfortable silence. "I hear you hurt yourself," she said softly.

"I don't think it's much," he said. It was odd how nervous she made him. "I'm sorry about the dish." It seemed like a lame apology but it was all he could think of to say.

"Can I take a look?" Her gentle hands were already touching his but she hesitated for a moment. Hearing no objection she began unwrapping Louie's handkerchief.

She was kneeling on the floor beside his chair and he could smell the soft flowery scent that drifted up from her hair. He leaned his head back in the chair in an effort to resist the attraction the smell always induced.

"Did I hurt you?"

"No, ma'am," he answered, sitting up again. He tried not to wince as her fingers probed the edges of the cut.

"Is there any chance there's still glass in there?" she asked, coming to her feet.

"No, ma'am."

"The bandages are in the kitchen. Come on in. I'll make us some coffee."

Winn listened in amazement to her footsteps as she left the room. Greg had been right. He couldn't hear it in her voice, but she was angry about the dish.

He touched a finger to the cut. It was slightly sticky. He was bleeding again, thanks to her tender care. If he wanted a bandage, he had to follow orders.

As he rose from the chair, he heard Greg's bare feet running down the stairs. A confused picture of shattered goblets and the child's bare feet brought him to the doorway in a second. "Greg!" he called.

Greg charged across the room. Winn went down on one knee and let the boy perch on the other. "Don't go near the front door and the table where I broke that bowl unless you're wearing shoes," he warned.

"I don't see no glass," Greg said.

"Any glass. Your mama's got to wipe the floor with a wet cloth to get the tiny pieces you can't see. Until she's had a chance to do that, you go through the kitchen door."

As he spoke he heard the soft tap of Cynthie's footsteps coming from the kitchen. "I'm just getting ready to take care of it now," she said.

"You wait until your mama's done and then you can go outside."

Winn started to lift Greg off his leg but the boy clung to his neck. "I'm not going outside unless you are." He had promised Winn that he would never go anywhere without him.

"Don't be silly," Winn said, hugging the small warm body. "Your mama's going to put a fresh bandage on my hand. I'll be fine."

"Then carry me out of the house." The little arms tightened around Winn's neck.

"You can't let a blind man carry you around. You'll get hurt." Winn could hear Cynthie's rag slide across the floor. Surely she would come and snatch the child away from him. He listened for an exclamation or hasty footsteps.

"I'll watch where we're going," the boy encouraged.

The rag continued to swish nearby. He even thought he heard Cynthie humming softly but wasn't sure. His own heart was pounding loud enough to drown out a thunderstorm.

"You're a crazy kid and deserve whatever happens to you," he muttered in the boy's ear as he stood up.

Greg giggled and leaned away, pointing. "Go that way."

"Greg!" Winn held him more tightly. He heard the panic in his own voice and couldn't understand why Cynthie didn't come rescue her baby.

He counted the steps to the kitchen door, trying his best to take normal-size steps, knowing he couldn't while holding the child. "Will we make it through the doorway?" he whispered.

"I can reach the top of the door!" called Greg.

Winn felt the jolt as the boy grabbed the upped sill and was glad he had been moving so slowly. "Don't do that," he pleaded. "There's no glass on the kitchen floor. You can walk now."

Greg threw his arms around Winn's neck. "There might be," he said solemnly.

Winn took a couple of steps into the kitchen. "There might be stickers outside. Do I have to carry you around everywhere?"

"Yes." The boy giggled, but he let go and Winn helped him gently to the floor.

Winn heard Cynthie come in behind him as Greg dashed out the back door, letting it slam behind him. He heard the sound of a stove lid dropping into place. "Have a seat, Mr. Sutton. I'll have the coffee on in a minute and we can get to your hand."

Winn gritted his teeth. Did she have any idea what he had just been through? Well, he would find a seat or trip over one. As he took a step forward, he realized that he already knew where the back door was. The sounds had helped him place both it and the stove. The table would have to be ahead and to the right.

He knew the room was small. One more step and he set his hand down on the edge of the table. A second later his other hand found the chair. He sat down and rested his arm on the table, feeling very proud of himself. He didn't realize that he was smiling.

Neither did he know that Cynthie had been watching and that her smile matched his. She went quickly back to the coffee preparations. "Louie or Peter will be taking us into town sometime this week," she began. She set something on the table. The soft thud wasn't enough to tell him what it was. "I think you should come with us."

He didn't want to go to town. He didn't want to stumble into people. He didn't want Cynthie to see how frightened he was by the whole idea.

She had taken his hand and turned it over. "This could sting," she warned. The next instant Winn jerked away as she proved her words to be correct.

Winn didn't know what she had used but it was probably unnecessary and definitely unappreciated.

He bit back a curse and let her wrap a bandage around his hand. Her touch was gentle and soothing, and her hair, as she bent so close to him, smelled fresh and sweet. And her heart could give a man frostbite, he reminded himself. She was about as predictable as Lullaby.

"You'll enjoy a trip in to Wichita," she said as she gently let his hand rest on the table.

Now she was even going to tell him what he enjoyed! He wondered if his face showed his irritation and decided he didn't much care. "Yes, ma'am," he said.

Cynthie studied her patient as she brought the cups to the table. He was obviously not happy with the idea. How could she make him see that getting out would be the best thing for him? Somehow she had to make him want to go to town.

Winn heard her set something on the table. China cups. He could tell by the clink they made against the saucers.

"There's always a lot going on in town," she said as she returned to the stove for the coffee. "Greg loves the noise and activity. I'm sure he'll want to show you around."

Winn pictured himself being dragged down crowded streets by a little boy, knocking over ladies with their arms full of packages, pushing aside men who might want to push back. He would certainly make a comical figure in a fistfight. Everyone in town would find it entertaining.

Winn heard the splash of coffee being poured and felt its warmth as the saucer was moved next to his fingers.

A moment later he heard the clang of the pot being returned to the stove, and Cynthie's voice came nearer as she spoke. "You must get rather bored here."

Winn took a careful sip of the hot coffee. It all seemed very strange. Here he was, trying to drink coffee in the dark with a woman he didn't know, trying to keep a handle on his life, which seemed to be slipping out of his grasp. What did she want him to say? Yes, I'd love to go to town and make a fool of myself. No, I'd rather stay here and make a fool of myself in private.

He set the cup back on the table. He didn't dare move his hand away from it; he might knock it over reaching for it again. He ran his other hand through his hair and instantly regretted the nervous gesture.

"There's a barber in town."

"What?" Winn was startled. Her tone had changed from conversational to nearly excited.

"I said there's a barber in town. Your beard showed care when you came here. Wouldn't you like to have someone trim it?"

"You're pleased with yourself for thinking of that, aren't you?" He hadn't meant to say it aloud, but the change in her voice had been remarkable. To his surprise, she laughed.

"You listen better than I realize. Yes, I am pleased, or I will be if you agree to go."

"I may be getting a little shaggy, at that," he said. He had been thinking the same thing that morning. He automatically felt his face and realized he had let go of the coffee cup.

As he began a search for it, he found his hand captured between Cynthie's soft palms. "I know it will be hard for you, but you have to keep trying. It would be too easy to hide here. Can't you see that?"

Winn wanted to tell her that he didn't *see* anything. That was the problem. How could she possibly know how hard it would be for him?

He was saved from making any sort of reply by Greg, who burst through the front door and sprinted into the kitchen. Winn found the soft hands replaced quickly by the china cup.

"There's a rider comin'," the child announced. "What's there to eat?"

"You ate enough at the church picnic to last most people a week," he mother said. "Besides, I'm all out of sweets."

Greg had quickly climbed onto Winn's lap. It looked like a well-practiced routine. "Then I'll drink Winn's coffee." He giggled.

Winn kept a firm grip on the cup. "Little boys don't drink coffee."

"Cowboys do." He hooked a small finger in the cup's handle, unaware of the danger of spilling the hot liquid.

Winn had both hands around the cup in anticipation of the child's action. "It'll keep you awake, and you only grow while you sleep."

Greg let go and looked up at his friend. "Really?"

"Sure," Winn answered. He used his left arm to pull the boy against him. "When you get as big as you want to get, then you can start drinking coffee."

Cynthie watched the exchange with a mixture of pleasure and jealousy. She wasn't often witness to their conversations and she was glad to see them so at ease with one another. It was a clear contrast to her own conversations with Winn. She left the room with the certainty that she wouldn't be missed and went to the porch to wait for the visitor.

Chapter Five

"Who's here?" Winn whispered in Greg's ear.

The boy on his lap shrugged and whispered back, "Let's go see."

They stepped out onto the porch as the hoofbeats ceased and, with a creak of leather, the rider dismounted. Gravel crunched as the visitor came forward. Winn could feel Cynthie standing near him on the porch. She had not gone to meet the visitor.

"Afternoon, ma'am." The voice was familiar. It was the neighbor who had given them the ride out from town the day Winn had been brought to the ranch.

"Afternoon, Mr. Ott," he heard Cynthie say. Yes. Reuben Ott. He remembered now.

"Good to see you, Mr. Sutton. You're looking better."

Winn smiled warmly, hoping his friendliness would irritate Cynthie. He remembered quite clearly her obvious dislike for Mr. Ott. "I'm feeling better, too, thanks to Mrs. Franklin's care." He took a careful step forward and stretched his hand toward the voice, forgetting about the bandage.

Ott came quickly up the porch steps. His firm handshake made Winn's hand sting, but it was easily ignored.

"How can I help you, Mr. Ott?" Cynthie's voice was cold and formal.

Ott took a step backward, putting himself, Winn was sure, dangerously close to the steps. "I brought that payment, ma'am." Winn heard the whisper of paper going from hand to hand in front of him.

He was tempted to invite Ott in for coffee. There was a whole pot inside that had hardly been touched. He decided against it. He was opening himself up to considerable discomfort if he annoyed his hostess.

"I'll get the receipt." Cynthie went inside and closed the door. Mr. Ott wasn't even to be invited inside to wait.

Greg slipped his hand out of Winn's and sent the swing to squeaking. "You live near here, Mr. Ott?" Winn asked.

"Yeah, I'm about Mrs. Franklin's closest neighbor except maybe for Kyle Dempsey. You know him?"

Winn shook his head. "He was here one day but I didn't meet him."

Greg piped up, "I don't like him."

Winn was startled but Ott only laughed. "He doesn't know how to buy a boy's affection." Suddenly the swing was silent.

Winn laughed. "What did you get?"

"Cherry ball," Greg said, taking the candy from his mouth to show it to Winn before he remembered that he couldn't see it.

"I don't think Mrs. Franklin likes me to do it, but I try to bring the boy something when I come. Don't want him thinking his neighbors don't care about him."

Winn wondered what there was between Ott and Cynthie. He reminded himself that he didn't want to know any more about her affairs than he had to.

Ott didn't let the silence last. "Don't suppose you know how long you'll be staying here."

Winn shook his head. He hadn't thought he would be here this long.

"It's a good thing you had a cousin here so close when you had the accident."

Winn was momentarily startled. Cousin must have been Cynthie's story. "I've thought of that myself," he said. Ott was obviously curious about his blindness and Winn wondered how far he'd go with his questions. His conversation, however, took a different turn.

"Might consider staying. It's a nice place to settle, the area, I mean. To hear some of those fellas in town talk, Wichita's going to be a regular city some day. They're trying to get a railroad and everything. There's always something going on in Wichita."

"So I hear."

"Yeah," Ott continued. "I'm glad to light here. I tended other folks' cattle for a lot of years. It's good to be working for myself for a change."

When Winn didn't respond, Ott continued, "I'm not saying it's been easy. I saved all my life and it still took me two years to scrape money together to finally get the place free and clear. Life never is easy, though. Well, you know that as well as anybody, I'd imagine. There are always problems, even if you've got money. Like Mrs. Franklin here. Awful thing, losing her husband like that last summer."

Winn could only nod in agreement. A cousin would already know the answers to all the questions he wanted to ask. He decided it was just as well. Learning about other people's problems tended to make a person part of them, and he had problems enough of his own.

Ott, however, didn't need much encouragement to keep talking. "Seems to me it would set easier with a young widow if she at least knew who killed her husband." Winn hoped he didn't look surprised. "Awful thing," Ott repeated.

Cynthie returned to the porch, preventing him from hearing any more intriguing information. "I believe this is all you need, Mr. Ott."

Winn heard the rustle of papers as the man examined them and then tucked them away in a pocket. "Yes, ma'am," he said. "It's been a pleasure doing business with you. Don't be a stranger, Sutton." He clapped Winn on the shoulder and ruffled Greg's hair before leaving the porch.

"'Bye," called Greg around the shrinking candy.

When the sound of hoofbeats turned from a walk into an easy canter Cynthie let out a slow sigh of relief.

"If Mama's your cousin, am I your cousin, too?" Greg slipped a sticky hand into Winn's.

Winn heard Cynthie's tiny gasp and grinned. "That's what I've been led to understand."

"Goody!" yelled the boy. He jumped down the steps and headed toward the barn, eager to spread the news to Louie and Peter.

"Lies can get you into trouble," he said softly.

"What was I supposed to tell people?" she snapped. Her mind was still on Ott and the things that she had heard about him. She could not be around that man without feeling angry.

"Am I hard on your reputation?" He might have meant to tease but he wasn't smiling.

Cynthie watched him for a moment before deciding not to answer. Ott always upset her. Winn was angry with her about the proposed trip to town. It wasn't a good time to talk. She turned to go inside but he seemed to anticipate her move and stepped toward the door. She tried to brush past him but he caught her shoulders.

"Why am I here?" he demanded.

His voice was low, his body only inches from hers. He was too close for her to think straight. She wanted to demand that he let her go, but his hands were so gentle she should have been able to slip away easily. She didn't try.

"You needed help," she said finally. She could barely hear her own voice above the pounding in her ears.

"But why here? Why you? And don't tell me I'm your cousin." In frustration, he wanted to shake her.

He didn't know why he had waited this long to ask or why it was suddenly so important to know. The narrow shoulders under his hands didn't fit his picture of a coldhearted prison guard. The fresh smell of her hair brought a sudden memory of her soft body in his arms and he could almost feel the clap of thunder. He let his hands drop to his sides.

"Sit down, Mr. Sutton," she said softly.

Her sympathetic tone took him by surprise. "Sit down?"

She led him to the porch swing, her hands feeling warm against skin that had turned suddenly cold. She leaned against the rail in front of him. "I don't want you to read anything into this," she began.

"Read anything into what?" He laughed but it was a nervous laugh. "Just tell me why I'm here."

Cynthie took a deep breath. "When your friends brought you into Wichita, Dr. Gordon sent for me."

Winn nodded. He knew that already. "Why?"

"My father was blind."

It took a second for the statement to register but when it did the full implications hit him like a blow. She was supposed to be his teacher. They never expected him to see again!

Cynthie watched the blood drain from his face. He slowly shook his head. "He lied to me."

She quickly moved to the swing beside him. "I know what you're thinking. That's why I didn't tell you before, but—"

He didn't let her finish. "*You* lied to me."

"No! Please listen." She put her hands on top of his. He didn't even feel them.

"You're supposed to teach me how to be blind. What did you think? By the time you told me I'd never see again, I wouldn't care?" His voice was deceptively quiet, but Cynthie could feel the tension in the big hands under hers.

"Winn, listen."

"No, I think I'd rather believe we're cousins."

"Dr. Gordon wouldn't lie to us. He just thought I'd be more understanding because I've had some experience."

Winn turned his face toward her, as if he needed to see if she was telling the truth. Those pale blue eyes tore at her heart. Her hand was halfway to his face before she caught herself.

Winn took a deep breath and let it out slowly. "I always thought I was a patient man, and I've had to accept some changes before. But this..." He shook his head.

Leaning closer, Cynthie squeezed his hand. "Then don't accept it yet. Just realize it's a possibility. I've written to a doctor in New York, and Dr. Gordon said..."

"I know what he said."

Cynthie felt tears form in her eyes. She hoped they wouldn't make her voice shake. She swallowed hard before she spoke. "Do you have family somewhere? I can write them for you."

Winn thought about it a moment. The letters he got from his sister were always reassuring, but he knew it had to be a struggle for the family to survive on what was left of the home place. If Cora knew about this, she would want him to come home. She might even try to come and get him. "No," he said finally. "There's no one."

Cynthie noticed it had taken him some time to answer. She decided to let it go for now. She gave his hand a pat as she came to her feet. "Shall we go finish our coffee?" she asked, trying for a cheerful tone.

"No, thanks," he said. "I think I'll just stay out here a while."

At the door she turned toward him again. "It's too early to give up hope," she said.

Cynthie carried her boots out of the bedroom and padded down the stairs in her stocking feet. It was still early but she couldn't sleep. She was hoping a morning ride would clear her head enough that she could tackle the books again before they left for town.

Maybe she was wrong to insist that Winn come with them to town. He had been quiet yesterday, and it made her worry. But then, he was usually quiet. He never gave her much sign of what he felt. The trip to town would give him something to do, and something to think about. Mostly, she hoped, it would give him more confidence.

She closed the stairway door behind her and started across the front room. She stopped suddenly when she saw the silhouette of a man on the porch. She recognized Winn and didn't even glance toward the bedroom to confirm it. She stopped long enough to pull on her boots before she joined him outside.

Winn was leaning against the porch post when he heard the door open behind him. He had heard tiny sounds from inside the house already, sounds of doors and floorboards that told him someone was up. He didn't turn to greet her. He couldn't have seen her anyway.

"You're up early," she said softly.

"If you say so," he answered.

She stepped up beside him. "The sun is just barely turning the horizon gray. Everything's still in shadows."

Winn didn't answer. He was used to getting up before dawn, but sometimes now he had trouble knowing what time it was. He hated relying on the damned clock chimes.

"I was going for a ride. Do you want to come?"

The suggestion took him by surprise, and he couldn't stop the humorless laugh that escaped from his chest.

"No, I'm serious," she added almost urgently. "My father used to ride."

Winn pictured himself on a tired old nag being led around a corral. "No, thanks," he said.

Cynthie decided not to push. He might not be ready to ride yet. She wished she knew the circumstances of the accident. That could help her know how to proceed. For now, she would let it go. "The horizon will be streaked with color soon," she said softly. "Would you like me to describe it?"

"No, thanks," he repeated, a little more firmly.

"It might help you picture it."

He wanted to shout at her, "I don't want to picture it. I don't want to hear you describe it. I don't want to think that that's the only way I'll ever see a sunrise again!" Instead he took a deep breath and let it out slowly. "Go on and enjoy your ride," he said softly. "I'll enjoy the morning in my own way."

Off to their right, the shells clattered in the breeze. A bird called and was answered. Cynthie stood so close, he could feel her heavy riding skirt brush against his leg. "All right," she said finally. He felt her hand touch his shoulder and heard her feet tap down the steps and crunch across the gravel.

He heard the hinges squeak as the barn door was opened. He stood listening for several minutes, wondering if the sky had colored and if there were clouds catching the first rays of light. He heard Cynthie ride out of the yard and wondered if she appreciated the freedom she enjoyed.

The shells, the birds, the whinny of a horse were all peaceful sounds but he didn't feel a part of them. Each new sound, the buzz of an insect, the slam of the bunkhouse door, made him feel more alone, more separate—even from the morning. He felt the sting of tears and brushed them away quickly. It seemed his eyes had found another way to betray him.

Winn stood at the river, Greg's hand clasped firmly in his own, and listened to the harness chain rattle and clink as the team was unhitched. Peter had been appointed to drive them into town, and he talked softly to the horses as he led them onto the ferry.

Cynthie stood nearby. He could hear the wind rustle her skirts. His feelings toward her were more confused than ever. He had entertained some rather morbid ideas about why he was staying with her. He had thought that perhaps she was so ugly the only man she could ever catch would have to be a blind man. He had even pictured himself as her prisoner. Somehow the truth was more chilling.

Her father had been blind. How could he have been anything more than a beggar? Had Cynthie married Franklin for his money then, as a way to look after her father? His head was full of questions about this other blind man. Questions that he was afraid to ask.

"I don't like the ferry," a small voice whimpered. Winn realized that Greg's grip had become unusually tight.

"I don't like them much myself," Winn said, going down on one knee.

Cynthie had bent down beside the boy, as well. Winn felt her skirt brush his leg and smelled her lilac perfume on the breeze. He wished he knew what she looked like, what thoughts he might read on her face.

"I don't like the ferry," Greg repeated, dropping Winn's hand in favor of his mother. "I wanted to be brave for Winn." The shy little confession was muffled, Winn guessed, against his mother's shoulder.

"Winn understands," Cynthie said.

Winn had been listening with divided attention to the voices of the ferryman and Peter calling to one another as they rolled the wagon onto the ferry. He realized that it was almost time to board.

"Believe me, Greg, I understand." Winn was still on one knee. Cynthie and her son were so close to him that he could hear their clothing brush together and the child's muffled breathing.

"Carry me." The plea was meant for his mother's ears alone.

"You're just too heavy, baby. Here, I'll hold your hand." When she tried to pry him loose, he turned quickly toward Winn and locked his trembling arms around the big man's neck.

The child was obviously terrified. Winn didn't hesitate. "Make sure I don't stumble," he said, coming to his feet. It was strange how Cynthie's light touch on his arm had such a steadying effect. She led him onto the ferry, where he stood with his feet braced apart. Greg's face was buried in Winn's neck and Cynthie's hand stayed reassuringly on Winn's arm.

"Has he always been this frightened of water?" Winn asked. The ferry gave an initial lurch and Cynthie's grip tightened.

"Not water," Cynthie said softly. "Just the ferry. And no, he hasn't always been afraid. It just started about a year ago."

"I'm not afraid," Greg protested in a voice choked with tears. "I just don't like them!"

Winn rubbed the tiny back. "All right, about a year ago you got big enough to have some sense."

"Yeah." Greg didn't raise his head but Winn noticed he had stopped shaking.

Cynthie, at Winn's side, seemed to move and sway easily with the ferry. Winn, however, felt like he would fall at any moment. With no horizon to watch, he didn't know how to compensate for the ferry's movement and he experienced some vertigo. If this ride lasted long enough, he'd be seasick.

Only Cynthie's hand let him keep his equilibrium. Though she pulled away or leaned toward him as the ferry rocked, she was always touching him, always stabilizing him.

Finally her hand tightened and she warned him that the ferry was about to touch the landing on the town side of the river. After she had helped him regain his balance, threatened by the sudden stop, she led him off the ferry. Peter was there at his other arm to help him onto solid ground. He listened to the young man's steps as he walked back onto the ferry to lead the horses off.

Greg allowed himself to be lowered to the ground and ran to join Peter. Now that the ferry had docked, it no longer frightened him, and he let Peter swing him onto the wagon for the ride.

Cynthie watched this activity, perplexed. How could he be terrified of the ferry just a moment ago and not at all concerned now? And he used to like the ferry. "Thanks for your help, Mr. Sutton. Sometimes that boy's a riddle."

Greg's fear didn't seem inappropriate to Winn. He hated boats himself, and Greg was only a child. But it wasn't his place to interfere so he kept quiet.

A short time later they were in the wagon again, moving down the rutted streets toward the center of town. Winn was in the back. Greg was sometimes on his lap and sometimes at the other side of the wagon exclaiming over some sight or other.

The sounds around the wagon seemed too numerous and varied for Winn to sort out so he concentrated instead on Greg. From the child he learned that there were hunters, Indians and ladies in town as well as a gentleman with a tall hat who seemed to be dressed in a much more peculiar manner than anyone else.

"Are we going to the store?" Greg asked his mother.

"Peter's going to the store. I'm going to the bank, and you're going to take Mr. Sutton to the barbershop."

"I want to go to the store," Greg said cheerfully. "I don't like the barbershop."

Winn had caught the child on his lap for the moment. If he didn't like the barbershop the same way he didn't like the ferry, Winn hoped they could revise the plan. "How would it be if you and Peter get me to the barbershop then you can go to the store together?"

"You won't get lonely?" Greg asked with real concern.

"I'll be fine, son. What are you going to do at the store?"

Greg leaned close and whispered loudly, "I'm gonna pick out some candy."

"Now I see why you don't like barbershops," Winn teased.

"Naw. Barbershops are itchy."

That particular description came back to Winn later as he sat in the shop waiting for his turn. Besides the barber and the man getting a haircut, there seemed to be two others in the shop. Winn guessed that they were just there to visit, because the barber had told Peter that Winn would be next. "You can expect him to be done in about half an hour," the barber had said.

Winn had introduced himself when he came in but since the others had not, their identities remained a mystery. All conversation had stopped when the boys had led him in. While it had resumed fairly quickly afterward, Winn was sure it was quieter than when Greg had first opened the door. He decided the atmosphere was definitely itchy.

The two men in the corner were discussing the railroad in quiet generalities. The smell of cigar smoke drifted from that direction. The barber and his customer were speaking in more confidential tones. Winn was paying little attention to either conversation until he heard the barber say, "...blind man." It seemed to hang in the air as the other conversation died away.

The customer in the chair didn't seem to notice the quiet. "Wasn't that the Frank—"

"Say, Phillips," interrupted one of the men from the corner. "What do you think about this railroad?"

If the barber minded having the topic of discussion changed, he didn't show it. He began to expound at length on the benefits of the railroad. The man in the chair tried to interrupt with his objections but had little success. Finally Phillips ended with, "What's good for the town will be good for us all."

He must have finished the haircut the same time he finished the speech. Winn heard the snap of a cloth being shaken and the creak of the chair as the customer rose. "I hope all that new business will bring in another barber," he grumbled. "Then you might have to lower your prices." The man sounded serious to Winn, but everyone else laughed.

As the customer left, the barber came toward Winn, his footsteps drowned out by the sound of the door.

He leaned toward Winn and nearly shouted, "Ready for you now."

Winn was sure he jumped six inches. One of the men in the corner said, "He's blind, not deaf, Phillips." The other man laughed.

Phillips mumbled an apology as he led Winn to the chair and awkwardly helped him into it. "In fact," said the man who had laughed, "I hear it works the other way." He walked across the room, his spurs jingling almost like bells as they hit the floor. He brought the smell of cigar smoke with him. "I've heard that if you lose your sight your hearing gets better."

"I haven't noticed that it has," Winn said. He wished the two men would leave. The foolish barber hovering over him was bad enough without an audience besides.

"Well, Phillips here probably undid all that just now, yellin' in the fella's ear." This came with a laugh from the man in the corner.

"That's enough now, Bert. I didn't yell, I just startled him. Why don't you go hang around somewheres else?"

"Well, I was goin' to get my hair cut," said Bert, stomping across the room, "but it'll likely all turn gray afore you get round to me."

An uncomfortable silence followed the slam of the door. Phillips filled it as quickly as he could by asking Winn what he could do for him. Winn asked for a trim and, since he normally cut his own beard, he tried to tell the barber what he was used to doing. He realized that he probably sounded very fussy to the other two men.

As Phillips began to cut, Winn listened to the man with the cigar. He was still standing. He could hear his spurs as he moved around some. Spanish spurs, probably, with large rowels. The man stayed near the door and Winn guessed there was a window there. Perhaps the man was also waiting for a haircut and was as angry at losing his turn as the one who had left. He might be watching for someone; perhaps he had a limited amount of time to spend here.

Winn hated getting special treatment. In the army some of his fellow officers had expected it, even demanded it. It had always embarrassed Winn. For an officer during a war, however, it was sometimes necessary. This was not. He felt like he should apologize to the man who was waiting, but he hadn't asked for it, and an apology would embarrass the barber even more.

The barber, who had talked so freely to the last customer, was quiet now. He cleared his throat occasionally as if he wanted to say something but he never spoke beyond instructions to turn this way or that. Once he told Winn to look up. He cleared his throat twice after that.

Finally he was satisfied and removed the cloth from Winn's shoulders. He lifted something from the counter and, clearing his throat, set it down again. Winn thought he heard a ghost of a chuckle from the cigar smoker.

Winn paid with a coin and was pocketing the change when the door opened. "It's your young friend," the barber said, as if he was talking to a two-year-old.

"He'll help you now." Winn mumbled his thanks and followed Peter out of the shop.

As the door closed behind them, Phillips sighed with relief. "I'm sure sorry to keep you waiting, Mr. Dempsey, but I just didn't know what to do, that boy leading him around and coming back for him and all."

"No problem," Kyle said. He let the curtain drop across the window and stepped toward the chair. "If you hadn't done it, I would have." He was glad to get Sutton out of that shop as soon as possible. He didn't want anyone else to know that Cynthie had a man living in her house. Even if he had gotten his own haircut first, he would have hung around the shop until Sutton was gone. He would never have left the men alone to talk about whatever they chose.

He looked at his reflection in the large mirror over Phillips's counter. His dark blond hair barely showed a need for a trim but that was the way he liked to keep it. He gave Phillips's reflection a smile and eased into the chair.

From the window he had seen Cynthie and the child waiting at the wagon. The Merlin boy would probably get them out of town soon. Maybe a casual observer would think that the stranger was another hired hand. Kyle didn't really believe it, but anything was better than having the drifter's living arrangements openly discussed in the barbershop. He still couldn't believe Cynthie would be so foolish.

He felt lucky to have been here when that old man recognized Cynthie's son. It was also lucky he knew of Phillips's proclivity toward expounding on the railroad. Yes, he had defused this situation pretty well.

He'd have to ride out to the ranch and convince Cynthie that the man was well enough to move on. There was no doubt that Sutton was the reason his last visit with Cynthie had been so short. She was overworked and trying to do something she wasn't qualified to do. Two more reasons for the man to leave.

Kyle relaxed in the barber chair and closed his eyes. He was confident he could convince Cynthie to see things his way.

Chapter Six

From the wagon seat Cynthie watched Peter cross the street to the barbershop. Greg was behind her, trying to move the purchases around to make room for Winn. He had refused to go to the barbershop with Peter but wouldn't say why. Now he chattered about the lunch they would eat on the way home and how Winn would like the candy he had picked out for him. He announced proudly that he had gotten extra candy because Mr. Ott had been in the store. Cynthie wondered how Mr. Ott ever got his work done when it seemed he was always in town.

She looked across the street, and all her irritation at Ott was forgotten. Peter was leading Winn out of the shop and onto the boardwalk. Peter seemed so young to Cynthie, but he walked with an air of confidence, unembarrassed by the big man's hand on his shoulder. He said something and they stopped for a moment to let a wagon pass before starting across the street.

Peter had chosen his path carefully to avoid the worst ruts in the street, but even so, Cynthie realized, it was a dangerous place for Winn. He was nearly across the street before she stopped worrying that he might fall and began really looking at him. He walked behind Peter and a little to the right but stood a good head taller than the youth. He had left his hat in the wagon and the sun warmed his face, bringing color to his pale cheeks. The wind tousled his shortened curls and blew a lock across his forehead. He walked with his head up, trusting Peter's lead—or at least appearing to.

Peter brought him to the wagon and went to see about the horses. Greg greeted his friend by leaning over the sideboard and throwing his arms around his neck. Winn hugged back, bracing himself against the wagon. Cynthie watched from her seat above them and tried to read the emotions on Winn's face.

He looked tired and strained. Evidently he hadn't had an easy time of it. He hugged Greg with such a fierceness that she could almost believe he was getting back from Greg some of the comfort he had given on the ferry ride. Surely a trip to the barbershop couldn't have been that bad.

As Winn loosened his hold on the small boy, the tension eased. Greg pulled away and held the bearded face in his hands. Standing in the wagon put Greg at about eye level with Winn. "Did you like getting your hair cut?"

Winn grinned at the boy's question. "It was pretty itchy," he said.

Cynthie experienced a pang of jealousy. They each sought help from the other, and they left her out completely. She was being unreasonable, she thought. Greg didn't leave her out, and she wasn't jealous of their relationship.

But if she was going to be honest with herself, she had to admit she was indeed feeling jealousy of a sort.

She sat there and watched Winn wrap his arms around Greg, knowing how good it always felt to hold the small warm body against her own. But what she wanted was to be in Greg's place. She could feel her cheeks growing warm at the thought and comforted herself with the knowledge that Winn, at least, couldn't see them.

She wondered if she had made some small noise because Winn chose that moment to turn toward her. He was still smiling, his dimples easily visible beneath the newly trimmed beard. She watched the wind dance in his hair, his locks highlighted by the sun's kiss.

"Am I more presentable, ma'am?"

Cynthie swallowed hard. How could she answer that question without letting him hear a tremor in her voice? "Hmm," she said, pretending to think it over.

The dimples deepened. "Now remember, it was your idea."

She realized with a feeling of wonder how easily she could fall in love with him. She couldn't watch him with her son and not be fond of him. She was certain that he was more of a friend to the boy than Victor would ever have been.

But also, she couldn't be near him and not feel a strong physical attraction. Although she knew from experience that those feelings only led to disappointment, it didn't seem to help. At some point, she had stopped reminding herself that such thoughts were inappropriate.

He was still facing her, more serious now, waiting for an answer. Very softly she said, "You look wonderful, Winn."

If he was startled, he covered it well. "Thank you, ma'am," he said, grinning at her.

"Ready," Peter said, startling them both. Winn turned toward the back of the wagon and Cynthie turned toward the front. She tried to pull herself together. How could she let the man do this to her? She glanced behind her. How could she not?

She hardly noticed when Peter climbed aboard and started the wagon moving toward the ferry. She was lost in thought when a wheel hit a particularly large rut and sent her rocking into Peter. "Whee," yelled Greg from the back. She heard Winn's answering chuckle and felt herself growing warm again.

The ferry was ready when they arrived and Peter began unhitching the horses as soon as he had helped Cynthie down. She walked to the back of the wagon where Winn and Greg were climbing out.

"Winn says he'll hold me again," Greg announced. He didn't seem at all frightened.

"Perhaps you should sit on the wagon as we cross," Cynthie suggested. "You won't have to worry about falling, that way."

"That's a good idea, ma'am," Winn answered. It probably was, from her point of view. He would be holding her baby, after all. But he hated boats and he hated wagons on boats even more. He decided he didn't want to tell her that.

Greg had found something to look at. Winn listened to him humming a short distance away. As Peter and the ferryman began pushing the wagon onto the ferry, Greg moved closer to Winn. By the time all was ready for them to come aboard, the little boy was once again clinging to Winn's hand.

"Come on, son." Winn lifted the boy into his arms. He didn't seem quite as frightened this time. Perhaps knowing ahead of time how he was going to handle the ride made the difference.

Cynthie took his arm and led him onto the ferry and to the wagon. He sat down at the back and Greg straddled his lap, the little arms securely wrapped around his neck. Cynthie made sure they were comfortable and moved away.

Winn took a deep breath as the ferry lurched away from the bank. This was safer than standing, he told himself. He didn't have to worry about falling. No, all he had to worry about was the wagon rolling off the ferry and into the river! He tried to brush the thought away. Sitting down, he didn't experience the dizzy feeling he had felt before. The rocking was more gentle this way.

He didn't care that it was more comfortable or even that it was safer. The question was not the strength of the wagon as opposed to the strength of his knees. The difference between this trip and the last was Cynthie. He had been worried enough on the first crossing to overlook the fact that he actually enjoyed her touch on his arm.

Cynthie, with the flower-scented hair and narrow shoulders, had made him feel safe. Cynthie, with the cool manners and warm voice, had even called him by his given name....

Louie was inspecting the corral fence when he heard the wagon coming. It was nothing urgent, but the fence could use some attention. He hated to see anything fall into disrepair, and Mrs. Franklin deserved to have the place looking nice.

He left the fence to meet the wagon. "Betts and Emery got back from Abilene," he said, offering Cynthie a hand.

"Good," she said and wondered why she didn't feel like it was good. She had to keep her mind on business. "Send Betts up to see me in a few minutes." She started toward the house.

Winn, walking a few steps behind her, gave words to her thoughts. "My friends should be returning, as well."

She stopped and turned to let him catch up with her. He was walking slowly, aware of the small strides of the child beside him. Greg wore a somber expression as if he realized that something serious had happened even if he didn't know what it was. She looked at the little hand held securely in the big one and wondered what Greg would feel if Winn left. No, *when* he left. They had never meant for it to be any other way.

"What will you do?" she asked when Greg stopped him near her.

"I don't know. I had a job on the Double M, a year-round job, not just roundup help. I might be able to go back there and stay until my sight returns. I just don't know." He paused for a moment, shifting his weight to the other foot. "I should have written them sooner, I suppose, but I thought I'd see by now."

The little boy looked from his friend to his mother. "He'll stay here with us, won't he, Mama?"

Cynthie wasn't sure how to answer him. Finally she said, "Winn will have to decide what is best."

"But he's our cousin," the child insisted. "This is his home."

Winn went down on one knee and let Greg climb onto the other. "Sometimes cousins aren't exactly close relatives, and this isn't really my home. Your mama took me in to look after me. Don't you remember how sick I was when I first came?''

Greg looked seriously into the big man's face. "Will you see sooner if you go away?"

It was a question only a child would ask, but it made Winn realize something. He would be no more use at the Double M than he was here. At least here he knew his way around and had Greg to help him. He would only be in the way back in Texas, and possibly not even welcome. But he didn't belong here, either.

The child waited patiently for an answer. "No, Greg, I won't," he said softly. "But I may have to go anyway." He wondered why he had added the qualifier, to make it easier on the boy, perhaps?

Cynthie watched the exchange with a growing sense of alarm. *Talk him out of it!* her mind screamed. *Find an acceptable reason for him to stay!*

She knelt beside the two of them and watched Greg's face pucker up to cry. "Greg," she whispered softly.

The boy jumped from Winn's knee and made a mad dash for the barn. Winn lost his balance for a second and Cynthie's hand was there to catch him. They both came slowly to their feet. She kept her hand on his arm a moment longer than was necessary.

"I'm sorry, ma'am. I never meant to hurt the boy. I shouldn't have spent so much time with him, I guess."

"Don't be silly, Mr. Sutton. You can't avoid friendship because you know it may have to end someday." She wondered if that applied to love, as well. They were talking about Greg, she reminded herself. "You've been very good for him."

Winn nodded. So he was Mr. Sutton again. Well, apparently she wouldn't be sorry to see him go, and he shouldn't be sorry to leave her, either. Except the thought of never again hearing her voice or smelling her lilac-scented hair seemed somehow unthinkable. As unthinkable as never seeing again.

"You'll excuse me," she said. "I have to talk to Mr. Betts." She turned quickly and walked away from him.

Winn stood for a few minutes thinking about his situation. Until now, he had thought of his friends' arrival as his salvation. They would take him home and things would be normal again. But he hadn't counted on still being blind when they came for him. And he hadn't counted on attachments here.

What if he did decide to go with them? What if they planned to take care of him? Did he really want that? And how would he travel? He hadn't even tried to ride yet. He was definitely not ready for Lullaby. He might never be.

He wasn't going to decide anything now. He'd talk it over with Slim and Mike when they got here. Mike would have a suggestion. He'd been around and was probably already giving it some thought.

He took a step forward and realized that he didn't know exactly where he was. He tried to remember what Cynthie's footsteps had sounded like. Which way had she gone? It seemed like it was straight away in the direction he was facing. He took a couple of tentative steps and heard a familiar tinkling. The shells!

He took small steps toward the sound, trying to remember the angle the sound came from when he was at the bottom of the steps. A couple more steps and he reached out for the handrail. It took some groping, but he found it slightly to the right of where he had expected it to be.

His left hand on the rail, he felt with his toe for the step, but it wasn't there. He was sure this was the handrail. He felt again. The step was not there.

He stood still, his hand on the rail, and listened to the shells. He tried to picture the house according to what he knew of it. The porch had a swing at one side, then the door, with the steps in front of it at the center. The shells hung on the far end, on the swing side. The steps came down, three steps, with a handrail on either side.

Winn wanted to laugh. There were two handrails! He had almost missed the steps after all. He moved to his left, putting his right hand on the rail, and walked easily up the stairs. He felt very good about this accomplishment. His sense of direction and distance from the shells had proven to be reliable.

He went inside and crossed to the door of the room he had been using. He paused for a moment, listening for Cynthie's presence in the house. He heard a rustle of paper near the door to the kitchen. Cynthie must be working there. He waited a moment, but she didn't speak. He went quietly into the bedroom, closing the door behind him so gently it didn't quite latch.

Cynthie was sitting at her desk when she heard Winn come in. She watched him cross the room and pause at his door. She wanted to say something, at least to greet him, but she was afraid to speak. If she said anything at all she might start begging him to stay. In a moment he went inside and she breathed a shaky sigh.

It seemed like everything conspired against her when it came to making sense of Victor's books. It was hard enough to concentrate under normal conditions, but when her mind was in such a turmoil it was impossible. The best she could hope to do today was find the right page and record the sale when Betts arrived.

She didn't have long to wait. A few minutes after Winn came in, Jeremiah Betts tapped on the front door. "I got the sales money, Mrs. Franklin," he said when Cynthie opened the door. "Mr. Louie said I was to come up here." He held a thick envelope out to her.

"Yes, of course," Cynthie said, opening the door wider. "Please come inside."

Jeremiah hesitated a moment. He wasn't invited into white folks' homes much and, though he had worked for the Franklins since they started the ranch, he'd never been inside. Finally he removed his hat, exposing a head of graying nap, and followed Mrs. Franklin.

Cynthie took the envelope and, turning toward the desk, asked over her shoulder, "Did you have any trouble, Mr. Betts?"

"Mister" always sounded good when she said it. "No, ma'am, I didn't have trouble neither with the stock nor the men." He was proud to get to say it and hoped she understood what it meant to him.

Cynthie turned and smiled. "I'm glad," she said and he knew she was.

She started to lift the ledger and changed her mind. Instead, she brought a chair from the kitchen and set it down. Casually she motioned to it and took her own seat at the desk.

Jeremiah looked at the chair across the room and at the woman's back. Did she mean for him to sit there beside her?

"I need a little information," she said as if she hadn't noticed his hesitation. He quickly crossed the room and sat down, easing the chair a little farther away before sitting in it.

"First, Mr. Betts, did the cook we hired work out all right?"

"Pretty good, ma'am, but it is good to be home." He saw her smile and was glad he hadn't told her that the cook wouldn't take orders from him and he had had to put Emery in charge of telling him where to make camp.

Cynthie bent over the ledger. "Did you lose any cattle on the trail?"

One question was followed by another. As Jeremiah sat stiffly in the chair and answered them, several questions of his own were going through his mind. Was she trying to find something wrong with the way he had done the job? Was she really going to pay him a dollar and a quarter a day instead of a dollar like the rest of the drovers? If she didn't, was he going to argue or just put up with it? It seemed he had been putting up with things like that all his life. He kept reminding himself that she had always treated him fairly. It didn't completely eliminate his fears.

Finally Cynthie leaned back in the chair. "It sounds like you didn't have any trouble at all."

"Well, ma'am, none but a little with the buyer. He wasn't shore he should give the money to no Nigra, but Billy Emery and the others backed me up and he gave in."

"The buyer," Cynthie mumbled to herself. "I should have thought of that."

Jeremiah was sure she should have, too. She would realize now that she had made a mistake, and he'd never get this chance again. But being in charge one time had been so good. Maybe one time was enough.

"You did a fine job, Mr. Betts. You said you paid the others. Did you collect your own pay, as well?"

"Oh, no, ma'am." Jeremiah was shocked at the suggestion. As she opened the envelope, he couldn't help worrying that she would find less there than she expected and accuse him of stealing. He tried to think back on their conversation to see if he had made any mistakes or left anything out.

To his amazement, she began counting out his pay. And she did remember he was due an extra twenty-five cents a day. Only after his pile of bills had been placed in his hand did she begin to count the rest. She wrote the amount in her big book and put the bills back in the envelope.

"There's one more thing I'd like you to do for me today, Mr. Betts."

"Yes, ma'am," he responded quickly, looking at the pretty face and then averting his eyes out of old habit.

"Could you take this in to the bank for me?"

She seemed to wait for an answer. Could she possibly think he would say no? "I'll do whatever you say, ma'am."

She smiled again. "I'll write out instructions for the banker." She bent over the desk and Jeremiah was able to watch her again. "He will give you a receipt that says the amount. Be sure he gives it to you."

"Yes, ma'am."

"Good." Cynthie folded the note, put it in the envelope with the money and handed it to Jeremiah. "I wouldn't want that banker trying to cheat us."

Jeremiah was so amazed that he almost forgot to reach out and take the envelope. "You want me to go right now?" he asked coming to his feet because she was rising.

"Yes, I do. I know you should have the rest of the day off since you just got back, but it is important that this get to the bank."

"Yes, ma'am."

"Now remember, Mr. Betts," she said, taking his arm as she walked toward the door. "As soon as that money's in the bank, you have the rest of the day off."

A slow smile spread across the dark face. Cynthie opened the door and teased, "Say hello to Mary for me."

Jeremiah tried not to look too eager or surprised. "Yes, ma'am. I'll shore do that." He started to step outside and stopped for a moment. "I want to thank you for letting me do this, be the trail boss, I mean."

Cynthie smiled. "Louie recommended you and I didn't doubt for a moment that you could do it."

The grin grew wide again. He nodded his thanks and stepped out onto the porch. Louie sat waiting on the bottom step. He rose when he heard the door open behind him. Jeremiah grinned at him, as well, before placing his hat on his head and hurrying toward the corral.

Louie and Cynthie watched him go then looked at one another. "Must have gone all right," Louie suggested.

"I've sent him to town."

Louie chuckled. "Then things went all right." He walked slowly up the steps. "Can I talk to you?"

Cynthie stepped back to let him in. "New problem?" she asked.

"More like an old one." He came inside far enough to close the door. "Now that the boys are back, I'd like to have a better look around."

"What do you expect to find that you didn't find before?" She hadn't meant to sound so discouraged.

"Don't know. Nothin' maybe. But we were looking for cattle before and had new riders and all. I'd like to get out there and check for signs of old camps, fires and such. Maybe figure out how somebody made off with the cattle."

"We don't even know that that happened. I haven't..." She made a motion toward the ledgers on the desk. "Oh, what's the use! I can't make heads or tails of those books anyway."

"Ma'am, I don't know nothin' about what the books'll say, but I know what should have been out on that prairie and wasn't. I'll likely be gone two or three days."

He was no longer asking for permission. Cynthie hadn't wanted to stop him, anyway. "Good luck," she said.

"I'll leave early tomorrow and take Emery with me if you don't mind." He tipped his hat and let himself out.

Cynthie sighed. When was she going to admit that she couldn't run this ranch by herself? She should turn it all over to Louie's better judgment. He was convinced they had been robbed, and he was in a better position to know than she was.

Even Kyle agreed with that. Kyle, in fact, offered a suspect.

Her thoughts were interrupted by the creak of the door as Winn stepped into the front room. "I didn't mean to be eavesdropping, ma'am."

Cynthie was momentarily startled but shrugged. "It's a small house," she said.

"Ma'am?" He stepped forward. "Louie was talking about stolen cattle. I didn't realize that you were having any trouble. I'd like to help."

"I appreciate that, but I don't know what you can do," Cynthie said, returning to her desk.

"If you'd let me, I could go through the books. I mean I could help you understand them, maybe." He paused for a moment then went on in a hurry as if he were afraid she would answer before she understood. "I may be leaving soon, and I've got no way to repay you for looking after me unless you'll let me try to help."

The urgency in his voice was not lost on Cynthie. He was offering something that he wasn't at all sure he would be able to give. Cynthie felt a tug at her heart that she hesitated to identify. She knew she could no more deny him a chance to try than she could have denied Betts his chance as boss.

"I'm open to any suggestion," she said. She slapped the chair she had moved for Betts and watched him come toward it, nervous but smiling.

When he was seated safely in the chair, he leaned back and said, "Go back about three years and read me all the entries." He listened for the sound of pages turning. There was none. "Go ahead," he urged. "I'm good at this."

The tension in his body contradicted the confidence in his voice. Cynthie watched him for a moment then hastily flipped the pages to the beginning of the book. "Here. June, 1867. We had just moved out here."

She began reading the entries, numbers, prices, sellers and buyers. Winn interrupted occasionally to ask a question or interpret something. He could figure in his head and kept a running total of how many calves there should be and how many yearlings. In the end, he came to the same conclusion Louie had.

Cynthie tossed the pencil onto the ledger and sighed. "I guess I knew Louie was right. Even without adding up the numbers, he knew what he could expect. I was just hoping we'd discover that Victor had sold more than Louie realized."

"I guess I haven't been much help."

Cynthie smiled. "Why, because you came up with bad news?"

The humor in her voice surprised him. "No. I mean, I didn't really tell you anything you didn't already know."

"Well, the answer to our next question doesn't lie in these books. Do you think Louie will find anything?"

"That depends. It could be someone around here taking advantage of your husband's death and systematically taking a few head at a time. But it might be one outfit that came through, took them at once and is long gone. Did any of your neighbors lose cattle?"

"Not that I've heard about." Cynthie found herself having trouble keeping her mind on business.

Winn looked so earnest. She decided it was good for him to have something to think about.

"Your men check the herd, don't they?"

Cynthie smiled but tried to keep it out of her voice. "Louie takes care of all that." She realized that she was more interested in Winn than in what he had to say about her ranch.

Winn hated to think that Louie might be anything but trustworthy, so he didn't even suggest it. Another thought he didn't mention was that, while Mr. Franklin had kept good records, he hadn't made money. Even before the recent loss, he had needed to build up his herd but he hadn't made much effort to do that.

Cynthie watched Winn's face and wondered what was going on behind those sightless eyes. Was he really going to leave her soon? Would everything go back to the way it had been before he came? She knew it was too late for that. She had already fallen in love with him. The voice that should have scolded her for such thoughts was blissfully silent.

Chapter Seven

Cynthie smiled to herself and closed the book that contained the cattle records. "Since you're so good at this," she began, trying to sound worried, "maybe you could help me with these other ledgers." Setting the cattle records aside, she lifted two ledgers out of a drawer and opened the top one. She explained that it was the record of the loans her husband had made to small farmers in the area. She began with the first name. "I didn't even know he was doing this," she added.

It had sounded almost like an apology. "How long has there been a bank in Wichita?" he asked.

"It just opened this year."

"There, you see? Your husband was just filling a gap. There's nothing wrong with loaning money if you're honest."

Cynthie read on, grateful for the reassurance and grateful again when he commented that the interest charged had been fair. She wondered why she had thought it might be otherwise.

The entries were in order of transaction, loans to one individual followed by a payment by another. Suddenly she read a name and stopped. "Merlin," she repeated. "Willard Merlin?"

Winn felt as if he were doing a fairly good job of keeping track of each individual's payments and hoped that the distraction wouldn't make him lose it. "Who's Merlin?" he asked.

"Peter's father. Now why didn't Victor mention that? Even when Peter moved here, he never said a word."

She seemed to be talking more to herself than to Winn, so he didn't respond. He was thinking that it was especially curious in light of what Louie had said about the boy.

"Peter must own some land, then," she said.

"If it's homestead land, he'd have to be living on it."

Cynthie shook her head. "This is Osage Reserve. You have to buy it for two dollars an acre. Maybe they just squatted, but I doubt if they'd borrow money unless they owned the land."

Cynthie came out of her musings and shrugged. She read on until she came to the first foreclosure. "I remember them," she said. "They had a fire and then they just left. I guess Victor took their farm, but I doubt it was worth as much as he loaned them."

For a moment, Cynthie was rather pleased that her husband had tried to help the farmers until Winn said, "Except they had almost paid off the loan, with interest."

Cynthie looked at him a moment and read on. Winn continued to figure in his head. When she was done he offered no comment. Ott was the only one to pay off his loan, but the other six had come close, very close in some cases. The first farmer had been burned out. Peter's father had been shot. There was a pattern here Winn didn't like. He reminded himself that it was none of his business. Whatever had happened was over now, and Franklin was dead.

"I suppose I can close the book on these. Ott paid and the rest were settled before Victor died." Cynthie pushed the ledger into a drawer. "I would like to give Peter back his father's land when he's old enough."

Winn smiled. "That's easy enough to accomplish." He was forever having to revise his opinion of the woman. Maybe his first judgment of her had been based too much on her treatment of Reuben Ott.

She startled him by saying, "Funny how Ott's the only one that stayed." He had thought it was funny, too, but hadn't wanted to say so. Ott's had been the last loan and was only half repaid when Victor died. When Victor was murdered, he reminded himself.

Cynthie continued, "You know, he's the one Kyle thinks stole my cattle."

She saw Winn sit up straighter. "What does he base this on?"

Cynthie shrugged. "Who knows. Victor didn't trust Ott. He told me that. I guess I'm a little suspicious myself."

Winn made no comment. Cynthie watched him, trying to read something in his face, but he was too good at hiding what he was thinking. "Are you up to going through another ledger?"

"Another? What else was your husband up to?" The words left Winn's mouth before he could think. He hoped he hadn't sounded critical.

She didn't seem to take offense. "Well, this started out as my father's business. I guess Victor kept it going after he died."

Cynthie thought Winn looked more interested. When he said, "Sure, go ahead," she heard eagerness in his voice. She smiled to herself. She would enjoy the chance to talk to him about her father.

"A trading business," she clarified. "Father ran a shipping business back in New York. He left it in good hands and came out here with Victor and me. While Victor started the ranch, he started this business. I thought it had ended when he died, but I found this ledger and realized it had continued to operate."

She opened the last ledger and began to read. "You know, it's odd, but this book gives me the most trouble," she observed after a while. "I used to help with Father's books back home, but Victor kept these. He must have come up with his own code or something. I understand the purchases, payment to employees, most of the rest, but he threw in these letters once in a while. Do you know what they mean?"

Winn had wondered the same thing, but assumed she knew what they stood for. "If they aren't shipping terms, could they stand for people, drivers perhaps?"

"Maybe, but they aren't in capital letters." She flipped back to the first page and read only the initials.

Winn listened in amusement. She wasn't concerned about the business. It was over and he doubted if she had any thought of starting it again. She just didn't like a mystery. He paid less attention to the letters she read than to her voice, which he found himself liking more and more.

"Well," she concluded, "They aren't the drivers because there are no shipments labeled K or D for Kyle Dempsey and he drove a lot for Father, and for Victor, too, I'd guess."

Winn grinned, wanting her to continue speculating so he could listen to her voice while she mused aloud. It was soft and expressive and somehow less formal than what he usually heard. "Pick a letter and find out what is the same about all the entries that include it."

"Good idea!" She sounded so pleased he almost laughed. She was mumbling in earnest now and flipping pages. The enthusiasm tapered off quickly, however. "Only thing I can see is that all the entries with any letter made a better profit than the ones without a letter." She sounded disappointed.

Winn shrugged. "Maybe the letter was put there after the profit was figured and it was an indication to your husband of what was done right. Kind of a notice to do something again. If the profit was less there was no notation."

Cynthie looked at Winn as she closed the book. Suddenly she laughed. "I don't know what difference it makes now. I guess I just hate being left out. Is that silly?"

The dimples deepened under his beard. "I don't think it's silly." He wanted to say that her husband had been a fool for not telling her all his business deals. She could have been left with debts or commitments she didn't even known about. As it was, she had had a harder time taking over because she had to learn everything at once.

"Thank you for your help," she said softly. She tried to think of something to say to keep him here, talking to her, but she was out of books and out of excuses.

His face grew serious as she watched him. After a moment he asked cautiously, "Would you mind telling me a little about your father? Maybe you can understand why I'm curious."

"Of course!" she responded eagerly, then, afraid she would scare him off, she asked more quietly, "What would you like to know?"

Winn shrugged, feeling suddenly nervous. "I guess I want to know why he was blind. What he did before and after. I don't know."

Cynthie started slowly. "Father was about fifty when he started losing his sight. One eye began to get cloudy, then the other eye did the same. His doctor said it was cataracts."

Winn tried to imagine what it would be like, having the blindness come on slowly with no way to stop it. He wasn't sure whether it would be worse than sudden darkness or if there was some way to prepare for the inevitable. He didn't know how to put these thoughts into questions and decided Cynthie's father would be the only one who could have answered them anyway.

Cynthie was watching Winn's face as she talked. "Looking back, it seems like it all happened so fast, but he may not have told me about it until it had progressed. Anyway, by the time he couldn't see to write, he had hired a bookkeeper and later a foreman for the business. He said he was ready to retire anyway."

Winn listened uncomfortably. It was his own fault for asking. Had he thought she'd tell him everything had gone on as before? Had he hoped for some secret in this man's story that would make his own life easier? Was he still hoping for one? He realized that he wanted her to continue.

"I don't think he would have come west with us if he hadn't lost his sight. His company would have kept him back East, but since it was already being taken care of, he felt free to come. Father often told me he was glad he'd come so he could be with his grandson. Greg was just a baby when we left New York."

Winn smiled. "I imagine he kept your father busy."

"He has a tendency to do that to anyone near him." Suddenly Cynthie felt tears coming to her eyes. Winn was really going to leave them. How could she let him go before she had a chance to help him? Deep down she knew he had to help himself, and making his own decisions was a big part of that.

She knew, too, that helping him wasn't her only motivation. She wanted him to stay. She wanted him to fall in love with her. And worst of all, she didn't have the first idea of how to accomplish it.

She knew Winn was waiting for her to go on. There was so much more she wanted to tell him about her father. How he had taken care of himself, run the trading business, played checkers, and how she loved him and missed him. Tears were running down her face, and her voice would shake if she tried to talk. She had missed him terribly when he died, but it wasn't her father she was missing now.

"Excuse me," she said finally. "I better start supper."

She got up rather abruptly and went around Winn into the kitchen. Her hand trailed across his shoulder as she went by.

Winn sat for a moment listening to the busy sounds from the next room. She had given him a lot to think about this afternoon—disappearing cattle, loans that didn't quite get paid off and curious notations on shipment records. Mostly, though, he was thinking about the way she sounded when she mused aloud and the way she laughed at her own curiosity. In the end, he was sure he had made her cry. She had dug up painful memories for him, and when it hurt he had no comfort to offer her.

He rose and made his way across the room to the front door. He had nothing to offer her at all. She would be glad when Slim and Mike took him away. But he had nothing to offer anyone else, either.

The thought quickly faded as the sun touched the shoulder her hand had brushed a moment before. Even though he had caused her pain, she had responded with a gentle touch. She was, as he had already decided, unpredictable. Or maybe all this time

he had been misunderstanding her. Suddenly he
wanted very much to learn more about her. He wished
he would have the time.

He heard Greg call his name, a long call that vi-
brated with the beat of small running feet. In a moment the small body collided with Winn's legs, but he
was already braced for the impact.

"You got...to come...see Sorry," he said, trying
to catch his breath. "You haven't met her yet. She's
Peter's. She lives in the barn." As the child talked, he
was already leading Winn away. "Peter says she's
gonna have puppies. I think that will be great. Will
you want one of the puppies?"

Winn laughed at the boy's enthusiasm. Leaving was
going to be much more difficult than he had ever
imagined.

Greg didn't wait for Winn to answer. "I ain't giving them away to nobody, but you can have one."

Winn corrected and Greg dutifully repeated the
words. "I'm not giving them to anybody."

"But wait a minute," Winn said. "I thought this
was Peter's dog. How can you give her puppies
away?"

Greg had stopped so he could open the barn door.
"Peter said he'd give me all the puppies. But he don't
know how many 'cause she didn't tell him that."

"Doesn't know," Winn corrected.

"Doesn't know," Greg said leading Winn into the
barn. "It's dark in here," he cautioned.

"Good. That'll slow you down."

Greg giggled. "You got long legs, you should move
faster'n me."

"Yeah, but it's dark out there," Winn mimicked, and let Greg hold his hand out to meet a cool damp nose.

Greg and Winn were filling buckets with water for the wash. Winn worked the pump and Greg watched the bucket to tell him when it was full. Greg's attention was easily distracted, but the system worked as well as it needed to.

"Peter says if we was Indians, Mama'd wash the clothes at the creek and we wouldn't have to carry no water."

"Any water," Winn corrected absently. He was trying to learn how the bucket sounded when it was full. When he stopped to answer Greg he realized that he had been counting the pump strokes. It was becoming a habit. He counted everything. "Our clothes will get cleaner in the hot water than they would at the creek."

"We wouldn't care if they wasn't clean if we was Indians," argued the child. "And I'd never get a haircut. Stop!" Greg giggled. "More water always keeps coming after you stop pumping and it spills on my toes."

Winn laughed. Greg found fun in everything. "Let's get these buckets to the fire," he said, feeling for the handle of the bucket at the waterspout.

"I'll help you carry one," Greg said, but the water only spilled when he tried to help.

"Maybe you better take my other hand and lead me. We can come back for the second bucket."

Earlier, Cynthie had asked Winn to help her carry the heavy metal frame from the shed. Now she had her large pot suspended on it and a fire started underneath. She was going to take advantage of the pretty morning and get the laundry, sheets, blankets, everything clean.

Cynthie had listened to the exchange between Winn and Greg as she tended the fire, and couldn't help but marvel at how they got along together. Victor would never have thought of letting Greg help with anything. To be fair, Cynthie reminded herself, Greg had been only three when Victor died and therefore less able to help. Somehow she couldn't picture it, anyway. Victor wouldn't have been out here pumping water for her. He would have sent one of the hands to help her in the first place.

She watched Winn walk toward her, noting the confidence in his stride. She knew she watched him with more than a caretaker's eye. She noticed the width of his shoulders, the strength of the arm that carried the bucket and the gentleness of the hand that held her son's. She noticed the blue eyes, masculine jaw and dimples and found herself longing to touch him.

When he stopped in front of her, she offered to take the bucket. "Just guide it over the pot. I'll pour," he said.

Greg had already raced back to the well. Before she could talk herself out of it, Cynthie decided to take advantage of their moment alone. She stepped as close to him as possible and guided the bucket over the lip of the pot. The nearness made her heart race. She leaned closer still and let her arm touch his as she helped him tip the bucket up. His arm was warm from the sun and sent little tremors of heat through her body. Her shoulder brushed against his upper arm when he lowered the bucket to his side. She couldn't help but wonder if his body was reacting the way hers was to these briefest of touches.

He stepped away and she tried to not sigh in frustration. How could she flirt with a man who couldn't see her? She ought to know better anyway. It would just lead to disappointment, but it felt so good that she didn't want to be reasonable.

Winn turned and counted his steps back to the well. He hoped she would think he was grinning at Greg as they returned with the second bucket. He wasn't about to tell her that all she needed to do was get the bucket resting on the side of the pot. He could tell easily enough when it was empty. He wondered how many buckets of water it took to do the wash.

His guide deserted him suddenly, halfway to the fire. Cynthie was there to help him empty the second bucket. Her hair smelled the way it always did, sweet and fresh. The brief contact, which he did nothing to avoid, made him wonder more about the rest of her. What did she look like? What might she feel like in his arms, right now, right here, with the wind in her hair and the sun on her face? He decided it was probably a good thing that Greg interrupted them just as he lowered the bucket and Cynthie stepped away.

"Someone's coming," announced the boy. "Somebody's riding a horse but he's bringing another horse."

"Let's go see," Cynthie said. She took the child's hand quickly and grabbed Winn's hand before the child could. Winn dropped the bucket and the three of them went around the house to wait for the visitor. Cynthie was feeling very clever, but when they stopped she had no choice but to let his hand go. His fingers felt strong and hard and slightly cool from the water. She felt a moment of jealousy when Greg left her side to claim the hand she had just dropped.

"It's Kyle Dempsey," she said, unable to hide a touch of annoyance in her voice. "The horse is a beauty!"

Greg was clinging to Winn's arm and seemed to be almost edging behind him. He remembered the boy telling Ott that he didn't like Kyle Dempsey and wondered if that meant he was afraid of him. He tried to distract him. "Tell me about the horse, Greg."

"It's brown. It looks mean."

"Sorrel," the mother corrected. "And he's right. She looks at least half wild. She's got a saddle and a small pack of some kind hanging from the pommel."

Winn barely heard the last of her description. Could the half-wild sorrel mare be Lullaby? He started to take a step forward but Greg held him back. He heard the horses come to a stop a few yards away and the creak of leather as the rider dismounted. Fancy spurs jingled toward them and Greg pulled farther away.

"You must be Sutton," said the voice from the barbershop. Winn could smell the tobacco smoke that clung to his clothes. He would have offered to shake hands but he wasn't going to force Greg to let go.

Cynthie made the introductions and Winn nodded a greeting. This man had to remember him from yesterday. Why hadn't he bothered to introduce himself at the barbershop? If he was enough of a friend to Mrs. Franklin that he visited often, he must have recognized her son. And if he hadn't made the connection before, why didn't he mention the earlier meeting now? Did he think a blind man wouldn't remember him?

It made Winn wonder what the man was trying to hide, and he found himself disliking Kyle Dempsey. If Dempsey wanted to pretend he hadn't seen him before, Winn would go along.

"I guess I've got some things that belong to you," Dempsey said. "Friends of yours left your horse and gear in the livery stable yesterday afternoon."

Cynthie felt her head spin. This was it. His friends were in town and Winn would leave.

Kyle continued, "Seems they just left her there and headed on south." He hadn't seen Cynthie turn pale, nor did he notice now as she brightened first with relief and then with anger. He was watching Sutton for his reaction, and the man showed almost none. Maybe he was too stupid to grasp what this meant.

Well, Kyle could grasp it, and it made him furious! If he had been around when those men had left the horse at the livery, they wouldn't have left Wichita without taking Sutton; he would have seen to that. Rumor had it the two men had argued the whole time they were in town, with the older man threatening to leave the younger if he didn't do as he said. If Kyle had been there, he would have shot the one that wanted to leave the horse.

Winn could feel Greg trying to pull his hand out of Winn's and he wondered if the boy wasn't about to run and hide. He didn't much like standing there being watched by Kyle Dempsey, either. "Let's go see the horse," he said softly to Greg.

Kyle watched them walk away and turned his attention to Cynthie. She took his arm and led him toward the house.

"Couldn't you have broken the news more gently than that?" she whispered fiercely.

"I'm not the one who deserted him." When she would have stopped on the porch, he propelled her into the house. "I need to talk to you," he explained.

Cynthie took a deep breath and led the way to the kitchen. There was still coffee on the stove and she went to get the cups. Kyle took his usual place at the table. He was right, of course. She shouldn't blame him for bringing bad news. And it wasn't really bad news anyway. Maybe that was why she had reacted so strongly. She was trying to cover her own pleasure at what had to be a disappointment to Winn.

"What do you suppose he'll do now?" Kyle stretched his long legs under the table.

"I don't know." Cynthie brought the pot to the table and filled the cups. "I don't think it occurred to him that his friends might not return."

"Had it occurred to you?"

Cynthie watched Kyle for a moment. "Yes," she said, returning the pot to the stove. When she sat down across from him she clarified. "I thought they might not come and he might have to give up waiting for them. I didn't expect there to be a sudden message that they weren't ever coming. They must have learned he was still blind and decided not to find him.''

Kyle groaned. Had the whole town been questioned about the cowboy living with Mrs. Franklin?

Cynthie mistook the reaction for sympathy. ''I can't really blame them. What could he do if he went with them?''

Kyle asked the question Cynthie had been asking herself. ''What can he do here?''

Cynthie sipped the coffee thoughtfully. He had to make his own life somewhere. She was sure he had family he hadn't told her about. Maybe now he was ready to tell someone about the accident and would let her write to them. It wasn't reasonable to hope that he would find a life here.

When she gave no answer, Kyle continued, ''You could pay the man's train fare to get him home, wherever that is. I'd even be willing to get him as far as the station in Abilene.'' He saw the resistance on her face and added, ''If he doesn't want it from you, we could get the church to raise it. Would he object to that, do you think? The reverend would love a cause.''

Cynthie smiled. He was right about the last, at least. ''I don't know. I don't want to rush him into a decision.''

Kyle felt a surge of anger and knew he had to move carefully. ''Waiting too long to make a decision might be a mistake, too. You've done your part, honey. You took care of him. Now he's well. He needs to move on.''

Cynthie tried to control her indignation at his words because she saw the truth in them. She didn't want Winn to go but she had to let him. She studied Kyle for a moment through the steam from her coffee. He was quite handsome and had always been kind to her. Why did she have to keep reminding herself of these things?

Maybe she wasn't really in love with Winn. Maybe it was just an attraction to a handsome stranger. Maybe she felt sorry for him and wanted to mother him, or maybe she wanted to replace her father. Could it be just a fantasy or a game, a way of reliving the old girlish longings that her more mature heart now knew to be nothing more than dreams? And maybe she was head over heels in love and was angry at Kyle for coming and ruining her whole day. She didn't know.

She sighed and set the coffee cup in its saucer. Kyle reached across the table and took her hand. "I've missed you lately. You take too much on yourself, you know. This man is responsible for his own future." He trapped her hand between both of his and rubbed her wrist with his thumb as he added, "And you're responsible for mine." He looked up to watch her face. "You know it's true," he added softly.

Cynthie wanted to pull her hand away and laughed to cover her panic. "Now you're putting too much on me." She got up to get him a saucer for his cigar. It was an excuse to slip her hand free.

Kyle smiled and removed a cigar from his pocket. The faraway look on her face had concerned him but now he relaxed, feeling like he had just been invited to stay.

* * *

Winn and Greg walked toward the sorrel mare. Winn spoke softly and she tossed her head.

Greg didn't seem to be afraid of the horse; it must have been Dempsey that worried him. Winn didn't like the man himself and had been glad to hear the spurs jingle away from him. Then he realized that Dempsey had gone into the house with Cynthie, and he had wanted, for a moment, to go after them.

He was confused about many things and he didn't feel competent to make any clear judgments. He decided to take one thing at a time.

Lullaby nickered to get Winn's attention. He approached her carefully and she stretched her neck forward to nuzzle his shoulder. He realized with a little surprise that he was glad to have her with him again.

"Lullaby, what have you been up to?" He rubbed the soft head and when his hand found the bridle, he curled his fingers around it.

"Yours?" Peter had come from the barn to join them. His voice came from about Greg's height and Winn guessed he was checking the mare's hooves.

"Yeah," Winn answered. "I should blame her in part for my accident but I guess I don't."

"Let's get her inside." Peter waited for Winn to let the bridle go before leading the horse toward the barn. Greg took Winn's hand now that it was free again. "Can I ride her?"

"No!" Winn bent down to the boy and tried to soften the sharp reply. "She likes to buck. I can't let you ride her."

They followed Peter to the barn. Greg left Winn by Lullaby's new stall and ran to visit Sorry. Winn listened to the sounds of the horse breathing as Peter removed the saddle. In a few minutes Peter was beside him placing something in his hand. "Want to brush her down?"

Winn grinned and let Peter lead him forward. The boy knew more than horses, he decided. Brushing a horse he couldn't see seemed less strange than he would have thought. Often, at the end of a day's work, he had tended his horse in near darkness.

Greg joined them in a few minutes. "Does she bite?" he asked.

Winn was glad the boy had enough sense to stay back a little. "I've never known her to," he said. Peter brought some oats and the mare moved toward them. Winn was momentarily startled. He hadn't seen it coming.

"Why does she like to buck?" persisted the boy.

"I don't know. I guess I kind of liked the challenge and never tried too hard to break her of it."

Greg climbed halfway up the ladder to the loft and tried to turn around and sit down on a rung. "Whee!" he yelled as Peter swung him to the floor.

"I could break her," Peter said confidently. Winn wasn't so sure, but he left his doubts unspoken.

"Let's go back to the house," he suggested instead, and then returned the brush to Peter.

"No," responded Greg cheerfully and scampered up the ladder again.

Peter spoke softly near Winn. "Dempsey's still there."

So Peter had noticed the same fear in the child. Winn wanted to ask what he knew about Dempsey but Peter had already moved away.

"I'll go back to the well and finish that pumping." Maybe the sound of the pump would remind Dempsey that Cynthie had things to do. He didn't like Dempsey, and he especially didn't like him spending so much time with Cynthie. He hadn't gone three steps before Greg joined him and they walked to the well together.

Chapter Eight

Black clouds boiled up on the horizon, filling the sky and blocking out the sun. Sharp flashes of lightning stabbed the darkness, sending waves of thunder rolling across the plains and shaking the earth.

Winn was alone. When the lightning flash lit the sky he tried to look around him but there was nothing to see. From horizon to horizon there was nothing but darkness.

He called out but the wind blew the sound away to be swallowed by the darkness. The thunder answered like an angry drum demanding silence. He waited and the lightning came no more. Only the dark clouds were left, roiling closer, devouring the sky, the plains and finally him.

Winn sat up abruptly, breathing hard. The air around him felt thick and heavy like the clouds in his dream. He ran a shaky hand over his face. It was damp with sweat. He could feel the stirring of a breeze from the window and knew that it would be cooler outside.

As he passed through the front room on the way out, he could smell a trace of Dempsey's cigar smoke, which hung in the air as a reminder of the arrogant man.

In a moment he was outside, standing at the top of the steps with his bare shoulder against the porch post, breathing in the cool night air. He remembered how his mother had insisted the windows be closed at night, believing the night air to be unhealthy. He wondered what she would think of all the nights he had slept in the open. The thought brought a smile to his lips. She hated being wrong.

Winn tried to concentrate on pleasant memories but it was like holding back the clouds. Anger seemed to surround him, offering evidence that everything he thought he knew was wrong.

Mike and Slim would not be back to get him. They may have gotten him help when he had been hurt, but they had abandoned him in the end. They didn't want to be burdened with a blind man. He shouldn't blame them for that, but he did. They had returned his horse and belongings and had ridden away forever. They hadn't even come to see him, to tell him themselves that they were going on without him. Slim especially owed him that.

Anger shifted focus. It wasn't just his former friends that angered him. He would not see again. The pain was gone. The swelling was gone. He had to accept it. Hope was gone.

He felt his heart pounding and his breath quickened again. He couldn't let the anger swallow him whole. He needed a plan, a direction, something to keep the anger behind him.

He wondered if he should talk to Louie. He didn't really know the man but he seemed to be very practical and Winn was sure he could count on him to be honest. Louie would be gone for a couple more days, but he could wait that long, he hoped.

He did not want to talk to Cynthie but he would have to. He was her guest and, though it was time for him to go, he didn't know where or how. Her father had been blind; she might have the best advice.

She was also a woman and probably more emotional, although she hadn't done much to prove that so far. Maybe it wasn't her feelings he was afraid would get in the way. Maybe it was his own.

He was willing to admit he was attracted to her. He had been forced to realize that during the last few days. But was he a man reaching out to a woman or a helpless soul reaching out for comfort? He didn't know, and before he could find out, she always pulled away. Or he did.

In some ways she seemed like a complete stranger. She was always surprising him with a sudden change in tone or touch. Damn, he wished he could see her! If he could see her face, she'd be easier to understand. How often had he been completely mistaken about her because he couldn't read her face?

And Greg! Whatever his decision might be, he'd never forget the boy. It was going to be hard to leave him, too. Thinking of Greg made him smile. He wondered if the child would eventually drive him crazy or be the one thing to keep him sane.

At least he had something he could give Greg before he left. If all his gear from the wagon was still intact, the figures he had carved during the drive would still be in his saddle bags. He would pick out one for Greg and send the rest to Cora's children.

He would find a way to send them to her without letting her know he was in trouble. She and her family needed a blind man even less than Mike and Slim did. Maybe he would only send two of the figures now and save the rest for some future date. That would keep Cora from worrying about him for a little longer.

Winn heard small noises behind him that indicated someone was up. He sighed deeply. Was it morning already or was Cynthie on her way out for another predawn ride? He didn't want to talk to Cynthie now. He didn't want to be asked to make a decision or, worse yet, helped to make a decision.

He stood quietly, hoping no one was there. He heard bare feet slapping softly across the front room but they were not heading for the front door. At the same moment he realized the steps belonged to Greg, he heard the child's cry.

He turned quickly and fumbled for the doorknob. "Greg!" he whispered loudly, as if the child's cry hadn't awakened Cynthie already.

The moment he was through the door, Greg threw himself against Winn's legs. "I thought you left," the boy sobbed. "You said you would go and you were gone."

Winn pried the bare arms from around his legs and went down to the child's level, letting him wrap his arms around his neck this time. "I won't leave without saying goodbye."

"Daddy did." The boy sniffed.

"But your daddy didn't mean to leave." Winn wasn't at all sure he knew how to handle the sobbing child. He was relieved to hear running footsteps, and in a moment Cynthie was beside them.

"What happened, baby?" She put one hand on each of them, wanting to comfort and love them both. Greg clung to Winn all the harder.

"He came down to find me, I guess," Winn tried to explain. "I was outside and he thought I'd left." Her hand was resting on his shoulder, an intimate touch with no shirt to protect him.

Cynthie rubbed Greg's narrow back. "But you found him now. It's all right."

"No! He'll leave! He said he'd leave and now he has a horse and he'll ride away!"

Winn held back a bitter laugh. "I don't think I'll do that any time soon. I don't know what I'll do, but I'll tell you when I do, Greg. I won't just leave."

Greg had stopped sobbing but he still clung to Winn's neck. "I'm sorry," Cynthie whispered.

One warm soft hand continued to rest on Winn's shoulder as the other comforted her child. Her hair smelled like fresh air and laundry soap and it helped to dispel the smoke that still hung in the air.

The clock chimed and Greg pulled away to count. "One, two, three."

"Time to be asleep," his mother said.

"Promise you won't go?" he said, turning to Winn.

Cynthie wanted him to promise exactly that but she knew he would qualify it. "Not without saying good-bye," he said. "Promise." He solemnly put one hand on his heart.

Greg allowed his mother to take his hand and lead him toward the stairs. When he turned around to look at his friend, Cynthie looked, as well. Moonlight was streaming through the window by the door, leaving him in silhouette. He stood erect, his head cocked slightly to one side, listening for their footsteps. "Good night," she said softly.

"G'night," echoed Greg.

"Good night," Winn responded and heard them go up the stairs. He reached behind him to find the door and made sure it was closed. Using it to get his bearings, he went to the bedroom. He opened the window as wide as possible and returned to the bed.

He wanted to sleep but he didn't know what waited for him if he did. The nightmares had become more frequent. They were often violent and always disturbing. He didn't want to think about them but he had to admit that he didn't know what waited for him during the day, either.

He tried to empty his mind and listen only to the creaking of the house and the night sounds through the window. With a start he realized that the creaking he now heard was not coming from the house. Someone was opening the door to his room. It closed very gently and there was a whisper of bare feet on the floor. A moment later a tiny bit of weight was added to his mattress.

"Greg?" he whispered.

"Shh," was the reply.

Winn felt for the sheet to cover the child and moved to give him more room. Moments after the child was settled, Winn could hear his deep, even breathing. He envied his ability to relax so quickly. In a matter of minutes, however, he, too, fell into a dreamless sleep, eased by the child's serenity.

It was later than usual when Cynthie dragged herself into the kitchen. She had worked hard the previous day and had fallen into bed exhausted, only to be awakened in the night by her little boy's cry. Afterward, she had found it impossible to fall back to sleep. She had lain awake until the early morning hours thinking of Winn.

Through the window, she saw him making his way toward the door guided by the rope. She didn't want him to be startled when he came in and found her there, so she called out, "Good morning," before he opened the door.

"Morning, ma'am," he responded, coming inside and carefully closing the door.

"Have you seen Greg this morning?" she asked. Looking up from her breakfast preparations, she saw the muscles in his face tighten for a second. She was surprised. It was just a figure of speech. He had never reacted that way before, and she knew it had slipped out more than once.

After a moment he answered, "He's sleeping in your father's bed."

Cynthie wasn't sure what to make of him this morning. Surely it was Winn's bed by now. But he wasn't staying. She had to remember that. Maybe he hadn't gotten any more sleep than she had. "I'm sorry," she said softly.

"Don't be sorry. He didn't bother me."

There was a sharpness in his tone that made her look up again. Was he angry at her for not keeping her son out of his room or for saying she was sorry? She decided she'd let it go.

"Will you eat in here with us this morning?"

"No, thanks, ma'am."

She wondered why she bothered to ask. He never ate with them if he could avoid it. She had an idea. "You know, if you go back to your room now, you'll wake Greg. Why don't you have a seat here while you wait for him to get up? He never sleeps very late."

He seemed to think about it for a moment before he found the chair and sat down.

"Coffee?" she asked hopefully.

Winn laughed, but it was a laugh of resignation. "It sounds good."

"I'm glad." Cynthie got the cups and set them on the table. "It'll be ready in a couple of minutes."

Winn laughed again. "I suppose by the time my coffee's ready the rest of the breakfast will be, too."

"If I time it right."

"You know, for a woman who isn't very bossy, you sure seem to get your own way."

There was a teasing quality in his voice she had only heard him use with Greg. She liked it, and even more, she liked having Winn to herself. She hoped little Greg would sleep until noon.

She brought the coffee to the table as soon as it was ready and continued with the rest of the breakfast preparations. She watched him while she worked. Despite his teasing, he didn't seem particularly comfortable. He kept his hands wrapped around the china cup and sat rather stiffly.

Finally he let her know what he was thinking. "Ma'am, I've got to come to some decision but I just don't know what to do."

Cynthie slid the skillet off the hot stove and came to sit across from him. "How can I help you?"

"You've already helped me, but I can't stay here forever."

Cynthie poured herself a cup of coffee to give her shaking hands something to do. "Where will you go?" She was surprised her voice didn't shake as well.

"That's the problem, ma'am. I don't know."

"Listen," she said, putting one hand on his arm. "Don't be in too big a hurry. When you first came, I wrote my father's doctor in New York. I haven't heard from him yet. He may know of something we can do. Why don't you wait until we hear from him?"

Winn shook his head. "If he hasn't answered by now, I doubt that he will."

Cynthie got to her feet and returned to the stove, more out of a need to expend some restless energy than concern for their breakfast. "Well, you know how slow the mail can be. And doctors are slow, too." Her voice trailed away and she concentrated on saving the eggs that had soaked up too much grease while she was at the table.

Winn sighed then chuckled to himself. "I was waiting for the boys to get back. Now I'll wait for this letter. What do I wait for after that?"

Cynthie wanted to tell him she would have thought of something by then. Instead she scooped up the eggs and ham and brought them to the table. She told him quietly where everything was on his plate and sat down across from him.

He made no move to eat. "There's such a thing as waiting too long. It will just get harder to leave and I don't belong here."

"But you could."

Winn looked genuinely startled, and it made Cynthie blush. It hadn't been something she had meant to say aloud. "I mean whatever you decide to do with your life, you could do right here."

A flash of anger crossed Winn's features.

Cynthie wanted to explain. "I just think you should be thinking about the things that you can do instead of what you can't. When you know what you want to do with your life, you can think about where you want to go and when."

Winn's tone was cool. "What if I come up with nothing? What if there isn't anything I can do?"

Cynthie watched him for a moment, trying to get her own emotions in check in the face of his. When she was sure her voice would sound steady and assured she answered him. "That won't happen."

"What won't happen?" asked Greg, coming into the kitchen rubbing his eyes. He went straight to Winn and climbed up on his lap.

"Greg, Winn can't eat with you there."

"That's all right, ma'am. I'm not hungry." He lifted Greg off his lap and came to his feet. Greg climbed into the chair and reached for the plate as Winn started across the room.

Cynthie watched him leave thinking she'd like to slap him next time he called her ma'am. She focused her attention on Greg, who stood on the chair with one hand supporting his weight on the table, picking at the eggs with his fingers. "Use a fork, Greg," she said in exasperation.

Winn went through the front room and out the door. He stopped on the porch and leaned his shoulder against the post. He hadn't meant to fight with Cynthie. For some reason he was picturing this place as a prison once more, a prison with a very persuasive guard. She had trapped him here again, this time to wait for a letter. But it was easier to stay trapped and blame her than to do anything about it.

His stomach rumbled and he wanted to kick himself. If he spent the morning hungry he had nothing to blame but his own stubborn pride. It seemed like pride was about all he had left.

Pride and one crazy mare. He walked down the steps and started slowly across the yard. He would see if he could make it to the barn without breaking his neck.

Something in the wind made him change direction. He had gone several steps before he realized that his stomach was leading him toward the bunkhouse; the smells of breakfast there had caught his attention, but now he wasn't sure he should invite himself to join the men. But the decision was already out of his hands.

"Peter saw you comin' and sent me to fetch you in," called a voice. "I'm Jeremiah Betts. I been gone till just recent and didn't get the chance to meet you." He took Winn's arm and walked beside him.

"I'm Winn Sutton."

"That's what the boy said. He said you the one owns that pretty sorrel mare."

"I'm afraid she's mine, all right." They had come to the door and Jeremiah held it open and helped Winn inside.

"Peter's just gettin' started on breakfast. With Mr. Louie gone, we both just slept late somehow. Now you set yourself here. I let Peter do the cookin' but I got to watch him."

Winn took the seat and heard his guide slide a chair across the floor until it ended up nearby. There were sizzling and bubbling sounds from the direction of the stove, but Peter hadn't said a word.

"Now Peter here is good with eggs," Jeremiah continued. "He likes to eat 'em and he knows how to cook 'em, but 'sides that, he ain't got no real talent for cookin'."

"I can't say as I do, either," Winn said.

"No, me, neither," Jeremiah said quickly. "But the difference, see, is when I'm eatin' I can tell if it was cooked good or not. But Peter there, he just got no taste for nothin' but eggs."

Winn wasn't sure how he should respond. He couldn't tell how Peter felt about it. He thought it was probably a well-worn argument, if anything so one-sided could be called an argument.

In a moment Jeremiah went on. "Makes you wonder what the boy grew up eatin', don't it?" He leaned across the table and said in a lower voice, "He's just grinnin' at us. He knows I don't mean nothin'."

Winn tried to grin, too, but he felt very uncomfortable. He hadn't been around Peter much without Greg, and Jeremiah was new to him. Dropping in for breakfast hardly seemed right anyway. The silence was filled with cooking sounds. Finally Winn asked, "You were up at the house a day or so ago, weren't you?"

"Yes, sir, I was," Jeremiah said. "I went up to report on the drive. You was up there then, was you?"

"I heard your voice. Mrs. Franklin lets me use a room off the front room there."

"Then you heard about the drive, I guess."

Winn didn't see the hopeful look on the man's face. "No," he said. "I heard your voice when you first came in. I didn't mean to be listening anyway."

Peter brought Winn's plate to the table and Jeremiah got up to get his own. "Need help?" Peter asked quietly.

"Tell me where everything is."

Peter did and placed a fork in his hand before going back to the stove for his own plate. Jeremiah brought the coffee and Winn heard the sound of the tin cups being filled. The sense of relief he experienced at not having to worry about breaking a china cup was replaced with a pang almost like regret. It came as a surprise but he didn't have time to wonder about it.

"I'd like to ride Lullaby," Peter said.

Winn was quiet for a moment. He found the young man's tone interesting. He was stating a desire and asking permission but there was no fear or excitement in his voice, just calm assurance.

"Be my guest," he said after some consideration. "But be careful."

"Before you go risking your hide tryin' to break a horse, you best recollect Louie told us to get that corral fence mended. It looked to me like that would take most all day even without us startin' so late."

"Winn could help."

The statement hung in the air and Winn's fork hovered halfway to his mouth. He was afraid his hand was starting to shake so he set the fork down very carefully.

After what seemed like several minutes, Jeremiah spoke softly. "Mr. Louie give that job to us to do and we don't need to go asking Mrs. Franklin's guest to be doin' none of it."

For some reason that was as embarrassing as being called useless. He was eating a meal from their table; he ought to do something in return. Before he stopped to think, he found himself answering, "I'll be glad to help any way I can."

He didn't see the glances exchanged by his two companions. Jeremiah looked doubtfully at Peter, who smiled back before resuming his breakfast as if nothing had interrupted it. After a few minutes of thought, Jeremiah said, "Well, a strong back and an extra pair of hands would shore 'nough make the job easier. You real certain you don't mind, now?"

Winn answered truthfully, "If I can be of any help at all, I'll be happy to try."

Try is what he did for the next several hours. He was kept busy but he never got over the feeling that he was more in the way than anything else. While Peter and Jeremiah carried the lumber from the barn that would be used to replace the ruined rails, Winn was loaned a pair of gloves and trusted with a sawhorse.

Peter found the first rail that would need to be replaced and put Winn to work on it with a crowbar. He added a couple of nails to a loose board and found the next rail for Winn to work on. Jeremiah sawed the boards to replace the ones Winn removed, and Peter stacked the ruined ones to chop for kindling.

Greg joined them shortly after they started. "Are we fixin' the fence?" he asked.

Jeremiah was the first to answer. "We's fixin' it but you better be careful you don't get hit with nothin'."

"I'm gonna help Winn."

Winn had quit working as soon as he heard the boy's voice, afraid that he would misjudge the child's location. "I don't think you can help with this," he said.

"Nope," said Greg, trying to sound like the men. "Don't got no gloves."

"Hold my nails," Peter called and Greg scampered away.

Winn wondered if his own job was any different from Greg's. Surely it would be easier for Peter to pull off the boards himself than it was to get him started and wait until he finished.

When Winn had torn the ruined rails off one side of the fence, Peter led him back to where they had started. Winn and Jeremiah held the new boards in place and Peter nailed them securely. Winn felt the pull of muscles that had been unused for too long. The feeling wasn't altogether unpleasant.

Despite Jeremiah's predictions, they were more than halfway around the corral when they decided to quit for lunch. Greg ran to the house to tell his mother he was going to eat with the men.

"We're fixin' the fence," he reported when he found her in the garden.

"Where's Winn?" Cynthie came to her feet and brushed the dirt from her skirt.

"He's workin', too. Jerry's gonna see what he can rustle us up to eat." Cynthie smiled. She wondered what Jeremiah Betts thought of Greg's nickname for him.

Having dutifully reported to his mother, Greg was eager to get back to the bunkhouse. He darted away as soon as she said, "Be sure to do what you're told."

Cynthie looked after him and smiled. He loved to be with the men and they were all protective of him. She knew they would send him back to the house if he got in the way or if there was any danger. How long could she let him run loose, though? In a few more years, she would have to start teaching him to read and write.

There was more he needed to learn than horses and cattle.

If Victor were still alive, he would be taking the child with him whenever he could. He had always been good about that. Of course, Victor hadn't approved of Greg spending so much time with the hired hands and Cynthie had suspected that was why he was willing to take such a small child along on trips to town. He had told Cynthie once that he couldn't trust her to watch the child closely enough. She worried sometimes that he had been right.

She looked over the garden with a critical eye and decided she had earned her lunch. As she went inside, she was still thinking about her late husband. Had it ever crossed Victor's mind that he might die and leave her alone? She doubted it. He had always been too self-confident. She wondered if he would approve of her staying here and trying to run the ranch. He would at least be surprised.

The thought made her smile as she brought bread and leftover pot roast to the table for a quick lunch. She wasn't going to drive herself crazy trying to live her life to please someone who was gone. In a way, now she had a chance to prove what she could do, a chance to prove to herself and others she could survive on her own.

She had to admit she loved the freedom. Maybe she wasn't competent to run the ranch herself, but she would be the one to decide who would help her run it. Maybe she did spend too much time riding and not enough time cleaning, but it was her time. If she let her little boy run a little too free, well, this was the West; people came here to run free.

Thinking about her son in the bunkhouse made her think of Winn. Winn was never far from her thoughts anyway. Greg had said he was helping with the fence. She wondered what he was doing. She had to fight the urge to go down to the corral and watch them.

She sat down to her lunch, enjoying the quiet. Greg had a knack for interrupting her thoughts and it was nice to sit quietly and think of Winn. There had to be lots of things that he could do, some things that he enjoyed, and she had to help him find them.

She had heard him correct Greg's speech a time or two but never in a way that made the child feel bad. He was obviously well educated and so good with Greg that he would make a wonderful teacher. He couldn't teach someone to read if he couldn't see, though.

Cynthie cleared away the remains of her light lunch and washed the few dishes. She had never gotten over the Eastern habit of dinner at night. A snack was enough for her at noon, but she knew the men were used to more. With Louie gone, they were forced to, as Greg put it, rustle something up. Victor would have expected her to cook the noon meal for the hands but that would have meant spending the entire morning cooking. They hadn't asked and she hadn't offered, but she felt a little guilty about leaving them to their own devices.

Maybe she could fix something tonight and invite Jeremiah and Peter for dinner. Was she hoping to placate Victor's ghost? He certainly seemed to be haunting her today. She grinned to herself. She knew how to get around that. As soon as Greg got tired of fence mending, she'd take him fishing. If they caught enough fish, she'd feed everybody.

Chapter Nine

Peter nailed the last board in place and simply said, "Done." Jeremiah had already begun to put the tools away.

Winn removed the borrowed gloves and returned them to Peter. He stood by listening to the quiet activity that marked the end of the job and felt Greg's little hand slip into his. "That was hard work," sighed the little boy.

"Let's get out of the sun," Winn suggested. "Want to help me get my gear up to the house?"

They walked into the relative cool of the barn and Greg helped Winn find the knapsack and saddlebags. A rifle leaned against the wall nearby.

"What you gonna do with the rifle?" asked Greg, trying to lift it.

"You better leave it alone," Winn warned. "Put this up in the bunkhouse where you keep your own," he said to Jeremiah, who was in the barn when they arrived there.

"Yes, sir," he said, taking the rifle away.

Greg was soon distracted by the saddlebags. "What's in this thing?" asked the child, struggling with the bags.

Winn shouldered the knapsack and waited for Greg to take his hand and lead him out of the barn. "Not much of anything, really, but just about everything I own."

Greg laughed. "That sounds funny."

Winn laughed, too, seeing the child's point of view.

"Is there a gun in here?"

"As a matter of fact, there is," Winn said. "It was in my saddlebag when I was hurt."

"But I thought cowboys always weared their guns."

"Wore. And not all of us. Let's stop at the well before we go in the house. I could use a drink of cold water."

"Me, too," the boy answered with an exaggerated sigh.

Cynthie met them at the well and lifted the saddlebags from Greg's shoulder. "How about coming fishing with me?" she asked, ruffling the child's sweaty hair.

"Yippee!" he yelled. He turned immediately to Winn. "You want to come, too, don't you?"

Winn considered the alternatives as he worked the pump handle. He could listen to Peter as he worked with Lullaby, knowing that he would never ride her again, or he could do nothing. The morning's activity had kept his mind busy and the black clouds at bay, and he was reluctant to sit idle. "I haven't been fishing since . . . I can't remember when," he answered.

The smile he threw in her general direction made Cynthie's heart skip a beat. "Then I guess you've been working too hard," she said, returning a smile he could hear in her voice.

Greg ran to the garden to hunt for worms and grasshoppers. Cynthie called after him to be careful of her plants then turned with Winn to carry the bags into the house.

From the well, Winn could make it to the house and through to the room he was using without any help. He couldn't help but wish Cynthie didn't know that and would take his arm. He was, however, sweaty and dusty from working on the corral fence. He didn't expect her to want to be near him even in better conditions.

They deposited the bags in the corner of the room. "Are there things you would like to unpack?" Cynthie asked.

"There's not much there but a clean shirt or two." He grinned at her. "Or at least a cleaner shirt."

"Then let's go." She grabbed his hand and pulled him from the room. "You can wash up after we catch our dinner."

She found the poles in the shed. Winn wondered if there were other buildings around that he didn't even know about and if he would run into them if he roamed around by himself. He pushed the thought away and tried to concentrate on his cheerful companions.

"We only got two poles," Greg said. "Peter made them. You can share Mama's." Winn grinned at the boy's idea of generosity.

The walk, once they left the yard, got more difficult and Winn had trouble navigating the uneven ground and large clumps of grass. Cynthie tried to watch for him and steer him around the worst places, but the going was still slow. Greg ran ahead to find their favorite spot.

"I haven't met many women who like to go fishing," he observed. He hoped if they started a conversation, she wouldn't become irritated with his slow pace. Her hand was on his arm and he could feel her excitement.

"You haven't met many women who *get* to go fishing," she corrected. The heat that radiated from beneath her hand made her almost giddy. "I bet you never called on a lady and invited her down to the nearest fishing hole, unless you had other things on your mind."

Winn laughed, surprised at the suggestion in her quip. "You've got a point there. So how come you're so lucky to get to go fishing?"

Cynthie guided Winn around a gopher hole before she answered. "This is going to sound terrible, but I get to go fishing because I don't have a husband anymore."

She had sounded amused so he continued. "So it's a widows-only kind of thing?" This could become more dangerous ground than what he was walking on.

Cynthie laughed. "Well, husbands do tend to tell their wives what they should and shouldn't do. It can be very limiting." Talking about her dearly departed in such a way seemed wonderfully naughty, especially since she had been thinking of him all day.

"So, do old maids go fishing, too?" Winn nearly stumbled over something that rolled when his toe caught it. He made a conscious effort to pick up his feet a little higher. The stick must mean they were close to the creek. In fact, once he thought about it, he could hear the peculiar rustling sound of wind in the cottonwoods.

"Sure," replied Cynthie in answer to his question. "But that's why they're old maids." She sighed deeply. "They had to choose between fishing and a man. Who knows. Maybe they made the right decision."

Winn laughed and Cynthie smiled, loving the sound. In the silence that followed, the sound of the wind in the trees along the creek grew louder, and a moment later they felt the coolness of the shade.

Cynthie lead Winn to the place on the bank where she and Greg usually fished. Greg was walking along the bank, looking for more insects to use as bait. When he saw them coming, he sat down on some grass and Cynthie found a place for Winn to sit a few feet away. Cynthie baited the two hooks with the worms Greg handed her, and after tossing in Greg's line, she handed him the pole. He held it tightly and watched the spot where the line disappeared in the water with extreme concentration.

Cynthie tossed in the other line and sat down between her son and Winn. When she offered Winn the pole, he shook his head. "Actually," she said, recalling their conversation. "I started fishing because I had to raise a son without a father. I discovered last fall that I liked it. When Victor was alive, he sent Greg fishing with Peter a time or two, but Greg really just wanted to be with his father."

"I like Peter," Greg said. He was still staring at the string and the water moving slowly past it. His voice sounded almost groggy.

"I know you do," his mother said softly.

Winn tried to hear the sound of the water but couldn't separate it from the cottonwoods. Insects and birds added more noise. He tried to picture the scene around him and discovered it wasn't too difficult. He didn't know how big the creek was but he had some clues; it had to be big enough to support fish but small enough to be quiet. Maybe he was wrong, but the mental picture remained.

"How did the fence mending go?" Cynthie asked after a few minutes.

"All right, I guess. They got done anyway."

Cynthie reflected on his short answer. Why hadn't he said, "We got done"? When no more details seemed to be forthcoming, she said gently, "You know, Winn, I'm much less interested in the fence than I am in how you got along working out there with the other two men."

"I got along fine."

There was the same tightening in his muscles. For some reason he didn't want to talk about it so she let it go. She hoped Greg could provide a distraction but he had stretched out on the grass and had fallen asleep. She watched him for a moment and smiled. He looked so innocent, his dark head lying on one outstretched arm, his bare feet covered with dust. She loved her little boy so much she often wondered how she could be so lucky.

Nudging Winn with her elbow, she passed her fishing pole to him. "You get to share my pole after all. Greg's gone to sleep."

Winn took it gingerly in his hands. "What do I do if I get a bite?"

Cynthie grinned, picking up her child's pole. "Same thing you usually do."

Winn felt the anger surge to the surface again. Was she intentionally being cruel or hadn't she stopped to think? He tried to stay calm. This wasn't worth getting upset over. When he could trust his voice he said, "I'm going to have a little trouble catching hold of a string I can't see."

"I know," she said. "Just swing it over the bank and I'll take it off the hook."

"Swing it over the bank," he repeated.

"Yeah, that way." With her fingertip she drew an arrow on his chest pointing away from her.

The sweet touch of her finger changed everything. She wasn't setting him up for failure, they were just here to have fun. He knew by now that he could trust her. It was his own frustrations that caused him to worry. "That way?" he grinned, pointing toward her.

"If you flip a fish in my lap, I'll remember it at supper."

Winn laughed at the threat but sobered suddenly when he felt a tug on the line. Instinct told him to hold on to the pole and tug back. He struggled to his feet. Cynthie was yelling instructions that made very little sense. He could tell when the fish left the water because the flipping shook the pole. He brought it carefully around, afraid he'd lose it.

"I've got it," Cynthie said.

The excitement woke Greg. "That's a big one. Did you catch it, Winn? Where's my pole?"

"It's on the ground," began Cynthie looking up. "Grab it, Greg!"

The boy jumped on the pole that was only inches away from where he had been half sitting. He scrambled after it for several inches before he got a good grip and could start pulling back. "Help!" he screamed. "No, I got it. It's mine. No, help!"

Cynthie was laughing so hard it took her a while to come to her son's aid. Finally she caught the end of the pole and helped him hold on as he backed away from the bank. "You were great, Greg," she said, still laughing as she removed the fish from the hook.

"Wow! They're really bitin' today," Greg said. He eagerly handed his mother another worm to bait his hook so he could go back to fishing. When his line was in the water and he was staring at it again, she asked him for another worm for Winn's hook.

"It's a good thing you didn't roll over in your sleep," she said to Greg.

Winn had been laughing at the earlier excitement but felt himself turn cold with fear. She couldn't have left her baby sleeping where he might roll over into the water, could she?

Cynthie saw his expression change and clarified. "The worms are in his pocket."

Winn digested that for a moment then laughed. "My mother would never have stood for that," he said, sitting down on the bank.

"Well, his pockets have seen worse." She handed him the pole after she cast it and busied herself getting the two fish on a string to keep them in the water until they were ready to leave.

Winn was still laughing. "What's worse than a pocket full of worms?"

Cynthie thought about it a moment. She looked at her son, who covered his mouth to hide a guilty giggle. "Bird eggs," she said finally.

Cynthie was almost through cleaning the dishes left from dinner. The five of them had eaten together. Even Winn had not objected. She was glad to see him more at ease.

Something was bothering him, though. Jeremiah had talked about Peter's session with Lullaby, but Winn had shown very little interest. He seemed angry every time she tried to draw him into the conversation. She wondered what was wrong, but she couldn't make him talk if he didn't want to.

She heard horses coming into the yard and left the sink to see who it was. Winn and Greg had been on the porch and had started toward the rider ahead of her.

Louie was riding in leading another horse, but her attention was on the second man, draped across the saddle. Peter and Jeremiah were coming from the barn but somehow she got to Louie first. He caught her shoulders and when she looked into his face, he slowly shook his head.

"It's Billy Emery," said Jeremiah in amazement.

"What happened?" Winn was the only one who seemed calm enough to ask. Cynthie thought at first that it was because he couldn't see the horror of the lifeless body on the horse. She looked at his face and knew that wasn't the reason. He was feeling all the same things they were but he had taken on an authoritative calm necessary in emergencies. She wondered, vaguely, where he had learned it, before her attention was drawn back to Louie.

"I found him," Louie said. He sounded too tired to be on his feet. "Shot. I think he found out somethin' he shouldn't have."

Cynthie told them to bring the body into the house. Winn wanted to help, but all he could do was hold the horses for them. Greg stayed beside him, clutching his leg. When Peter came back for the horses, he said Jeremiah would ride into town and get the sheriff. Winn nodded to Peter and, taking the child's hand, went back to the house.

Cynthie met them at the kitchen door and led Greg away to clean him up for bed. Louie had been coaxed into having something to eat and Winn sat down at the table with him. Louie looked at the younger man and didn't wait for him to ask.

"There's been cattle stolen off Mrs. Franklin's land. I don't know if you heard about that or not. I was out there looking for evidence of old camps. Found a couple, too. They might mean nothin', but whatever Emery found meant something to somebody. He was lyin' near a camp that looked to have been deserted in a hurry. My guess is he caught somebody in the act."

"Changing brands?" Winn guessed. "Did they leave anything behind that would tell you anything about them?"

Louie was quiet, and Winn wondered if he might have nodded or shaken his head. He listened to Cynthie's light footsteps on the stairs. "I'll tell you later," Louie said and took a gulp of coffee.

Cynthie entered the kitchen. "I better take care of the body tonight," she said.

"The sheriff will want to see him first. I'll wait and help you," Louie said.

Cynthie shook her head. "He'll want to talk to you and then you better turn in. You've had a long day."

Winn knew there was no way he could help so he didn't offer, but he resolved to stay with her for company at the very least. He took the coffee Cynthie offered. Peter came to the front door with Emery's best clothes and offered to sit up with the rest. Cynthie thanked him but firmly sent him off to bed. She returned to the others and they sat drinking coffee and talking quietly while they waited for Jeremiah to get back with the sheriff.

It was completely dark by the time they arrived. Cynthie lit a lamp in the front room while Louie let the sheriff in. Winn stood by and listened to the other two men talk, and Cynthie came to stand near him.

Louie didn't tell the sheriff anything he hadn't already told Winn except the location of the camp and how he and Emery had separated in an effort to cover more ground. Whatever it was Louie had found, he was keeping it from the sheriff as well as his boss.

The sheriff watched Louie go through the man's pockets and asked about kin. Louie knew of a brother but they hadn't been close, and Emery himself probably didn't know where to reach him. The sheriff said, in that case, his things would belong to Mrs. Franklin.

Cynthie cleared her throat. "We'll worry about that later," she said.

Winn wanted to put an arm around her and pull her close so she could lean against him. She sounded small and frightened. She was close enough to touch, but he didn't dare.

In a few minutes the sheriff was ready to leave. Louie renewed his offer to help, but Cynthie refused. After promising to be back after a few hours' sleep, he left Cynthie and Winn alone.

"I think it'll be quiet enough now that you can go to bed," she said.

Winn shook his head. "I'll stay if you'll let me."

Cynthie sighed with relief. "Thank you," she whispered. She knew the task would be hard enough to face without being alone, as well.

She removed the poor man's dirty and bloody clothing, calling occasionally on Winn to help her lift him. She washed the body the best she could, and began dressing him for burial. "I didn't know him very well," she said as she worked. "He hasn't been here as long as Louie or Jeremiah, and he usually kept to himself."

Winn heard a tremor in her voice and stepped closer to her. He knew strong men who would get squeamish doing what she had to do. What would he do if she fainted?

"Somebody who loved him should be doing this," she said.

Winn reached out and touched her shoulder. "Wouldn't it be harder on them?"

"I don't know." Cynthie's hands were trembling and she gripped them tightly together. "It's hard when it's someone you love but...I wish...I should have..." She started to sob, and Winn turned her into his arms. She twisted her fingers into his shirt and gave in to the tears.

Winn pulled the silky head against him and caressed the narrow back. He wanted to comfort her, to stop the heartbreaking little sounds that she muffled against his chest. At the same time, he wanted to hold her forever, amazed at the wonderful feeling of having her in his arms.

Eventually the tears were spent and she was no longer shaking. He bent to kiss the top of her head. "Feel better?" he whispered.

She nodded against his chest but didn't pull away. He kept his arms around her, waiting for a sign from her that she wanted him to let her go. He wanted to touch her for as long as she would allow it.

"This doesn't have anything to do with him." Her voice was so soft he barely heard her.

"But it brings back memories," he suggested softly.

She nodded. "I remember exactly how I felt when Louie brought Victor home. It seems as if it was just yesterday instead of nearly a year ago."

"Do you want to tell me about it?" His lips were still close to her hair. He wanted to kiss her again but he knew he mustn't. She would think he was taking advantage of her, and she wouldn't be completely wrong.

"Louie found him." She pulled away but only a little. One hand toyed with a button on his shirt. "He brought him in on his horse. He'd been shot, almost exactly like this." She shuddered as she sighed. "I better finish," she said more firmly, and Winn let her go.

She finished dressing the body without saying anything more except to instruct Winn when she needed his help. Finally she said, "I'll send someone into town to tell the pastor in the morning. The funeral will probably be in the afternoon. I don't suppose there'll be too many folks out for it."

She was quiet for a moment then stepped closer. "Winn," she began. "About earlier..."

He knew by her voice where she stood and he knew exactly how tall she was. His hands reached out and easily found her shoulders. "Please don't apologize," he said.

"All right." She moved closer and put one hand on the damp circle her tears had left on his shirt. The warmth of her hand quickly soaked through to his cool skin. "Let me thank you, then," she whispered.

She looked up into the gentle face only inches away. Those lips had already kissed her hair, small difference now if they kissed her lips. She smiled to herself, wondering if he would make any move toward her. He didn't, but he didn't pull away, either. She slipped her hand up and around his neck, pulling his head toward her as she rose on tiptoe to meet him.

Winn felt her lips, warm against his, and wanted more. He wanted to pull her toward him and wrap his arms around her. The slight brush of her body against his made him long to mold it against him. He kept his hands on her shoulders and didn't dare think about what he wanted.

He let her decide when the kiss was over; it was, after all, her thank-you. When she slid her hands from around his neck, he raised his head and let his hands drop from her shoulders.

They stood near each other for a moment, each waiting for the other to speak. Finally Cynthie said, "You might as well get some rest. I'll sit with the body until Louie comes.'

"I can do that, Cynthie." He knew he wouldn't sleep anyway. Too many things had happened during the day and few of them would help him sleep, the sweet torturous kiss the least of all.

Cynthie watched the flickering lamplight play on the handsome face. She wanted to suggest they stay up together, but knew it made more sense for her to rest. "Call me if you need anything," she said. He still stood where he had been when she kissed him, waiting for her to leave. There could be no more procrastinating. "Good night," she whispered as she walked past him.

"Good night."

She waited on the stairs a moment listening, but the room was quiet. She checked to see that Greg was sleeping soundly before she went to her own room.

There she lit a lamp and, after changing into a nightgown, she sat down at her dressing table and brushed her long black hair. She stared at her reflection in the mirror and touched a finger to her lips.

A moment later she frowned. That had been the most polite kiss she had ever experienced. Polite was exactly the word for it. She got up quickly, turned away from the mirror and put out the lamp. She didn't want to see the tears that were falling again, this time for herself.

"Behold, what manner of love the Father hath bestowed upon us, that we should be called the sons of God. Therefore the world knoweth us not, because it knew Him not. Beloved, now are we the sons of God..."

Greg clung tightly to Winn's hand. They had gathered in a small fenced cemetery a short distance from Cynthie's house. More people had come than Cynthie had expected, and they all brought food that filled the tables that had been set up in the yard. Winn knew it was respect for Cynthie that brought most of them here.

Winn was sure Louie was standing near him, probably Peter, too. When Dempsey arrived, he had moved Cynthie away and Winn had lost them in the crowd. He would have liked to have been near her, but she had the right to choose her own companions. In truth, it wouldn't have mattered to Winn at all, had it been anyone but Dempsey.

"Little children, let no man deceive you. He that doeth righteousness is righteous. He that committeth sin is of the devil. For the devil sinneth from the beginning. For this purpose the Son of God was manifested...."

Winn tried to keep his attention on the pastor, but this seemed like such an odd funeral to him. He had never met the man they were burying, but he was pretty sure several others here could say the same. He couldn't see the casket. He couldn't see the mourners. Greg's tiny hand was all that seemed real.

The poor man's body had seemed real enough last night, however. The threat to Cynthie that this death implied was very real, as well. Winn wished he knew how to protect her.

He tried to pull himself back to the funeral. The pastor's voice was a little too comforting to keep his attention.

"For this is the message that ye heard from the beginning, that we should love one another. Not as Cain, who was of that wicked one, and slew his brother. And wherefore slew he him? Because his own works were evil, and his brother's righteous."

Was that why the pastor had chosen this passage? Did he think that the murderer was in the gathering? The message would probably be lost on him if he were, Winn thought.

"We know that we have passed from death unto life, because we love the brethren. He that loveth not his brother abideth in death. Whosoever hateth his brother is a murderer...."

Billy Emery had a brother, they said. One who didn't even know of his death. It was a sad thing to come to the end and be buried by strangers. Winn had a sudden picture of himself in the casket. Cora would never know. He searched his memory for something in his belongings that would lead them to Cora. He pictured Cynthie saying, "He may have had family but we don't know how to reach them."

Greg was leaning against Winn's leg; he bent down and lifted the child. Winn was surprised at how attentive the boy seemed to be. At four, Winn was sure he would have been easily distracted. Perhaps Greg reflected the mood he saw around him without understanding what was going on. Winn wondered if the child could remember his father's funeral or if they had sent him away until it was over.

"And whatsoever we ask, we receive of Him, because we keep His Commandments, and do those things that are pleasing in His sight. And this is His Commandment, that we should believe in the name of His Son Jesus Christ, and love one another...."

Winn was almost convinced that the pastor had chosen the longest chapter in the Bible. At last he concluded, "And hereby we know that He abideth in us, by the Spirit which He hath given us. First John, chapter three."

Cynthie watched the pastor gently close the leather-bound volume, but she was more aware of Winn across from her. She wondered what her neighbors thought of Greg clinging so tightly to him. She would have liked to be beside them both but Greg didn't want to be with Kyle and she was beginning to wonder if it was mutual. Kyle had his hand possessively on her back and she couldn't shake it off discreetly.

The pastor began to sing "Rock of Ages" and the mourners joined in. Cynthie meant to keep her eyes on the casket and remember why she was here, but a strong, deep voice rose above the others and made her lift her eyes.

Winn's voice had caught the attention of a few others in the gathering, as well. By the time they began the third verse, several voices were dropping off, unsure of the words, but Winn sang as if a hymnal were in front of him. By the final verse he was nearly singing a solo. Cynthie wondered if the others hadn't quit singing to listen.

> While I draw this fleeting breath,
> When my eyelids close in death,
> When I soar to worlds unknown,
> See Thee on Thy judgment throne,
> Rock of Ages, cleft for me,
> Let me hide myself in Thee.

Everyone joined again for a very firm amen. If Winn knew he had become the center of attention he didn't show it. He held Greg in his arms, rocking him gently, while the boy rested his head on his shoulder, ready to fall asleep.

Kyle was aware of it, though. She could feel his body tense beside her. She didn't have to look into his face to know he was angry. She didn't want to. She wanted to watch Winn.

As the mourners started to leave the cemetery, Cynthie took a step toward Winn, but Kyle grabbed her arm to hold her back. She saw Louie and Peter appear on either side of Winn to walk with him out of the cemetery. She wanted to jerk her arm out of Kyle's hand, but the pastor was beside her and she wouldn't make a scene.

Louie and Peter helped Winn put Greg to bed in the bunkhouse. Jeremiah was there ahead of them and Winn wondered if he had stayed near the ranch yard during the service. Peter and Jeremiah had slipped away, but Louie stayed beside him.

"Want something to eat?" Louie asked. Winn shook his head.

Louie seemed nervous, as if he was uncertain of something. Winn had noticed it last night, as well. Around two in the morning, Louie had joined Winn in Cynthie's front room, but hadn't said anything more about Emery's death. Winn had waited for Louie to mention what he had found, what he hadn't told the sheriff. Instead, the older man had finally said, "You best get some rest," and Winn had followed his advice.

Now they stood in the shade of the bunkhouse where Louie could watch the people gathered near the house. The sounds of the crowd were distant and subdued.

"I found cigar butts out there," Louie said suddenly.

Winn thought immediately of Dempsey, but a lot of other men smoked cigars. He knew his mistrust of Dempsey might be purely personal.

Louie went on in a quiet voice. "I tried to like Dempsey 'cause Mrs. Franklin does but I can't do it. There's things I haven't told her on account o' not bein' sure. Some things, too, I guess I decided didn't matter anymore.''

Winn waited for him to continue, hoping he would go back and explain about the things he'd kept to himself. Instead Louie changed the subject. "Do you have any influence over Mrs. Franklin?''

Winn was startled into a laugh. "I don't think so.''

Louie sighed. He watched the crowd for a moment, found Cynthie and noted Dempsey beside her. He had hoped there was something between his boss and young Sutton.

"Well," he started again. "I'm not sure I did right, but I just wanted to protect Mrs. Franklin. Maybe it don't make any difference now, but I just can't be sure.''

Winn didn't speak, and after a moment Louie went on, lowering his voice still more. "I know that Franklin was selling guns down in the Nation. Sometimes the wagons was kept here before goin' south. Dempsey was his driver. I don't see how he couldn't know. Well, I didn't think I could go squealing on my boss, and he wasn't asking me to take part in nothing illegal, so I tried to forget it. Anyway, Franklin died and it was over.

"Except it wasn't over 'cause somebody killed Franklin and we never found out who. Now Dempsey's here all the time and I find myself keeping quiet again to protect Mrs. Franklin. But I got to figure a way to protect her from Dempsey, too.''

"Do you think Dempsey's been stealing her cattle?'' Winn asked. "Why?''

"It don't figure, I know. Seems like if he wants her cattle all he has to do is marry her, unless maybe she don't want to marry him."

There was a hopeful note in Louie's voice that seemed to ask Winn if he knew the woman's heart. Winn wished he could give him the answer he wanted. Instead he remembered something she had said. "Dempsey's been telling Cynthie that it's Ott who took her cattle."

"Well, that don't surprise me. He's playin' on a feud that her husband started. Goes back to that loan Franklin made. Dempsey was mixed up in that, too, I'd just about bet on it."

Winn thought of something else. "Did you know Peter's father borrowed money from Franklin?"

"No," Louie said quickly. "Borrowed money and died. Are you sure?"

"It's in Franklin's ledgers," Winn said. "Merlin's debt was nearly paid off. His land now belongs to Mrs. Franklin."

"I guess there's been a lot of things I just didn't pay attention to."

They were quiet for a time. A young couple bid Cynthie goodbye and headed toward the barn. Louie knew Peter would help them hitch their buggy. By the way Winn turned his head, Louie guessed he was listening to them leave. When they were well past, Winn asked, "What are you going to do?"

Louie sighed. "The sheriff and I are to go out to that camp today. He ought to see the cigar butts the same as me. Tomorrow, I'll take the boys and we'll round up what cattle's left and bring them in close. We can keep 'em here till the grass runs out. I hope the sheriff ends this before then.''

Several people seemed to have decided to leave at once. Their voices grew nearer and passed on. "I better help the boys with the hitchin'," Louie said.

Winn stood alone, listening to horses, harnesses and voices. He was afraid to go very far from the bunkhouse without his little guide who was still sleeping inside.

Cynthie's gaze kept returning to Winn. As the mourners left, she could see them glance in his direction, obviously curious about his blindness or perhaps his presence at the ranch. Only Ott and the pastor bothered to turn aside and greet him.

How she longed to leave the last remaining guests and run to his side. She wanted to tell him how glad she was that he had held her little boy in his strong arms and comforted him. She wanted to say that his singing had been wonderful and she wanted to hear it again. She wanted to tell him that she loved him.

Chapter Ten

Winn sat on the porch swing wrapped in the night. There were more differences in day and night sounds than he had ever realized. It seemed as if even the wind sounded different at night, Winn mused, perhaps because at night it was free to go where it pleased. He tried to empty his mind of all thoughts except the sounds around him.

He heard an owl hoot somewhere near the barn. The wind kept the shells clattering almost constantly. He knew he would never forget the sound of those shells.

That wasn't the only thing he would never forget. It had been a week since Billy Emery's funeral, a week since he had held Cynthie and kissed her. Whenever he thought of her, he thought of her soft body wrapped in his arms. Now, as always, when he thought of it, he tried to think of something else.

The day after the funeral, Greg had taken him to the cemetery to show him where his father and grandfather were buried. Emery's death seemed to have affected him, but he was more curious than unhappy.

Winn had traced his fingers over the carved stones to read the inscriptions. Victor G. Franklin had died in August of 1869, not quite a year ago. He had been forty-five years old. Cynthie's father had been named Tyler Randolph, and he had died in January of the same year and had been fifty-two.

He thought of Cynthie burying her father and husband in little over half a year. He wished he could have been around to comfort her.

He was thinking about her again. There was no getting around it. All week he had tried to avoid her but it hadn't helped. Of course, she was probably glad to avoid him herself, as ill-tempered as he was becoming. He didn't actually lose his temper, but anyone around him was bound to notice how touchy he had become.

He was ashamed of it, but the anger would come on suddenly. He would think of something he wanted to do and instantly realize that he couldn't possibly do it, would probably never be able to do it. It was then that he would feel the surge of anger. He tried to control it by forgetting about what he had wanted in the first place. It didn't work.

The strongest desires always involved Cynthie. He wanted to help her. He wanted to find out who had murdered her hired man and who had stolen her cattle. He wanted to check the campsite himself to see if he might find something the others had missed. It was all so impossible. He wanted, at the very least, to talk to Louie about the murder and what the sheriff might have found, but Louie had been busy all week with the cattle. He and Jeremiah were taking turns as guard, and of course Winn couldn't help there, either.

He should go inside and sleep, give his mind a rest, but the house smelled like Dempsey's cigar smoke and he couldn't turn his thoughts off anyway. "Think about what you can do," the lady had said. Right now he couldn't think of a thing.

Upstairs, Cynthie stood by the window, half listening to the same night sounds. She felt a mood almost of despair coming over her. She hadn't felt this bad since she had lost Victor. She supposed that the death of Billy Emery had stirred up a lot of old feelings.

But a lot of it was due to her present situation. What could she do to save her ranch? Someone wanted her cattle enough to kill for them. She wished whoever it was would just take them and not hurt anyone else. She was worried for Louie and Jeremiah. She was glad, at least, that Louie wasn't letting Peter take a turn guarding the cattle.

It was time she faced the fact that she couldn't run this ranch herself. Kyle had been telling her the same thing the last few days. She didn't need it anyway, not really. She still owned Father's shipping business in New York, and she and Greg could live comfortably anywhere.

Maybe that's what she should do, sell the ranch before anyone else got hurt. Maybe she could keep the house and still live here, raise a few horses. Could she manage that with the help of Louie, Jeremiah and Peter? She knew she wanted to stay out here on the prairie. She and Greg had become part of it and she didn't want to leave it.

She looked down at the letter in her hand. She didn't know how to plan her future. She wanted desperately to include Winn some way, but she knew she was just daydreaming.

There wasn't enough moonlight to read the letter through again. She didn't want to anyway. "If his sight has not returned by the time you receive this, there is nothing I can do. Nerves were probably damaged in the accident and can only heal on their own."

How was she going to tell Winn? He seemed so moody lately and spent more time by himself. She didn't know how to help him. She had been such a fool to think she could, just because her father had been blind. Father had lost his sight gradually, had been given time to prepare for it, and in all likelihood had hidden any anger or despair from his daughter.

Winn's life, on the other hand, had changed so suddenly he didn't know what to do with it anymore. Maybe she could teach him how to live with his blindness but she couldn't make him want to learn. He had to do that himself, and she was afraid he wouldn't.

The doctor had mentioned a school for the blind in Boston. It had been established nearly forty years ago and would probably be very good for Winn. Would he let her send him there? Did she want to send him away?

Anything would be better than watching him like this, she decided. She would tell him about the letter soon. Soon. She felt like a coward. Maybe she could try one more time to get him busy. He was always better when he had been doing something.

She smiled, remembering church last Sunday. It hadn't been hard to talk him into going. The week before he wouldn't even consider it. Surely that was a good sign. They had sat with Greg between them and Winn hadn't seemed uncomfortable at all.

And he had sung. She loved to hear it. So had the rest of the congregation. He had told the pastor that as long as they sang familiar hymns he wouldn't need a hymnal. He had laughed when the pastor told him that the church didn't own any hymnals yet.

But the happy mood hadn't lasted, and by the time they were home he had been quiet and sad again. When she managed to be alone with him, she would see his face harden with anger and he would leave. What did he blame her for? How could she make him tell her what she had done?

She tossed the letter on her dressing table. "Arrogant doctor," she muttered. "If you were going to wait this long, you shouldn't have written at all."

She flung herself on the bed. What could she do to make Winn laugh? There had to be something she hadn't tried yet that would give him confidence, burn some energy, fill up some time. She would think of something if she had to lie awake all night. She was not going to give up yet.

"I think this is crazy," Winn said for at least the third time.

"It'll be fun," Greg said. He tugged at Winn's hand, trying to make him walk faster.

"Fun for you, maybe. You get to watch."

Greg giggled and Winn was sure he heard Cynthie laugh, as well. He turned in her direction. "I want you to remember that this was your idea."

"I can't blame it on Greg?" she teased.

"You help him, Mama. I'm gonna tell Peter."

"Oh, good. Peter's going to watch, too."

"Well, he's got to saddle her for you." She took the arm that Greg had dropped and walked along beside him. She wasn't feeling nearly as confident as she pretended. This might turn out to be a poor idea but it was all she had been able to come up with last night.

"Tell me about this horse, again," Winn said. "I think Greg was exaggerating."

"No, really. All you have to do is sing. She was trained by somebody, God knows who or how long ago, but she walks when you sing. You stop singing, she stops walking. You start singing again, she turns around and comes back where you started."

"I can think of a lot of cases where that wouldn't be very handy."

Cynthie laughed. "You can rein her like any other horse, too, except she's pretty old and won't run, no matter what. Victor found her for Greg and had the boy riding her before he learned to walk."

Inside the barn Peter was saddling the old mare and Greg was playing with Sorry. When he saw them come in, he brought Sorry over to Winn.

"Does that dog ever go outside?" Winn asked, scratching the furry head that leaned against his leg.

"She's not exactly a watchdog, is she?" Cynthie agreed.

"Peter says not all dogs got to be watchdogs," Greg said. "Some dogs is just friends."

"Are friends," Winn said, and Greg dutifully repeated it. Winn had noticed some time ago that he was always hearing about things Peter said but hardly ever heard Peter say anything himself.

"Ready."

He heard Peter going by, leading the horse. He felt her warmth and smelled the distinctive scent that was horse. With Greg's hand in his, he followed the horse outside.

He was really going to ride again. He felt both excited and frightened. At the same time, he wanted to pretend it didn't matter. It was a way of protecting himself, just in case he couldn't do it.

He took a few minutes to get to know the horse who was supposed to teach him how to ride again. She didn't seem as old as Cynthie had indicated. He had expected some poor old nag with her head hanging to the ground.

They had put his own saddle on her. The stirrups shouldn't need adjusting. He had a habit of tightening the cinch just before he mounted, but he was afraid if he did it now, it would look as if he didn't trust Peter. Or that he was procrastinating which he probably was.

He grabbed the saddle horn, grateful no one had offered to help him up. After two tries, he used his left hand to guide his foot into the stirrup.

Finally he swung into the saddle—and almost off the other side! Peter caught him before he fell, but he couldn't quite gain his balance. Having his right foot guided into the other stirrup didn't help as much as he thought it would.

"Stand up in the stirrups," Cynthie instructed.

She had to be kidding. He'd feel even less secure if he tried that.

"Stand up in the stirrups," she repeated. She was close to the horse, her hand on his thigh. "When you sit back down, you'll have your directions straight again."

Directions he took to mean up and down. He followed her instructions and felt better when he was seated again. He gave himself a couple seconds to get used to the feeling. "I think I'm all right now," he said, trying to relax. "Here goes," he mumbled.

"Oh, come along boys and listen to my tale;
I'll tell you of my troubles on the Old Chisholm trail.
Come a ti-yi-yippy, yippy, ya! Yippy ya!
Come a ti-yi-yippy, yippy ya!"

The mare had started walking as soon as he had started singing, just as Cynthie had predicted. He was afraid to stop singing even to catch his breath, for fear she would stop and go back.

"I woke up one mornin' on the Ol' Chisholm Trail
A rope in my hand and a cow by the tail."

He thought he heard someone call out. He had a feeling Greg had decided to run along behind.

"Oh, it's bacon and beans most—"

Something seemed to grab at his face. He raised his arms to fend it off. Tree branches! The old gal had decided to get rid of him! He had stopped singing, but she was still walking slowly. He kicked his boots free of the stirrups and took the fall.

Greg ran up, out of breath, moments after he hit the ground. Winn rolled over and came to a sitting position.

"Peter says, when you fall off, you got to get right back on again."

"Shut up, Greg." It had been an instinctive reaction. "Sorry," he mumbled, coming to his feet.

Cynthie was beside them in a moment. "Are you hurt?" A finger touched a scratch on his face and he pulled away.

"No, I'm all right, I guess." He dusted away dirt he couldn't see and ran his fingers through his hair. "I bet that's the only tree in two hundred miles of prairie and that horse just had to walk under it."

Cynthie laughed then covered her mouth.

He heard the sound as she muffled it and tried to picture how she looked. "Well, I'm glad you enjoyed it."

Cynthie saw a hint of a smile in his dimples and let herself laugh with relief. "Well, you're supposed to hear the tree."

"Hear the tree?" he asked, incredulously. "What do trees say?"

Cynthie laughed even harder. Greg's small fists punched at her legs but she hardly noticed. "If you didn't sing so loud, you'd know." The dimples deepened in earnest, and she wanted to throw her arms around his neck, she was so glad to see them.

Peter led the mare up to the little group under the tree. "Wanna ride her back?" he asked.

"Shut up, Peter," Greg said.

"Greg…" Cynthie scolded, but Winn stopped her.

"No, that's my fault," he said. "And Peter's right. I'll ride her back."

Mounting was just as difficult the second time, except he got his bearings faster using Cynthie's trick of standing in the stirrups.

The trouble this time was he wouldn't know when to stop her and she might just walk right past the house and yard. He tried to make her start with the usual heel in the ribs but she stood patiently, waiting for him to sing. He gave in to her wishes and sang two more verses of "The Old Chisholm Trail." This time he sang softer, and when he heard a shout behind him he stopped and waited for the others to catch up.

After he had dismounted, Greg wanted a ride. Peter lifted him up and went back to the barn. Winn stood with Cynthie as she watched her little boy on the back of the big horse. He was singing his own version of Winn's song, making up any words that he couldn't remember.

"I should put something on those scratches," she said softly.

"No hurry. Mostly, I bruised my, uh, dignity."

Cynthie laughed again and covered her mouth too late. "I'm sorry," she said. "It's just that…" She covered her mouth to stifle another giggle.

"It's just that I looked really funny. Did you know all along that would happen?"

He was smiling again, and it made her heart race. She had been so frightened when she had seen him fall that she had laughed in relief when she knew he wasn't hurt. She turned away to watch her little boy. He had stopped singing for a moment and now he and the mare were on their way back. When she turned toward Winn she was serious.

"I know it isn't quite like the riding you're used to. But it's a first step. It's got to be better than nothing."

Winn was quiet. Cynthie decided he wasn't going to answer and she turned to watch Greg again. Unwilling to end his ride so soon, Greg turned the horse away and started singing again.

"It may be better than nothing," Winn said finally. "But it reminds me of what I can't do."

"But don't you think about it anyway?"

That was certainly true. Trying to forget hadn't worked at all. He intended to remain silent, to let her think she was helping him, but the frustration boiled over inside. "What do you expect me to do, tell you all the things I want to do and let you teach me how to do them halfway?" What would she think if he told her that what he wanted most was her? Would she let him love her halfway? Could she love half a man?

The bitterness in his voice frightened Cynthie. She had no answer to his question; she had no answers at all. She stood silently and watched her son ride around the yard until he tired of the game. Winn stood just as silently beside her, following the movement of the boy and horse by the child's song.

When Greg was safely on the ground again, she took the mare to the barn and unsaddled her and rubbed her down. She had to keep busy, too. She was feeling as lost and bitter as Winn. There was nothing else she could do for him. She had tried everything she could think of. It was time to tell him about the letter and leave the decision up to him.

Cynthie tapped on Winn's door. "I want to talk to you," she said. It had taken longer than usual to get Greg washed and settled into bed and this was her first chance to be alone with Winn. She had heard him moving around while she tucked Greg in so she knew he hadn't been in bed very long.

After what seemed like a long hesitation he answered, "All right."

Cynthie carried a lamp into the room, knowing it would be dark. Once inside, she closed the door and turned to look at him. He was stretched across the bed on his back, his hands tucked under his head. He had removed his shirt and washed. Drops of water on his chest glistened in the lamplight, and the ends of his hair were damp.

"I got the letter," she began. He didn't move. It was like he hadn't heard. "From the doctor in New York."

After a long moment of silence he prompted, "And?"

Cynthie sighed. "And he's sorry."

She crossed the room and set the lamp on the table. She resisted the temptation to pace.

"He mentions a school." She watched for a reaction. "In Boston. We could send you there."

He seemed to be staring at the ceiling. She came to stand near the bed. "Would you go, Winn?"

He took a deep breath and let it out slowly. When he spoke his voice was very soft, almost too low to hear. "I'll do anything you want, Cynthie."

She sat down on the bed next to him and he turned his face toward her. "I can't help you any more," she said. "I just don't know what else to do."

Her fingers reached out and stroked his face. He caught them quickly with his own. "You've done a lot, Cynthie. Whatever happens, I want you to remember that. You've done more than most people would have."

Cynthie swallowed back the lump in her throat. "I'll write to the school tomorrow if you want me to."

Winn nodded. "I don't know how I'll pay for it."

"Don't worry about it." Cynthie sat for a moment and watched him. "I'll write to your family for you, too, if you want me to. Isn't there someone?"

He turned his face away from her. "Not that can afford a school like that."

"That's not what I meant, Winn. Isn't there someone who'd like to know where you are?"

He still held her fingers in his hand. He squeezed them a little tighter. After a moment he shook his head.

Reluctantly, Cynthie pulled her hand away and stood. "Good night," she said. She retrieved the lamp and left the room.

Winn lay for several minutes after Cynthie had gone, his fingers beating out a nervous rhythm on the bed. He rolled to a sitting position and ran his hands through his hair. Resting his elbows on his knees, he held his head, trying not to think about what Cynthie had just said or what he was about to do.

Finally he got up and took the three steps to the corner where his bags were. He felt under the larger knapsack for the saddlebags and brought them to the bed.

He tested the weight of each bag and chose one. He unbuckled the fastener, dumped the contents onto the bed and felt among the articles there, searching. Picket pins. They were what had fooled him. It must be on the other side.

He unbuckled the other fastener. The contents from that pouch followed the rest onto the bed with the noisy clang of metal hitting metal. He felt around again, more urgently. His fingers found a warm piece of wood and he stopped.

He picked up the little piece and held it with both hands. It was the last one he had done. At first it seemed like just a rounded chunk of wood, but he knew each little groove. He traced with his fingers the cuts he had made with the knife. Here were the ears, laid back across the body. There were the haunches, and there the round tail. He had been so proud of it, a little rabbit with no projections that little fingers might break. He held it for a moment more and then tossed it onto the bed and continued his search.

Finally he found what he was looking for. The gun. He always carried it in his saddlebag; he hadn't wanted to wear it since the War. His rifle, in the scabbard of his saddle, was needed more often on a cattle drive than a pistol, he had reasoned. People who wore pistols found reasons to use them.

He ran his fingers over the butt and barrel. He hated this gun. He couldn't hold it and not remember the War. The death and the blood and the pain.

He sank onto the bed beside his belongings. He slowly positioned the gun into his right hand, his finger on the trigger. The cylinder rotated with two ominous clicks when he pulled back the hammer. He sat for a long time before starting to raise it to his head. With a shaking hand, he lowered it onto his lap.

He couldn't do it here. He didn't want Cynthie to come in and find him. The picture made his stomach turn.

He'd walk away, a long way from the house. One of the men would find him. Surely they would understand. Louie could explain to Cynthie how impossible it was to live this way. Louie could explain to Cynthie and Greg.

Greg. Winn felt his head spin along with his stomach. No one would be able to explain something like this to Greg. He had promised Greg that he would say goodbye. Greg already had a father and grandfather buried on the prairie. He couldn't think of Greg and even consider doing this. As useless as he was, he still couldn't do it.

Holding the gun over the bed, he emptied the chambers, hearing the rattle of the cartridges as they dropped against one another. With his fingers, he counted them to be certain the gun was empty, then began gathering the articles from the bed. Rawhide string, picket pins and a picture of Cora all went haphazardly into the saddlebags; he didn't even notice what he shoved inside.

Feeling over the covers to make sure he had gotten everything, he inadvertently sent the little wooden rabbit rolling off the mattress and under the bed, the sound muffled by the discarded blanket.

The next morning, Cynthie was surprised to find Winn waiting for her in the kitchen. He stood when she entered the room. His saddlebags were lying on the table and his fingertips tapped them nervously.

She stood still and watched him. "You're up early," she said. She knew that he might have been up all night.

"I would have made coffee," he said, "but that seemed kind of hazardous. I did bring in some water."

"Thanks," she said. She realized that she had been standing in the doorway staring at him and quickly went to start the coffee.

"I need you to do something for me," he said. "In these bags somewhere is a pistol. I want you to find it before Greg does. Can you put it up someplace?"

"Of course," she answered, coming over to the table. She was standing near him. He wanted to reach out and touch her. He wanted to and couldn't and for once it didn't make him angry. It was as if the cloud he had been trying to outrun had caught up with him last night and now there was nothing left to run from.

Cynthie had opened one side of the saddlebags and tried to look inside. It was so full of things she had to reach in and feel for the gun. Her fingers touched something flat and square and she pulled it out without stopping to think. It was a picture of a woman in a silver frame. She was young and beautiful, her eyes sparkling merrily at the camera. At the bottom a careless hand had penned, "To Winter, with love." When he told her there was no one to write to, had he been thinking of this woman? Was this the Rosie he had called for in his dream?

She felt a stab of jealousy. She knew Winn was listening intently to her movements so she put the picture carefully away and opened the other pouch. Whoever she was, he had left her. Maybe he carried her picture with him and never forgot her, but he wasn't with her, was he? She was surprised at her dislike for someone she knew nothing about.

She found the pistol and made certain it was empty. "I'll put it in the top of the cupboard," she said, crossing the kitchen to do so.

"That will be fine," he said. He said the same when she invited him to eat breakfast in the kitchen with her and Greg. She wasn't particularly surprised; he was more and more willing to eat in their company.

But later she realized that the morning marked the beginning of a change in Winn's behavior. While she had worried before about his irritability, now she worried about his lack of it. He seemed to go along with anything that was suggested and, while he never seemed frustrated, he never seemed happy, either.

Greg didn't seem to notice. He played with his favorite companion and managed to keep them both busy.

Two days later, Winn helped Cynthie move the furniture while she cleaned underneath. She felt a little guilty about asking him to help. She didn't have any real reason to clean; it had never been a high priority anyway. It did, however, give her a chance to spend time with Winn.

She caught herself watching him push aside her desk instead of lending him a hand. He had no right to look so good. The attraction she had recognized a long time ago had only gotten stronger. She felt a need to let him know how she felt about him but she didn't know how to do it. The little flirtatious advances on wash day and since hadn't seemed to register. She couldn't quite bring herself to tell him how she felt. Nothing he had done indicated that her feelings were returned.

The muscles in his arms flexed as the desk slid across the floor. "That's far enough," she told him, hoping her voice sounded sweet and alluring.

He relaxed and turned to lean against the desk. With an inward sigh, Cynthie began to sweep where the desk had been. What excuse could she find to brush against him? She glanced at him. He stood silently listening. As she swept closer, paying little attention to any dirt on the floor, he casually stepped out of her way.

Cynthie wanted to swear. She swept away from him, gathering the dirt that she had earlier scattered. What had she expected? In the mood he was in lately, he probably wouldn't respond if she threw her arms around his neck and kissed him full on the mouth! She glanced at him as she reached for the dustpan. It might be worth a try.

She let the dustpan lie and propped the broom against the wall. She took three slow steps toward him. He looked like he was trying to guess what was happening by the sound.

"Winn?" she whispered softly.

"Winn!" they heard Greg yell. "Winn, guess what!"

Cynthie stepped away, embarrassed. The little boy burst into the room and ran straight for Winn who scooped him into his arms. "What's up, Greg?"

"You mean, 'sides me?" The boy giggled.

Cynthie snatched up the broom and dustpan and began vigorously cleaning the pile of dirt, scattering as much as she swept into the pan.

"Sorry had her puppies," Greg said. "You got to come see them." Before Winn could answer he hurried on. "I know you can't see them but I held one with my eyes closed and I could still see it."

Cynthie found herself smiling. "Go ahead, we can finish later."

Winn let the boy slide to the floor. He took the small hand but hesitated a moment. "Don't try to move that yourself," he said.

"It'll keep," she assured him.

He stood for a moment longer, as if there were something else he wanted to say. Finally the boy's insistent tugging won and they left the house.

Cynthie considered going with them but she was too frustrated to care about puppies. She went back to her sweeping, realizing the games she had been playing to gain Winn's attention had only caused her to clean the same area three times.

She should know better anyway. The more time she spent with Winn, the stronger her feelings for him became, and ultimately the deeper she would be hurt. She should avoid Winn whenever possible, she told herself.

Even as she thought it she knew she would ignore her own advice. In her heart she knew the attraction she felt for Winn was already too strong to ignore.

Chapter Eleven

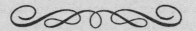

At dinner the next evening, Greg asked Winn if he knew how to play checkers.

"I used to," he said.

"I watched Peter and Jerry play checkers. I know how so I can help you 'member," Greg offered.

"Remembering isn't the problem," Winn said quietly.

Cynthie winked at her son. "After you eat you can get out Grandfather's set."

"I'm done," he said around his last mouthful of bread.

As the boy scampered off to find the game Cynthie began clearing the table. "Father had a special set made," she explained. "The board has pegs that the checkers sit on. There's a peg on the top of each checker, too, for a crown. One player's pieces have smooth edges and the other's have serrated so you can tell them apart."

She helped them set up the game on the table and then turned them loose to play while she washed dishes. Greg was confused at first because the checkers were all the same color.

"That makes the game more even," Winn said.

Greg tried to play with one hand over his eyes but he couldn't resist the urge to peek.

Cynthie listened to them play and tried to pinpoint what had been concerning her. Nothing Winn said really sounded wrong. The way he spoke to Greg was as patient as ever. He made sure the boy was happy, but that was where it ended. It was like he had no feelings of his own, anymore.

"I watched Peter and Jerry play. They was real serious," Greg said.

"Were serious," Winn corrected. "Maybe they were playing for money."

"Jerry said they *were* playing to see who was best."

Winn laughed. "We're just playing for fun, aren't we?"

Greg shrugged. "I get to jump you. Jerry says you don't know he's a colored man."

Cynthie looked at Greg sharply. She hadn't even thought of that, and it could very well make a difference to Winn.

"I kind of thought so by his speech." Winn felt the board to make sure the pieces were where he pictured them. "There are colored men working on the trail drives. They lost homes the same as a lot of others. Crown me."

"Ah, gee!" Greg dutifully put a captured checker on top.

Cynthie was almost disappointed. She might have preferred him to be upset.

The next afternoon Louie returned from town with a letter for Winn. He delivered it to the house with some groceries. Cynthie set it on the table and eyed it as she unpacked the box.

It was addressed to Mr. Winter Sutton, in care of Mrs. Franklin, Wichita, Kansas. Who would be writing to Winn that knew he was here? Had he found someone else to write to his family for him?

She picked up the envelope and studied it thoughtfully. The block letters had been carefully penned and looked almost like a child's. The postmark read Fort Worth, Texas. It must have been from one of Winn's companions from the cattle drive.

She smiled to herself as she dropped the letter to the table and returned to the supplies. This might be just what Winn needed to cheer him up. News from his friends would let him know he hadn't been abandoned after all.

She was setting a box of baking soda on the shelf when she froze. If it was news that Winn's friends were returning for him, it would plunge her into as deep a despair as Winn seemed to be in now. She stared at the letter from across the room. She was tempted to open it, read it, perhaps even answer it without letting Winn know it had arrived.

She heard Winn and Greg coming in the front door and scolded herself for her deceitful thoughts. She called Winn into the kitchen before she could change her mind.

"A letter came for you," she said.

Greg climbed on a chair and looked into the box his mother was unpacking. "Did a letter come for me, too?"

"No, silly." Cynthie ruffled his dark hair. "But Louie bought you a piece of hard candy. I think I lost it, though."

Greg laughed. "No, you didn't."

Cynthie smiled at the little boy. "No, I didn't." She produced the candy from her apron pocket. "Can't fool you, can I? Now run and thank Louie."

In a second, the back door slammed behind the little boy.

Cynthie took a knife from a drawer and slit the envelope. Winn had taken a seat at the table and waited patiently during her conversation with Greg. She glanced at him as she dropped the knife in its place and withdrew the letter. Either he was very good at hiding his feelings or he didn't care at all about the letter.

She cleared her throat. "It's from a Theodore Jackson, Junior."

"Slim," Winn provided.

She took a step toward him and, with an effort, drew her eyes back to the letter. "Dear Winn," she began. She scanned the letter quickly, noting several misspellings. It was all in the same careful block letters and not difficult to read. "I did not want to leave you alone but Mike would not wait and I do not know how to get home. I will speak to Mother and Father. When they know that you saved my life they will let you come live with us. I must hurry now or Mike will leave without me."

She looked from the letter to Winn. "His address is at the bottom," she added. Her heart ached for him but his expression was closed and she didn't know how to comfort him.

When he said nothing she whispered, "You saved his life?"

Winn shrugged. After a moment he managed a small smile. "Nice of him to write."

Cynthie watched him closely. He had a choice now, though she prayed he wouldn't go. After a moment, she asked, "Shall I answer the letter?"

Winn sighed. "Not yet. Let me think about it."

Cynthie watched him rise and leave the kitchen. In a moment she heard the door to his room close quietly. She reread the letter and shook her head. What could she do for him? How could she make him happy? In a few days there would be an Independence Day celebration in Wichita. Winn was going along with her and Greg. She had a feeling that wouldn't make any difference to Winn, since nothing else did.

"Can you hear all the people, Winn?" Greg was too excited to sit still. Winn had held Greg as they crossed the river and now they were on their way to the livery stable to leave the horse and wagon. "Have you ever celebrated 'Pendence Day?"

Winn grinned. "Every year," he lied. He hadn't celebrated anything during the War, least of all Independence Day. "But every place does it differently so this will be new." He didn't say that almost everything seemed new to him now.

Greg had come and sat down beside Winn to talk to him. In a moment, though, something else caught his attention and he scrambled across the wagon bed to get a better look.

He was the first one out of the wagon at the livery stable and was practically jumping up and down, waiting for the others to be ready to go. Finally, he was walking toward the source of all the noise and excitement with his mother on one side and Winn on the other. From the smile on his face anyone would have thought he was the happiest boy in the world.

Peter was trailing a short distance behind carrying the basket with plates and utensils for the four of them and the cake Cynthie had baked as her contribution to dinner. Louie had chosen to stay behind, unwilling to have everyone away from the ranch at once. Jeremiah had gone in early to get Mary so they could attend the celebration together.

At Waterman's Grove a plank stage had been constructed and the orator of the day, William S. Jay of Emporia, was already drawing a crowd. Cynthie led her group to the table that had been set up to hold the food.

"I'm glad you made it."

Cynthie turned at the familiar voice. "Good morning, Kyle." She smiled at her little boy and added, "We wouldn't have missed this for anything." She turned away from Kyle, toward Peter, and opened the basket.

Winn's attention was centered on Cynthie's voice. Had that cheerful greeting been meant for Dempsey? He felt a wave of anger just as Greg pulled away. Winn tried to catch the little hand but it was gone before he knew it. "Greg?" The lack of an answer might not mean he was gone, just not answering.

"I still think you should have let me bring you," Kyle said. He glanced at her companions. A little child, a blind man and a half-grown orphan. He didn't think they were proper escorts for a beautiful woman, but he knew better than to say so.

Cynthie was trying to take the cake out of the basket Peter held open for her while Kyle stood so irritatingly close she could hardly move. It wasn't all Kyle's fault. She knew she would be having a completely different response had it been Winn standing so close.

"Greg?" The boy always ran away from Dempsey. Winn should have anticipated it when he first heard the man's voice instead of letting his jealousy get the upper hand. "Greg!" Winn called again, louder this time.

Cynthie's head come up at the sound of his voice. She looked around quickly but didn't see her child. "What happened?" she asked, making her way to Winn.

"I don't know. He just let go. You don't see him?" Winn wished he could think about this calmly but he couldn't go look for the child. With the river so near, and every type of person imaginable crowding into town, the child could be in danger.

"I'll find him," Peter said.

Winn felt the youth brush past him. Cynthie's hand was on his arm. "Don't worry," she said.

He tried to relax. She could see what the crowd and the area looked like. If she wasn't worried, he shouldn't be.

Kyle tried to make his way to where Cynthie was talking to Sutton. Peter had thrust the basket into his hands before he took off and then the crowd had seemed to work at pushing him farther away from Cynthie. By the time he was at her side, she was comforting Sutton as if it hadn't been his fault at all.

"Why didn't you hang on to the boy?" Dempsey demanded.

Every muscle in Winn's body tensed. If it weren't for Dempsey, Greg wouldn't have run away. He tried to hold his temper for Cynthie's sake.

"Peter will find him," Cynthie said, turning to Kyle and opening the basket again. "I don't think he'll wander very far."

Sutton's very presence here filled Kyle with frustration. Must she advertise the fact that she had taken in a stranger? What was she telling everyone about him? "Well, this is no place for a child anyway," he grumbled.

As he said it, Winn could hear a squeal of laughter that could only have been produced by a little girl, followed by a boyish shout. Obviously Greg wasn't the only child at the celebration. Winn hoped Cynthie heard the voices, too.

"How could you leave a blind man to watch your child?" Kyle continued. He had lowered his voice, and Winn knew he wasn't expected to hear it. The condescending tone the man was using on Cynthie infuriated him. His feelings were aggravated by the knowledge that the man had a point. If anything happened to Greg, it would be his fault.

Winn heard the fancy spurs jingle. "I need to talk to you, Cynthie." The voice was a little farther away. Winn guessed he was following Cynthie to the table.

"Go ahead and talk, Kyle." Now Cynthie's voice was coming toward him.

"Alone." Winn could smell the cigar smoke. He thought he heard the basket pass from one person to the other.

"Kyle," Cynthie said softly. "I can't just leave Winn."

Kyle knew if he let the anger he was feeling show, Cynthie would turn stubborn; sometimes she wasn't easy to control. But he had had all he could stand of Sutton. Anger overruled caution and he grabbed her arm, making her gasp and the dishes in the basket clatter. "If he needs a keeper, how in the hell could you put him in charge of your son?"

Winn lost control. Jealousy, worry and anger combined to make him reckless. He threw a punch directly at the voice. He felt the barest contact and knew Kyle had dodged the blow or else he had misjudged the man's location. He heard Kyle's surprised laugh and knew a frustration worse than any he had experienced before.

"Winn!" Cynthie had his arm. "What's gotten into you?"

He wanted to tell her that he didn't like Kyle touching her or talking to her but he had no right to tell her anything of the kind.

"Kyle," she said and Winn heard a warning in her tone. So the bastard was ready to hit him back. He wished Cynthie hadn't stopped him.

Cynthie looked from one to the other, angry with both of them. Her son was lost and all these two wanted to do was fight with each other. The best thing to do was separate them. If she knew Winn was safe she could talk to Kyle alone and then get rid of him. She looked quickly around and found a bench at the end of the long table.

"Come sit over here," she said to Winn.

Winn heard the hardness in her voice and knew she was angry. He couldn't blame her; he had acted like a fool. No doubt he had looked ridiculous throwing a punch at someone he couldn't see. There was really nothing he could say to defend himself.

Kyle followed behind them. Cynthie slapped the bench and he raised his eyes heavenward in disgust. He would have liked to show Sutton where it was by bodily throwing him onto it.

Once Winn was seated, Cynthie gave him a pat on the shoulder. "Stay here a minute. I'll be right back."

Kyle couldn't watch this anymore. He grabbed Cynthie's arm, setting the basket she carried next to Sutton, and nearly dragged her away.

"What is the matter with you?" Cynthie demanded when he brought her to a stop under a tree near the bank of the river.

"Can't you guess?" He dropped his voice to its most seductive. "I can't stand seeing you with Sutton."

"Kyle, you were rude and insulting. You had no right to talk to Winn like that."

"The fool lost your child."

At the stricken look on her face, Kyle decided to change his tactics. "I'm sorry. I'm just worried about little Greg. And I can't help but feel jealous. When is that man going to leave?"

"I've written to the Perkins School for the Blind. It's in Boston. If they'll take him, he'll go." Maybe saying the words would help her accept them. She looked across the river without seeing it.

Kyle saw the sadness in her face and knew a moment of blinding fury. He glanced toward the table where they had left the object of his anger. There were too many people moving around to see him.

"He's taking advantage of you," he said. "He's been here for weeks."

"Where's he supposed to go?" Cynthie looked toward the table but Kyle grabbed her shoulders and pulled her around to look at him.

"He's made excuses to stay. If you can't see that you're as blind as he is."

"Let me go," she said. She tried to pull away but he wouldn't let her.

"No! You have to listen to me." Kyle struggled for control. "I can't watch you make a fool of yourself over that invalid."

"He's not an invalid!" Cynthie wanted to slap his face but he held her too tightly. Suddenly she wished Winn's punch had landed square on Kyle's nose.

"Face facts, girl! He's using you. He is an invalid and he knows it. He's found a good thing with you and wants to keep it. Tell me, has he made advances?''

''No,'' she answered, too quickly. She could feel the blood rushing to her face.

''I don't believe you.''

Cynthie looked at Kyle and knew her face had betrayed her. ''This is none of your business,'' she said.

''The hell it isn't! You know by now how I feel about you. Marry me.''

''I can't.'' He had finally loosened his hold on her shoulders and she pulled away.

Kyle watched her closely. What did she mean, can't? Horror gripped him. ''Have you and he already...''

''No. Of course not, Kyle.''

He took her shoulders again, this time very gently. ''It doesn't matter if you have. I love you, Cynthie.''

''Kyle, please...''

His hands tightened again, frustration at her making him reckless. ''You better think about it, girl. You're bound to lose everything.''

''What do you mean?'' she asked, shaking off his hands.

''Don't you know why you're the only target around here for those cattle thieves? It's because your ranch is the most vulnerable. A woman alone, an old man as foreman. It's too damn tempting. If you don't do something quick, Ott will just pick off the rest of your men, one by one.''

''And by doing something, you mean marry you?''

Kyle was too self-absorbed to notice the incredulity in her voice. ''Yes! He'd think twice about hitting a ranch run by a man.''

Cynthie was so angry she couldn't answer. She turned sharply away and stomped toward the crowd. Kyle watched her go feeling somewhat bewildered. He had enough sense not to follow.

Winn listened to the spurs as Dempsey and Cynthie moved away from him. He felt absolutely helpless. He didn't want Dempsey talking to Cynthie, though he knew he had no right to object. The thought of Dempsey touching her left Winn fairly shaking with rage.

At the same time he couldn't help but worry about Greg. It had been his fault that the boy had run away. If he had been thinking about the child's feelings when Dempsey had arrived, he could have reassured him. At the very least he could have kept a better grip on Greg's hand. Instead he had been thinking like a jealous lover.

The noises around him were confusing. Cynthie's voice wasn't among them and he knew she and Dempsey had gone quite a distance to talk. He pictured them strolling along beside a tree-lined river and forced the image away.

He needed to keep his mind on Greg. Where might he have gone? What sound around him might indicate an attraction for the boy? His imagination conjured up all kinds of things from the sounds he heard.

His visions of Greg facing one terrible danger or another were interrupted by a tap on his shoulder and a voice near his ear. "Excuse me. We've got to move this bench."

Winn wasn't sure what to do. He didn't want to point out to these strangers that he was blind and needed help going somewhere else.

"They're bringing in another table for the food, and you have to move," the voice added.

Winn mumbled an apology. At least the voice didn't sound impatient with him. He stood up and started to edge away. There were people all around him. If he moved slowly he wouldn't knock anyone over, he hoped.

"Is this your basket?"

"Ah, yes." He reached a hand toward it and the basket handle was placed over his arm, which mildly irritated him as he had expected to grab the handle. He heard the dishes inside clatter before he steadied it with his other hand.

He walked farther away, hoping to get clear of the men moving the table but sure he was putting himself into someone else's path. If he moved away from the noise, he reasoned, he would be moving away from the crowd and therefore out of everyone's way. In a few minutes he stopped and listened, realizing that all the noise was well behind him. He was far enough away that he could no longer smell the food.

He turned around and tried to pick out different sounds. The orator was still expounding but he was too far away for Winn to make out the topic. The sounds of the crowd around the tables of food were even softer than the speaker, which must mean they were farther away. He was sure he was still close enough and tall enough that Cynthie would find him if he just stood here.

Something was thumping against the hard-packed earth. It was a steady beat he recognized as a walking horse and it was coming toward him. He heard the rattle of a chain and knew it pulled a wagon. "Hey! Get out of the way!" a voice yelled.

Winn didn't take time to consider where he should go. He walked quickly at a right angle away from the moving sound. "What are you, blind?" the voice called after him.

Winn had crossed a street away from the celebration. He didn't know what he might run into here if he walked around. He decided he would recross and try to tell by the surface under his boots when he was off the street. He listened for sounds of more wagons or horses and heard none; perhaps the noise from across the street merely drowned them out.

He asked himself why he should care if a wagon did run him down. What difference would it make? In fact, it might be the best solution since he was too big a coward to shoot himself.

Peter met Cynthie before she got back to the crowd. "Is Greg back?" he asked.

"No!" Cynthie whispered, her fight with Kyle forgotten. "Maybe he's with Winn."

She and Peter hurried to where she had left him. A new table had been placed end to end with the first and was already filling up with food. She looked around but couldn't find Winn. She couldn't even see the bench.

"Excuse me, did you see a man sitting on the bench over here?" she asked one stranger after another. Pe-

ter left to resume his search. Cynthie prayed that they
were together, for both their sakes.

Finally she found the man who had asked Winn to
move. "I didn't know he was blind," he said apolo-
getically. "I just thought he was kinda . . ." The man
shrugged and tapped his head.

Cynthie didn't waste time being angry with him, but
went at a run in the direction he had pointed. She tried
to look all around her at once. Finally she came to the
end of the grove and turned in a circle to look behind
her again. Where could he have gone?

She spun around to look across Waco Street and
saw him. He was ready to start across at such an angle that it could put him in the intersection with
Douglas Street. She didn't even look for traffic.
"Winn!" she yelled as she ran toward him.

When Winn heard her voice, he knew the answer to
his question. As long as she was anywhere near him,
he wanted desperately to live. She was at his side in a
moment and leading him off the street. She took the
basket from his hands and set it on the ground with a
clatter. The next moment, her arms were around his
neck and she was pressed up against him. He wrapped
his own arms around her and ignored the voice that
told him he had no right.

"I was so scared," she said into his shoulder. "Why
did you leave?"

"I didn't mean to," he began.

"I know, I know. That man made you get up. But
you came so far."

"I kind of got pushed here and there. I seem to get
in the way easily."

To his complete surprise, she laughed. She slipped out of his arms. "Come on back. I have to look for Greg."

Winn remembered the basket and reached for it where he had heard her drop it. She helped him find the handle and they started across the street. He realized that she was walking in a much different angle than he would have taken.

"I was hoping Peter had found Greg by now," he said when he felt grass beneath his feet again.

"He's probably found someplace to play and doesn't even know he's lost," she said.

"He always takes off when Dempsey's around." Winn regretted the comment the moment he said it. He hadn't meant to remind her of his own bad behavior where Dempsey was concerned. Besides, it sounded like he was trying to place the blame for the boy's disappearance on someone else.

Cynthie surprised him by answering softly, "I know."

They returned to the area near the table where they had been when Greg ran off. There were long tables not far away, waiting for people who were ready to eat. Cynthie led Winn to the end of one of these and set the basket nearby.

"I'm sure Peter can find you here," she said. "I'll come back in a little while to see if he's found Greg."

Winn nodded and prepared for a long wait.

"Hi." The little voice made Winn jump. In a moment Greg was climbing onto his lap.

"Where have you been?" Winn was too relieved to scold. He'd leave that to his mother.

"Over there," came the reasonable answer.

Winn had to laugh. "Why did you decide to go over there?"

"'Cause I don't like Kyle Dempsey."

Winn nodded in agreement. "Tell me why you don't like Dempsey."

"'Cause he's bad."

Winn wasn't sure what he was hoping to find out from the boy but, since he had started, he wanted to continue. "What did he do that was bad?"

"He made Daddy scared of the ferry." Greg's little hands began patting out a rhythm on the tabletop.

"Is that why you're afraid of the ferry?" Winn asked.

Greg's hands stilled and he gave an exasperated sigh. "I'm not afraid of the ferry," he said slowly as if he were explaining something that anyone should know. "I don't like the ferry."

"All right," Winn acknowledged. "Is Dempsey the reason you don't like the ferry?"

"Yeah," said Greg. Winn could hear a frown in his voice as if he were trying to figure something out. "He said some bad things to Daddy on the ferry and made him afraid. There's Mama!"

Cynthie ran up when she saw her child on Winn's lap. She hugged him tightly. "You scared us, Greg," she said. "Stay with us now, all right?" She slipped into the seat across the table.

"Sure," said the boy, settling himself into Winn's lap as if he expected to be there forever. Winn was glad she hadn't scolded him.

Anyway, Winn thought, Cynthie probably blamed him for the child's disappearance. After all he had done this afternoon, she was probably saving all her anger for him.

Peter arrived a few minutes later, smiled at Greg's greeting, and took the seat next to Winn.

"The buffalo's rotten," Peter said.

"That's a shame," Cynthie said but she was so glad to have her family together again that she couldn't bring herself to care.

"What buffalo?" asked Winn and Greg together.

Cynthie explained. "They were going to roast a buffalo whole like you would a pig. What happened?"

Peter shrugged.

"I'd think a buffalo would be a little big to roast that slowly," Winn suggested. "There would be almost no fat, either."

"They dumped it in the river," Peter said.

Cynthie wrinkled her nose. "There's plenty of food anyway," she said.

Winn heard a jingle of spurs and wrapped his arms around Greg just as he started to squirm. "Stay right here," he whispered. "You're with me, remember?"

Cynthie saw her son relax but wondered why Winn thought he had to hold him so tightly. He could let him get down off his lap; he wasn't going to wander off again, surely. She was about to say something when she heard Kyle behind her.

"Can I talk to you, Cynthie?"

She glared at him a moment then nodded, making no move to get up.

He tried to stifle his irritation at having to talk to her in front of her three misfit charges. She had been angry enough when she stomped away from him earlier that he decided not to push his luck. He gave her his most charming smile. "There's to be a ball tonight to dedicate the new hotel. Would you come with me?"

"I can't keep Greg out that late," she said.

He looked over at the boy who was glaring at him with open animosity. That nosy Sutton was hanging on every word. "Send these three home, then. I'm sure Peter can see to their safety. I'll bring you home later."

"Thank you, Kyle, but I think I'll pass. I'm sure it'll be a terrible crowd." She saw the disappointment on his face and for once didn't feel guilty. She knew he was hoping to get her alone and decided it was a safe bet to add, "There's to be dancing this afternoon, though."

Kyle glanced again at her three companions. "I'm afraid I have business to take care of this afternoon." He bade them goodbye and walked away. If he couldn't have Cynthie to himself, he'd wait until another time. An afternoon spent watching over what amounted to three children would probably bring her to her senses better than anything he could say.

Cynthie watched him go with no regret at all. She smiled across the table at her son. "Who wants to eat?"

Just before dark, Peter went to the livery stable and hitched the wagon. Cynthie, with Winn and a very tired Greg, followed more slowly. Greg settled into the back of the wagon with his head on Winn's lap and was asleep before they got to the ferry.

As Peter started the team moving on the west side of the river, Cynthie heard the whistle and pop of the first fireworks of the evening. She wanted to wake Greg so he could watch but she hesitated, unsure of what she would say to Winn.

When she looked behind her Winn was already shaking the boy's shoulder. "Greg, look," he said softly. "You're missing the fireworks."

Greg set up slowly, rubbing his eyes, then gave a little start as the next rocket burst and seemed to shower the town with sparks.

"Watch for me, Greg. Tell me the colors."

Greg climbed into Winn's lap and, with the strong arms around him, exclaimed over each explosion until he became too tired to care.

Cynthie listened and thought her heart would break. What must Winn be feeling, hearing about something he'd never see? She remembered her own glib offer to describe a sunrise. How could she have thought it would be appreciated?

Today must have been awful for Winn. Kyle had been so rude. She didn't blame Winn for taking a punch at him, but it must have been humiliating to miss. He had been quiet all afternoon and she wished she had let him stay at the ranch with Louie.

Realizing that she had failed to help a blind man was one thing. Feeling the man she loved slip away from her was quite another. There must be something she could do that she hadn't yet tried. She glanced over her shoulder at Winn. The lamp on the corner of the wagon gave enough light for her to see that he was awake. Greg slept peacefully on his lap, his little hands folded in Winn's large ones. Cynthie sighed. How many nights had she lain awake already trying to think of a solution?

Chapter Twelve

Winn stood on the porch, his bare shoulder resting against the post. Being out here at night was becoming a habit. He had heard the clock chime once when he crossed the front room and once again a moment ago. Did that mean it had been half past twelve and was now one o'clock, or one and now one-thirty? Either way, it was a long time before sunrise.

He had been awakened by another nightmare. He should learn to go back to sleep after them but they always brought him so thoroughly awake that there was no chance of sleeping. He would be tired tomorrow, and end up napping like little Greg.

What difference did it make? There wasn't anything he needed to do anyway. Greg would take him along as he played. Peter or Louie might find a job for him, just to keep him busy. Even Cynthie would try to keep him from getting bored. Nothing would go undone without him.

It seemed like a useless existence but perhaps no more so than his old life had been. He had a sudden picture of himself pushing cattle past Wichita year after year, never meeting Cynthie and Greg. Perhaps he would even have passed close enough to see the ranch and never discover who lived there.

Would fate have been kind enough to allow him to meet her if he hadn't lost his sight? He pictured himself being sent into Wichita for supplies and bumping into Cynthie at the store. Would she even have noticed him? Or would they each have passed the other by and continued on their separate ways?

Winn found the vision more disturbing than his nightmares. Lately he had been able to imagine going through life blind but found it impossible to imagine living without Cynthie. Yet she deserved more than he could offer. He remembered the school she had mentioned and tried to tell himself he could learn to be useful. Would Cynthie wait for him while he was gone? There wasn't much chance of that with Dempsey around.

Dempsey! Winn shifted his weight to his other leg and adjusted his shoulder on the post. Any thought of that man set him on edge. He thought again of his conversation with Greg. What could have happened on the ferry that made Franklin afraid? Greg said his father was afraid of the ferry. Could Franklin have been afraid of Dempsey? Winn couldn't help but wonder if he was just looking for an excuse to discredit Dempsey.

Sounds inside the house told him someone was up. In a moment, the door behind him opened. He knew it was Cynthie but wasn't sure how he knew. Her steps were different from Greg's, though tonight she was barefoot like her son.

She came to stand beside him. He could smell her, could feel her beside him without touching her. He thought perhaps he could recognize her breathing or his heart somehow knew the special rhythm of hers.

"I heard you come out," she said.

He had been outside for more than thirty minutes. Had she been awake that long?

A light breeze came to life, cooling the air around them and clattering the shells. Cynthie wondered for a moment if she was making the right decision. She had stood by her window, knowing Winn had gone to the porch, picturing him there. She had been afraid for so long that he would leave but now it seemed she had lost him anyway. It was as if he had retreated inside himself and slammed the door. The futile punch at Kyle seemed to have taken the last fight out of him.

She didn't know what to do. Should she comfort him, challenge him, declare her love for him? What would make him want to live?

Even as she had tried to decide what she should do, she had found herself coming to him. The longing in her heart had become too strong to deny. Reason had told her she would only find heartbreak if he didn't return her love, but she decided to ignore it. Experience told her she would only be disappointed even if he did, but her yearning had outshouted that voice as well.

Now she stood beside him, feeling the familiar skip of her heart and the quickening of her breath and knew she had been right to come. "You come out here at night a lot, don't you?" she asked, finally.

"Quite a bit, I guess," he answered.

"Why?"

Winn smiled. "I don't know. I can't sleep. It seems like day and night make less difference now."

"Do you still have the nightmares?" she asked, after a minute.

"Some."

"Do you want to talk about them?"

He thought about it for a moment. He imagined himself telling her the dream he had just experienced standing here fully awake. "Do you think that would help?"

Cynthie took a deep breath. "I don't know, Winn. But if it might, it's worth a try."

Winn smiled. Was she worried about him or curious about his dreams? His mother had had a friend who thought dreams told the future.

She laid her hand on his bare arm. "Please, Winn, I want to help."

Her touch was like a lightning bolt. She had no idea what she did to him or she wouldn't be out here alone with him. "They're pretty bad," he warned, hoping she would run to the safety of her room, praying she would not.

Cynthie tensed, wondering what on earth she had gotten herself into. But if it might help Winn, she was willing to try anything, anything at all. "Go ahead," she said.

He turned toward her, leaning his back on the post. "They're just dreams," he reminded her.

"But if you talk about them, maybe they won't come back," she urged.

"They're never the same, Cynthie." He was amazed at her persistence. Maybe he should just tell her he dreamed of angry cattle and skittish mares and let her go back to bed.

Cynthie watched his face almost disappear as clouds blocked the moon. She tried to imagine what it would be like to be in darkness like this all the time. She reached up toward the face she could barely see but stopped short of touching him. "Did you have these dreams before the accident?"

Winn shook his head. "The first time I heard your voice I dreamed of angels." He wasn't sure why he'd said it; perhaps to warn her there was more he wanted than comfort.

The breeze brought the cool promise of rain. They heard the low rumble of distant thunder. After a long minute, Winn asked, "What do you look like?"

Cynthie's heart skipped a beat. She couldn't speak around the lump in her throat. She found his hands and brought them to her face. She felt a heat in her body that had more to do with desire than the warmth of his touch.

He touched her cheeks thinking how soft the skin was under his rough fingers. He let his left hand cradle the side of her face while his right hand traced the curve of her ear. He caught a lock of hair between his thumb and forefinger and gently followed it down to its end.

"What color is your hair?"

"Black," she whispered.

"As black as the night?" he asked, running his fingers through it to feel its silky texture.

"At least," she said.

"Then I can see it as well as anybody." His hand went back to exploring her face. He traced a finger over her nose and brow. Her bones seemed small beneath his fingers, the curves of her features gentle and soft. She must be beautiful, he thought with a pang of longing. His voice turned husky when he asked, "What color are your eyes?"

"Brown," she said. The touch of his fingers and the sound of his voice were making her knees weak. She leaned toward him, seeking his support.

"There are lots of browns. Brown like what?" He had to keep some sort of reason in the conversation.

Cynthie laughed self-consciously. "I don't know," she said.

"Brown like Lullaby?" His hands were cupping her face, his thumbs gently rubbing her cheeks.

Cynthie hesitated. "I don't think so."

"Brown like a thrush," he suggested.

"Darker," she said and laughed again. "About like your saddlebags."

Winn chuckled softly. "That dark, huh?" His thumbs worked their way down her face. "And what shade of pink are your lips?" He felt as if he had just stepped over a thin line he had thought he was avoiding.

Cynthie's breath caught in her throat. "I . . . I don't know."

His voice dropped to just above a whisper. "I can't tell much about them with just my fingers."

Cynthie leaned toward him, so slightly she wasn't even conscious of it. It was all the invitation Winn needed. He lowered his head and touched his lips to hers but only for a second. "They taste just like I remember them," he whispered.

"Better be sure," she breathed.

Winn thought he must not have heard her right, but there were no other sounds that could have confused him. Slowly she leaned into his body and brought her lips back to his.

Winn felt her silky gown brush against his bare chest and fought the urge to pull her more tightly against him. He had no right to this woman. She wasn't offering what she seemed to be. She was... Hell, he didn't know what she was doing. He wondered if she did. He kept the kiss soft and gentle as long as he could. When his need for her threatened to control him, he pulled away.

She sighed softly and whispered, "I don't think you've studied them enough."

She leaned toward him again but he caught her shoulders. "I don't think you realize what you're doing."

"Of course I do, Winn." She tried to lean against him but he stopped her.

"Cynthie." Frustration tinged his voice with anger. "I may be blind but I'm still a man. Go back to your room before it's too late." He dropped his hands from the soft shoulders and realized he was still praying she would stay.

"I love you, Winn," she whispered softly, leaning against him. "Only a blind man wouldn't see it."

Winn wasn't sure which startled him the most, her declaration of love, her teasing or the soft body he suddenly found pressed against him. When her lips found his again, he gave up and gathered her into his arms. Minutes later, he took her hand and led her into the house and through the dark to his bedroom.

He stopped with his leg touching the side of his bed and turned her into his arms. Without some solid object for reference, he was afraid he would lose track of where he was if he kissed her again, and he wanted very much to kiss her again. But first he had to know. "Are you sure, Cynthie?"

Cynthie ran her hands slowly up his bare chest, feeling the soft hairs, the strong muscles and the hard collarbone. When her hands were on his shoulders, she used them to lift herself upward and planted a soft kiss on his lips as an answer to his question.

Winn gathered her into his arms, nearly bringing her feet off the floor. She clasped her arms around his neck and held him as tightly as he held her. After a moment his arms relaxed and she came slowly back to earth.

His fingers sought the front of her gown for ribbons to loosen and she delighted in the warm touch. Her hands trailed down his chest to the waist of his trousers and began to undo the buttons.

Winn inhaled sharply. "You have an advantage," he rasped. "I can't see the fasteners."

Cynthie heard the hint of frustration in his voice and giggled softly. "Not true. It's dark in here." She brushed his fingers away and quickly found the ribbons.

Winn heard the whisper of cloth as her gown slid from her shoulders and onto the floor. He knew she stood before him naked, truly offering herself to him, and wondered for a second if this was just another dream. If he awoke now to find himself alone it would be the cruelest nightmare of all.

Cynthie gave him a tantalizing kiss at the base of his throat and lay down on the bed. In a moment he followed gingerly, afraid of hurting her. When she was nestled against the length of his body he stroked her hair and whispered, "I think I fell in love with you the first time I heard your voice, I just didn't know it until later."

The words warmed Cynthie's heart and her lips sought his again. She clung to his neck as he slowly rolled her to her back and covered her body with his.

Winn's senses were so filled with the smell and taste and feel of her that, had he been able to see, he was sure he would have closed his eyes to savor the other sensations. His fingers explored the curves of her body. He tasted the skin on her neck and felt her pulse under his lips. He inhaled the scent of her hair as if it were life itself.

The wonderful sensations that had spread to every part of Cynthie's body seemed more intense than any she had felt before. At first she tried to tell herself to hold back, not to let the feelings overwhelm her, that it would only leave her more disappointed when it ended. But Winn's touch was too sweet to resist and soon she was beyond hearing any call but that of desire.

Winn marveled at the fact that this woman could love him. He could feel the truth of it in every touch. She gave herself to him so freely, answering his passion with her own, that he thought his heart would burst.

Cynthie was past wondering, past thinking at all. She was part of Winn and he of her. Their bodies moved together in a victory dance while their lips drank a toast to love. The bonfire at the core of their being rose higher until it exploded like fireworks in a diffusion of pleasure.

For a long time afterward, while Cynthie slept in his arms, Winn lay awake and considered what had happened. How could he live up to the love she offered? Could he, Winn, the blind cowboy, become the man she deserved? He felt her snuggle closer to him and sigh in her sleep. He smiled and kissed the top of her head. Somehow he would find a way to do it.

Cynthie stood in the doorway in her nightgown. It was time she started breakfast, but she had to try once more to talk him out of this. "But you'll be more comfortable here," she argued.

"Comfort isn't the issue," he said calmly.

He was gathering up his things and she refused to make a move to help him. In fact, she considered taking things out of his bag as he put others into it. "And what is the issue?"

"I've got no right to be here. We proved that last night. It'll happen again if I stay."

"You make it sound like last night was some awful mistake!" If he said it was, she wouldn't believe him. She knew what they had shared was special; it hurt too much to even consider otherwise.

Winn stood still for a moment, facing her. "No, sweet, not exactly a mistake and certainly not awful," he said softly.

"Then I don't understand." She came toward him but he went back to his work. She watched him for a moment, trying to think of something persuasive to say. "The bunkhouse isn't far enough away to make a difference," she suggested.

Winn laughed. "Maybe not. But can't you see?" He stopped and took her shoulders. He had known exactly where she was by the sound of her voice. "I don't have any right to even court a woman like you, let alone . . ." He let his voice trail away.

"What?" she coaxed, leaning toward him.

He laughed again and let her go. "You know exactly what. Cynthie, you need to let me try to earn the right."

Cynthie wanted to ask if she was willing to grant him the right, what there was to earn, but she heard Greg running down the stairs. Winn heard him, too, and stopped packing to wait for him.

Greg paused a second in the doorway, taking in the bags on the bed. He ran in yelling, "Winn!" and collided with the man's leg. He locked his hands together around Winn's thigh, determined to keep him where he was.

Winn chuckled. "Good morning to you, too."

Greg knew he was being teased and didn't like it. "You said you wouldn't leave unless you said goodbye," he accused.

Winn pried the boy's arms loose and went down on his level to talk. "I'm only moving as far as the bunkhouse."

Greg took a moment to think about that. "I want to move to the bunkhouse, too."

"No, baby," Cynthie said before deciding to stay out of it. She didn't need to help Winn explain what he was doing. Maybe Greg could be on her side.

"You remember when I came here, I was sick? Well, I'm not sick anymore so I need to go back to work."

"I need to go to work, too," said Greg, puffing out his chest to show how strong he was.

"You'll have to stay here to look after your mama."

Greg scowled at Winn and then at his mother. "I'll still get to play with you every day, won't I? Will you have time to play?"

"I'll make time for you, Greg. Now help me get my things together. I think there's a comb on the stand by the bed."

Greg went to get it and in his hurry to bring it back to Winn he dropped it. "Oops," he said, getting down on his hands and knees to retrieve it. "What's this?" He started to crawl under the bed and came out with the wooden figure. "It's a bunny!" he yelled in delight, bringing it to his mother to see.

"Where did this come from?" She took the rabbit in her hands and looked at the detailed carving. She was as delighted as her son.

Winn realized what Greg had found. "It must have fallen out of my saddlebag sometime," he said, mustering a casual shrug. He remembered dumping the contents of his bags on the bed and suppressed a cold shudder at what he had been considering.

Cynthie brought him gratefully back to the present. "Did you make this, Winn?" He thought her voice expressed more wonder than the little figure deserved. He nodded and went back to his packing.

Cynthie caught his arm and stopped him. "Winn, have you tried to do this since..."

"No!" In a moment he added more calmly. "I haven't thought about it. I've tried not to think about it."

"But Winn, how much of this is done by feel anyway?" She placed the little figure in his hand. "Maybe you could still do this."

Winn held the rabbit, hardly daring to think about what she said. In a moment he smiled. After last night, he might dare a lot of things.

"Can I see the bunny?" Greg was standing back, wondering why the adults were acting so funny over a toy.

Winn turned toward the child's voice and went down on one knee. He held out the figure and Greg took it, climbing up on his lap the way he had done so often. "You can have the bunny," Winn said.

Greg gave Winn a quick hug and ran off to make the bunny hop across the porch. Cynthie picked up the comb her son had forgotten.

"I think that's everything," Winn said.

"If I find anything else, I know where to find you."

She had tried to sound seductive but Winn only nodded and began gathering up his bags. She made one last try. "If this is to protect my reputation..." she began.

Winn laughed. "Maybe it's to protect mine." He waited for her to step aside. When she didn't, he started around her.

She stepped in front of him again, placing a hand on his chest. "I love you," she said.

Winn smiled. He bent toward her and she rose to kiss his lips. "I know you think you do," he said softly. "Let's make sure it isn't pity you're feeling."

Cynthie thought about it for a moment before she stepped aside. She watched him walk out of the room and out of the house.

Greg stopped playing to go with his friend to the bunkhouse. Inside, Louie stood near the stove stirring up batter. At the table, Peter sat with a book open in front of him. Greg greeted them both as he came in and Winn nodded his hello.

Louie took in the knapsack and saddlebags and grinned at Greg. "Show him Emery's old bunk," he said.

Louie and Peter exchanged a look as Greg led Winn toward the back of the bunkhouse. "Betts ate early and relieved me at the herd," Louie said. "I'm just fixin' breakfast for myself and Peter, here. Care to join us?"

Winn had dropped his things on the bunk and let Greg lead him back to the other two. "That would be fine," he said. "Greg, you better get back up to the house for your own breakfast."

Greg let go of Winn's hand but made a side trip over to Peter and Louie on his way to the door. "See the bunny Winn made?" He showed them quickly, not wanting them to try to hold it. "It's mine," he emphasized just before he left.

Winn cleared his throat as he came forward, reaching for a chair. "I hope you don't mind, Louie."

"Nope," the older man answered. "Not my place to mind anyway."

Winn nodded. He had located the chair and moved around it to sit down. "That's not exactly right. Cyn...Mrs. Franklin says you do the hiring. I can't imagine I'll be worth much, but I can try."

Louie flipped a flapjack over. He grinned at Peter and said thoughtfully, "I heard about the fence. I reckon we can take you on, on a trial basis."

After breakfast Peter said, "I've been riding Lullaby."

"Oh?" Winn sat up straighter, revealing his interest. "How's she doing?"

"Good," said Peter, nodding thoughtfully.

"He's been riding her about every day," Louie said with pride in his voice. "She hasn't thrown him yet, has she, son?"

Peter shook his head. "Tried, though."

Winn knew what that was like. "Will she ever be safe for anyone else to ride?"

Louie laughed but Peter answered, "Sure." He grabbed the last flapjack, rolled it up and took it with him as he went to do the morning chores.

"Peter's taken a likin' to that horse," Louie said.

"So did I, when I was young and foolish."

Louie laughed. "Are you old and wise, now?"

Winn shook his head. "No, I'm afraid not. I still fall for the unpredictable ones."

Louie chuckled. "But we were talking about horses, weren't we?"

Winn shook his head and Louie chuckled some more. "You go out to the barn and holler at Peter. He'll put you to work. I got to get some sleep."

Winn complied. As he went out the door he heard Louie whistling as he cleared the dishes from the table.

Three days after Winn moved to the bunkhouse, he stuck the picture of Cora into his shirt pocket, gathered up his carved toys and counted the steps to Cynthie's kitchen door. He had left Greg playing with the four growing puppies. They would keep the boy busy enough to allow him a few minutes to talk to Cynthie.

"What's all this?" she asked as she met him at the door. He dumped his armload on the table and she picked up one of the little figures. "Oh, Winn! These are wonderful!"

"I came to ask a favor." He removed the picture from his pocket and handed it to Cynthie.

The smile faded from her lips as her attention went from the fat little raccoon in her hand to the picture in his. She felt her throat close and wasn't sure she could force her voice through it. She swallowed hard. "Who's this?"

Winn smiled. Was there a touch of jealousy in her voice. "Cynthie, meet Cora." She hadn't taken the picture from his hand. He extended it a little farther. "My sister."

"Oh!" Cynthie gasped, finally taking the picture. "Your sister." She studied the merry eyes and dimpled cheeks in the photograph and looked up at Winn. His face held a similar expression. "Winn, I should have guessed," she blurted before realizing that she had just given away the fact that she had seen this picture before. She didn't want him to think she had gone through his things. She added quickly, "I saw this the day you brought me your gun." He was still smiling so she continued. "I thought she was an old girlfriend, like Rosie."

"Rosie!" Winn's expression went from amused to stunned.

Cynthie bit her tongue. She didn't really want to talk about Rosie, but now she had to explain where she had heard the name. She got up quickly and moved to the cupboard, gathering two cups, hoping her action would cover her embarrassment. "You called to her in your sleep once."

She set the cups on the table, unable to look at Winn. She wanted to postpone his reply, even if it meant making a fool of herself. "When you first came, remember? The night of the storm."

Winn listened to the voice, the sounds of her steps, the coffee being poured. "Called to her in my sleep, huh?" He was trying not to laugh. "I can believe that. Rosie's shown up in more than one of my dreams."

Cynthie sank into a chair. "Coffee?" she offered, trying to sound cheerful.

Winn pulled out a chair and sat down. "You don't have to be jealous of Rosie." He couldn't help but laugh a little.

"Of course I'm not jealous, and you don't have to explain." She picked up the carved raccoon and tried not to think about throwing it at Winn. "Did you want me to send these to your sister?"

Winn was quiet, savoring the moment. Cynthie was jealous! It would last only as long as she didn't know who Rosie was. He'd let her find out along with Cora. "I want my sister's children to have the toys. Could you take down a letter, too?"

"Of course. I'll get paper and ink." Before she left, she moved the coffee cup into his hand.

He listened to her leave, smelled the coffee, enjoyed the feel of the warm smooth china and tried to think of what he would tell Cora. When Cynthie was ready, he began, "Dearest Cora, I hope this letter finds you and your family well."

Cynthie wrote the words carefully on the page and glanced up at Winn. His brow was drawn in concentration. "Take your time," she said gently.

Winn gave a short laugh. "This is harder than I thought it would be. Let's tell her who you are first. She's going to know it's not my handwriting and she'll be worried. We need to tell her right away that I'm all right."

Cynthie smiled. "I am well," she suggested. "Cynthie Franklin is writing for me because I cannot see"?

"Something like that," Winn said, raising the coffee cup to his lips. "Then I'll explain about the accident." He listened to the pen scratch the paper. When it was silent, he began again, speaking slowly as he chose each word.

"We were taking the herd to market in Abilene and had just left the Indian Nation when the accident occurred." He gave her a few seconds to catch up. "You will remember the young drover named Slim. He got himself into a mess and I was trying to get him out. He roped a cow he was trying to return to the herd and had her turn on him."

Out of the corner of her eye, Cynthie could see Winn's fingertip trace patterns on the tabletop as he tried to become accustomed to writing verbally.

"The cow had gored the horse and Slim was down before I got my rope on her, too. I regret to add that Lullaby was no better behaved than when last I wrote and—"

Cynthie interrupted, "Slow up a little."

"Sorry." Winn fought the urge to tap his finger. When her pen was quiet he asked her to read the last sentence and then he continued, "While I succeeded in distracting the cow, my horse threw me before we were safely away. You will be glad to hear that Slim is fine and my own injuries are all but healed. Mike's timely arrival made short work of—"

Cynthie caught up as Winn hesitated. "Of Rosie, which is what we named the cow."

Cynthie's pen was still poised over the paper. She was glad Winn couldn't see how embarrassed she was. After a full minute, she dipped the pen, reciting his words as she finished writing his last sentence. "So Rosie was the cow."

Winn grinned. "Still jealous?"

"Don't be silly," she said quickly. "What else do you want to say?"

"I want to say that you're probably very pretty when you're embarrassed."

"I mean in the letter." She tried to sound exasperated but it came out with a laugh.

"Ah, yes, the letter. Read back to me what we've written so far." She did, and he concluded, "Cora, dear, I've fallen in love with a wonderful woman. If I can prove to her that I am worthy of her love, I plan to stay here in Kansas. Hug the children for me. Your brother, Winn."

It seemed to take Cynthie a long time to write what he had told her. She was sure Cora would be able to tell that her hand was shaking as she wrote the words. Winn loved her! He was going to stay! Finally she helped him sign his own name to the page and dipped the pen in the ink again. She knew he would hear the scratch of the pen on the paper but she had to add a postscript. "He doesn't have to prove anything to me," she wrote and signed it, "C.F."

"The address is on the back of the picture," Winn explained. "I had Peter write it there for me right after Emery's funeral."

Cynthie wondered for a moment what might be inferred from that statement. "I'll get some paper and string to wrap these," she said, rising from the chair. Footsteps and the jingle of spurs on the front porch caught their attention. Cynthie nearly groaned aloud.

Winn stood. "I'd be obliged," he said. "Louie and I are going into town tomorrow, so I can mail the package then. I'll come by for it and a list of what you might need."

They heard Dempsey knock.

Winn spoke quickly. "I'll come back another time and we can write to Slim."

"You don't need to rush off, Winn," she said, laying a hand on his sleeve.

He didn't answer, just patted her hand and went out the door.

Dempsey knocked again. "Coming," Cynthie called. She scooped the letter, the picture and the figures from the table and deposited them on her desk, closing its lid quickly on her way to the door. She didn't want to listen to what Dempsey would say about any of them.

Chapter Thirteen

Winn couldn't get Dempsey out of his mind. From the time he walked out of Cynthie's kitchen until Dempsey rode out of her yard, Kyle Dempsey was all Winn could think about. This was the man's second visit since he had moved to the bunkhouse. He told himself he was glad to be far enough away that he didn't have to smell Dempsey's cigar smoke. However, he had come to notice that Dempsey spent more time with Cynthie than Winn did.

He was still thinking about him the next day when he and Louie were hitching the wagon. He decided he hated Kyle Dempsey from the tips of his fancy spurs to the end of his foul-smelling cigar. He was beginning to wonder if his idea of giving Cynthie some time to think had been such a good one after all.

Louie checked the chain Winn had fastened and said it was fine. Winn was sure Louie could have hitched the wagon faster without him, but he was determined to learn. Next time, he vowed, his efforts would really help.

"Go on up to the house and get Mrs. Franklin's list," Louie said. "We'll be ready to go in a couple minutes."

Winn nodded and began walking toward the house. At the back door he knocked, feeling as nervous as a schoolboy.

Greg opened the door and laughed at him. "Why didn't you just come in?" he teased.

Winn smiled at the boy as he stepped inside the door. "Is your mother here?" he asked.

"I'm here," she said. Her voice came from the table.

"I've come for the list, ma'am, and Cora's package. Louie and I are about ready to go."

Cynthie studied him for a moment. So she was "ma'am" again. She had been Cynthie just the day before. But then Dempsey had arrived. She refused to call him Mr. Sutton. If she was his employer now, she could call him what she wished.

She got up from the chair and crossed the room, pretending to check something in the cupboard. "The list is nearly ready, Winn," she said. She was stalling so she could watch him for a minute. He was trying to look very dignified but Greg was swinging one arm and he wasn't going to do anything that might hurt the boy's feelings. She was sure he realized that Greg couldn't understand the change that had occurred, literally, overnight.

She smiled thoughtfully. "Greg, honey, go check in Mama's sewing box to see if I have any more blue thread. I think I'm almost out."

The boy ran to comply and Cynthie moved nearer to Winn. "I forgot to ask you yesterday how the job is working out."

Winn detected a certain amount of humor in her voice. "Ain't fired me," he said, trying to sound like Peter.

Cynthie bit her lip to keep from laughing. "I can fire you, too, you know." She stepped even closer.

"Thought so," he said.

Cynthie had to laugh out loud. "Here's my list." She put it slowly into his shirt pocket and patted it.

Winn asked in a very low voice, "You flirtin' with me, ma'am?"

Cynthie started to lean toward him. "I'll show you flirting," she whispered.

She jumped back as Greg came running into the room. "You got a whole new one and a little bit of another," he announced breathlessly.

Winn grinned. The list was in his pocket. She had already known she wasn't out of thread. He patted his shirt pocket the way Cynthie had, and she blushed. "Anything else, ma'am?" he drawled.

Cynthie ran a finger down his dimpled cheek. "Just your package," she whispered.

Winn waited, not moving, and Cynthie sighed.

Greg ran to the table. "I'll get it," he said. Cynthie stepped back as the boy put the package into Winn's hands.

"'Bye, Winn," he yelled after his friend as he went out the door.

* * *

At the river, Winn helped Louie unhitch the wagon and added his strength to the wheels when it was time to roll it on and off the ferry. As they bounced over the rutted streets of Wichita, he realized that at least part of the town was starting to feel familiar.

Louie pulled the wagon up beside the general store and set the brake. Winn followed him off the wagon and into the store by the sound of his steps. He waited just to one side of the door, enjoying the smells of the store. Coffee, pickles, leather and sawdust. Winn frowned at this last one; maybe he was mistaken.

Louie was giving the list to the storekeeper, who began directing him to the various items. Louie stepped in front of Winn. "Box weighs about forty pounds. Put it in the wagon."

Winn took the box and was grateful for the warning of its weight. He turned carefully and stepped out the door. He listened for footsteps. Hearing none, he crossed, found the wagon and placed the box safely in the bed.

He was smiling when he turned to go back into the store. He had taken only a couple of steps when he bumped into someone who seemed to be standing still. "Excuse me," he said, stepping back.

"See, I told you," a voice said to an invisible companion.

"Told him what?" Winn was smiling but there was a hard edge to his voice.

"That you can't see." There was laughter and a little shuffling of feet as if one companion had nudged the other.

Winn knew he was facing the source of the voice so he could pretend to look straight at him. He also knew that the man could be waving his hand in front of his eyes. He decided he didn't care. "Can't see what?" he persisted.

"Come on, Howie. Let's leave him alone." This was a new voice.

"Can't see nothin'," said the first, ignoring his friend.

"I can see you're an idiot," Winn said, knowing he was getting too reckless. He heard slow steady footfalls that ended beside him. He didn't know if someone was taking his side or if the bullies now had him surrounded.

"What did you say?" Howie was angry now.

"I think he called you an idiot," came a voice next to him. Ott! This was a surprise.

"And I think I'm agreeing with him." Louie spoke from the door of the store.

"Sorry, fella," said the second stranger and, with his grumbling companion, moved on down the walk.

"Good to see ya, Reuben," said Louie, coming forward.

Ott shook hands with both men. "Can I help you load the wagon?" he asked.

"I never turn down an offer like that," Winn said.

Ott followed them into the store and Louie indicated a sack of flour. As Ott lifted it he commented, "That new counter over yonder'll be nice when it's done but the place sure is a mess in the meantime."

Winn grinned. He hadn't been mistaken about the sawdust.

"What ya say, I buy you two some lunch?" Ott suggested.

"Now, *I* never turn down an offer like *that*," Louie said.

The café Ott chose hadn't yet begun to fill with the noon crowd. As soon as they found a table, Ott asked for the day's special, smothered pheasant. Winn considered declining but he knew he would be hungry later. Besides, he had to learn to do this sometime.

Louie seemed to sense his hesitation. "All the meat's off the bone and it's too good to pass up." He added to the waitress, "Make that two more."

When the waitress had gone Ott asked, "Know any more about who killed that cowhand of yours?"

Louie shook his head. "Nobody's tried anything else but we moved the cattle in close and posted a guard. That wouldn't stop a determined thief, though."

"It's such an awful thing. I can't help thinkin' it was a lot like Franklin's death."

Louie nodded. "Thought of that, myself."

"Course," Ott continued. "Franklin had some enemies."

Winn spoke for the first time. "Enemies?"

"Well, let's just say he made some folks mad." Ott was clearly hesitant to say what he had been thinking. He added hastily, "None of 'em would hold a grudge 'gainst Mrs. Franklin."

"It's hard to tell. If someone's mad enough he might," Winn said. "If you know anything, it could be important."

"I think a lot of Mrs. Franklin," Ott said. "She don't take to me, but that don't matter."

He was quiet for a moment as if considering what he should say. "Well, several of us around here found ourselves needin' money," he began. "And Victor Franklin seemed like the one to go to. His rates were reasonable and here he was a family man and all. Well, we all took our money and went to work, payin' it off like we should. Only thing was, after a while, Franklin sends Dempsey out to run us off."

"Exactly what did he do?" Winn asked.

"Well, he come out to my place and talks like this wasn't a healthy place to stay. You know, nothing real threatening, but there just the same." He leaned closer to his companions and lowered his voice. "Now I know for a fact that he threatened Merlin out there 'cause Merlin told me. Weren't long after that, Merlin was dead."

"Peter's father," mumbled Louie.

"But that can't have nothin' to do with this. Dempsey was workin' for Franklin. He didn't come back to bother me after Franklin died."

Louie shrugged. "I ain't good at figurin' other people's doin's. Kinda makes my head hurt."

Winn said, "I think Dempsey threatened Franklin."

"How would you know that?" Ott asked.

"Something Greg said. I've got a gut feeling Dempsey's into this up to his . . . cigar."

Louie laughed. "And the fact that he's courting Mrs. Franklin doesn't have anything to do with your gut feelin's."

"Not a bit," he said, and knew it was a lie.

The waitress brought their plates and Louie told Winn where everything was. He offered to cut the pheasant into smaller pieces and Winn accepted, feeling a little foolish but reminding himself that spilling all the food in an effort to cut it himself would prove even more embarrassing.

Winn wanted to hear more about Mr. Franklin and Dempsey but Louie and Ott confined their conversation to local politics and Winn had to concentrate on the meal. He could tell that the café was filling with customers and was glad when they were ready to leave.

Ott walked with them to the wagon and bade them good luck. When they reached the west side of the river, Dempsey was waiting to take the ferry into town.

"Afternoon, Mr. Dempsey," Louie said.

Dempsey didn't speak, but walked his horse past them with no more than a glance and a tipped hat.

Winn helped Louie hitch the wagon and when they had traveled a half mile from town he said, "Take me out to Dempsey's place."

Louie could think of a lot of arguments against it. In the time it took to travel to Dempsey's small cabin, he came close to mentioning three or four of them. Each time, though, he would look at Winn and decided to keep his misgivings to himself.

Finally he said, "It's just ahead here. What do you expect to find?"

"I don't know, a bunkhouse full of hired guns, maybe."

"I hope you're kidding," Louie said.

"If he's into something this bad, he'll keep any hired men a long way from here. If they were out here, people like Ott would know about it, which is the last thing he would want."

"I hope you're right." Louie stopped the wagon well away from the group of buildings. "Doesn't look like there's anyone around."

"Hello, the house!" Winn called. Louie jumped enough that Winn could feel the seat shake. "We're just being neighborly," Winn explained calmly.

While they waited for an answer, Louie eyed his companion skeptically. Finally he decided it was safe to move in closer. As he set the brake in front of the house, Winn said, "Tell me what you see."

"Well, there ain't much to recommend it, that's for sure. There's a slap-together cabin, a lean-to shelter what pretends to be a barn, and one shed."

"Let's start with the shed," Winn said, climbing out of the wagon.

"Start with the shed," Louie mumbled, coming around the wagon to lead Winn toward it. "The best thing I could do right now is fire you. You keep forgetting who's boss."

Winn just grinned. "You want to find something here as much as I do."

"Now that's where you're wrong," Louie said, leading Winn forward. "I want the sheriff to find somethin' here."

The shed was dark inside. Louie struck a match but found no lantern. Leaving the door wide open brought in enough light for him to see a little. "What are we lookin' for?"

"Let's start with branding irons. Could he turn the Franklin brand into his own?"

"Nope, won't work. Franklin's a rocking *F*. Dempsey uses a lazy *K*, which is seemin' more appropriate all the time." Louie was looking into the shadows of the little shed. Most of the tools stored there looked as if they hadn't been used in a while.

"Could he have another brand registered that you haven't seen?"

"We won't find out here," Louie said.

"We will if we find a second iron."

"Here they are." Louie found the irons hanging on the wall behind the door. "This one's the *K*. Here it is. Circle *P*."

"Would it fit?"

"I'd bet on it. But Winn, this ain't exactly proof."

Winn was thinking the same thing. "If we could find a rebranded cow, the hide would show it."

Louie shook his head. "Never seen a circle *P* cow. Chances are he brands 'em and heads them straight to market."

Winn wasn't discouraged. "At least we know who to watch."

Louie hung the irons back where he had found them and led Winn out of the shed, eager to be away. In the wagon, he asked, "You want to be the one to tell Mrs. Franklin what we found?"

"It'd be a pleasure," Winn answered.

Louie shook his head and mumbled, "You're crazy." He turned the wagon out of the yard and started toward home.

Louie's mention of proof was bothering Winn. He wanted to confront the man, force a confession from him. He was hardly in a position to do that.

They had traveled barely two miles from Dempsey's when he felt Louie tense beside him. It was all the warning he got. A moment later there was a buzz of a bullet over his head and the report of a rifle.

Louie whipped the horse into a run and Winn held tightly to the wagon seat. He felt Louie slump against him as the rifle cracked again.

Winn bent forward to find the reins in Louie's slack fingers. Another shot buzzed over his head, with the rifle report an instant later. Was it his imagination or was there a fraction more time between the whine of the bullet and the sound of the discharge? Perhaps the rifleman wasn't following. He kept himself low, holding the reins but letting the horse run.

Between the sounds of the running horse, rattling wagon and his own heartbeat, Winn couldn't tell if a rider might be coming behind him. When the horse was growing tired and there had been no more shots, he sat up enough to check the man beside him. The front of his shirt was warm and wet. "Louie," he said. "Hang on." But he was afraid it was already too late.

He hoped the horse would have sense enough to run for home. He had slowed some but, even at this speed, a wheel could hit a rock or hole and overturn the wagon. There would be no help for Louie if that happened. He pulled on the reins and brought the horses to a trot. "Home," he yelled and dropped the reins.

He took out his handkerchief and pressed it to the sticky hole in Louie's chest. He felt the wagon swerve and hoped it was the right direction. His sense of distance had been confused by the run. In a few minutes he heard a shout and the wagon was slowing.

"Peter?" he called, praying that the horse had brought him home.

"Here." Peter had brought the rig to a stop and was climbing up beside Louie.

"Oh, God! What happened?" It was Cynthie's voice. She had seen the wagon come in and was running from the house.

"Get Dr. Gordon, Peter," Winn said.

Peter didn't bother to answer. He ran for the corral to saddle a horse.

Cynthie was already beside the wagon. She felt quickly for a pulse.

Winn was still holding the handkerchief against Louie's chest. Blood was seeping between his fingers. "Is he . . . ?"

"Not yet," Cynthie answered. "Can you help me get him inside?"

Winn climbed down from the wagon. "The bunkhouse is closer."

Cynthie helped Louie into Winn's arms and led the way. Inside, they laid the man on his bunk. Winn had felt no sign of life and wondered if Cynthie knew for sure the man was still alive. He couldn't help but think that this had been his fault. He had underestimated his enemy, and now Louie was dying.

"Sit here beside him," Cynthie instructed. She took his hand and pressed it to the wound. "I'll get some water."

In a moment she was back. She moved Winn's hand away. "The bleeding's slowed," she said.

"Where's Greg?" Winn asked softly.

"He's asleep upstairs." Cynthie's mind was racing around in circles. She wanted Betts called in from the herd; it was too dangerous now. Should she have told Peter to bring the sheriff, as well? No, the doctor was the most important thing. Greg could wake up any minute. God, Louie looked awful!

"What happened, Winn?" she finally asked. "Who did this?"

Winn took a deep breath and let it out slowly. "Cynthie, I can't be sure, but I think it was Dempsey."

"That's impossible! He'd have no reason!"

"Louie and I went out to his place to look around," Winn started to explain.

"You what! Why?"

"Cynthie, there are things that you don't know. Things that Louie and Ott..."

"Ott! Did he put you up to something? I'd bet he did this."

"Cynthie, please. You need to listen to me."

"You couldn't see who did it."

Winn didn't need to be reminded. Louie had seen someone, he was sure of that, but Louie might not live to tell. "I didn't mean for this to happen," he said softly.

Cynthie didn't want to fight with Winn. She didn't want Louie to die. She didn't know what she should be doing to try to save him. "Greg could wake up any minute," she whispered, her voice shaking.

Winn knew Cynthie was crying and he wanted to take her into his arms and promise to protect her. It wasn't a promise he could keep.

"I better wash the blood off my hands and go to the house. I'm afraid I can't help you much here." He got up and left the bunkhouse while Cynthie's soft sobs tore at his heart.

He was opening the front door when he heard Greg's hurried footsteps on the stairs. Greg ran to Winn to be lifted into strong arms.

"Did you get any candy in town?" asked the boy, giving Winn a hug.

"You bet. Can you help me unload the wagon?"

Greg slid to the floor and puffed out his chest. "Yeah," he said, taking Winn's hand and walking out the door. "Where's Mama? Why's the wagon so far from the house?"

Winn decided to take one question at a time. "Help me move the wagon closer."

After the run from Dempsey's place, moving the wagon in the yard didn't seem like too big a problem, especially with Greg to tell him when to stop. When the wagon was close to the back door, Winn climbed down. "You'll have to help me decide what goes in here and what needs to go to the bunkhouse."

"Sure," Greg said, climbing into the wagon bed. "You 'member what Mama wanted?'

"Louie told the storekeeper to put your candy in your mama's box."

When the box was sitting on the kitchen table, Winn and Greg climbed onto the wagon and drove it into the barn. "We'll take the things to the bunkhouse later.

Now you'll have to help me rub down the horse,''
Winn said as he climbed down.

"Where's Peter?''

Winn took a deep breath. He had been putting this
off and it wasn't getting any easier. "He went for a
doctor, Greg. Louie's hurt. Your mama's with him in
the bunkhouse.''

"Oh." Greg climbed out of the wagon and slipped
his hand into Winn's. "How did he get hurt?''

Winn knelt to Greg's level and the boy climbed onto
his knee. "He was shot, Greg.''

"Like Billy?''

Winn wished to God he could see the child's face.
How would he know when he had said enough and
when he was saying too much? "Yes, but Louie isn't
dead." He didn't want to add that Louie could be dead
in a very short time, possibly was already.

Greg didn't speak or move.

"Do you understand what I said?'' Winn asked.

Greg squirmed a little. "I want Mama so I can cry,''
he said in a small choked voice.

"Son, your mama's doing all she can for Louie and
Doc Gordon should be here soon. You know how Peter can ride. But when Peter gets here with the doctor,
he'll be tired and we need to help him by taking care
of the horse. He had a run, too, and needs to be fed
and watered and rubbed down. Do you think you can
help me?''

Greg slid off his knee and took his hand. They were
unhitching the horse when they heard Peter ride in
with the doctor. Winn wanted to go to the bunkhouse
to hear what the doctor said, to be with Cynthie

whether the news was good or bad. He knew he needed to stay with Greg instead. In a few minutes, Peter came to the barn. He took care of his own horse and the doctor's then helped Winn.

When they were done Peter went to saddle a fresh horse. "I'm to bring Betts in," was all he said.

Winn took Greg's hand and they walked to the bunkhouse. They sat on the bench there and waited for word.

"I'm hungry," Greg said after a while.

Winn wasn't sure what to do. Maybe he should take the boy to the house and see if he could find something to eat. The thought almost made him panic. "Your mama won't be much longer," he said.

"I want Mama," Greg insisted and Winn realized that the child was probably scared as well as hungry. He wished he could assure him that Louie would be all right but he knew that wouldn't be fair.

"I'll see if your mama can come out. You wait here." He patted the boy's leg and stood, making his way to the bunkhouse door.

Inside he stopped and listened for a moment. He could hear voices across the room at Louie's bed. If Gordon was removing the bullet and needed Cynthie's help, he didn't want to interrupt. In a moment he heard Cynthie say his name.

"I didn't mean to bother you but your son is asking for you," he said.

"Go ahead," Gordon told her. "I'm about done here."

Winn could hear the splash of water as Cynthie washed. In a moment he heard her shoes tapping across the room. She paused beside him before leaving the bunkhouse without a word.

Winn wanted to go with her but he knew she didn't want him to. He shouldn't have gone to Dempsey's. She had every right to be furious with him. It was his fault Louie was shot and probably dying. He had made her more upset by blaming Dempsey.

He heard the splash of water again. "How is he?" he asked.

Doc Gordon sighed. "He's bad, I won't pretend he isn't, but he might live. I've done what I can."

"Thank you." Winn listened to the doctor as he gathered up his instruments. He wanted to ask how he could help but knew there was nothing he could do. "Would you send the sheriff out when you get back to town?" he asked, and Doc agreed.

The door behind Winn opened. He could hear Betts's voice but knew there were two people who entered. Peter, he guessed. Betts hung back near Winn but Peter crossed the room quickly.

Betts tapped Winn's arm and they left the bunkhouse as the doctor began to tell Peter how to care for Louie.

Chapter Fourteen

It was almost dusk. Winn sat on the bench outside the
bunkhouse whittling. The small piece of pine that he
stroked so carefully with his knife would be a toy for
Greg. He had decided to try something simple, a ball
on a string with a cup to catch it in. He was working
on the handle; it couldn't get more simple than that.
Louie had found the wood for him.

Louie. Louie still hadn't stirred.

He sighed. His attention wasn't on the wood at all.
He couldn't help turning toward the house, listening
for sounds, wishing he could see what was going on.

The sheriff had talked with him. Winn told him
about the branding irons as well as everything he had
heard from both Ott and Louie. The sheriff had listened but hadn't seemed too eager to act. Winn had to
admit that a blind man wouldn't make the best witness.

A young woman named Mary had followed the
doctor out from town. She had heard that someone
else at the Franklin place had been shot and hurried
out, afraid it might be Jeremiah Betts. She stayed and

gave Peter further instructions for Louie's care, visited with Cynthie and cooked the evening meal. Winn sat outside and whittled.

Cynthie hadn't wanted to talk to him. Or listen to him. He had questioned the wisdom of bringing Jeremiah in from the herd but she had replied that the herd didn't matter now.

He touched the rough surface of the wood. It was getting smoother. It was too thick yet anyway. He tried to concentrate on the wood and forget everything else, but he couldn't.

Dempsey was in the house with Cynthie. He had come in the late afternoon and had been there for an hour, maybe more. Winn didn't think he was a good judge of time in a case like this.

He felt a presence at his side and heard Peter say, "Hi."

"Hi, yourself," he said, stilling the knife. "You're as quiet as an Indian."

Peter sat down beside him and asked, "Dempsey did it, didn't he?"

The question didn't surprise Winn as much as it might have. The boy wasn't known for small talk. "I can't prove it, son," he said, "but that's my guess."

Peter was quiet and Winn resumed his whittling. After several minutes, Peter said, "Saw Franklin pay Dempsey once. Dempsey said, 'If you make this too difficult, I may decide there are things I want more than your money.' "

Blackmail? Winn had never heard Peter put that many words together at one time. It made him all the more certain the boy was quoting exactly. "Did you tell anyone about it?"

"Didn't suppose nobody'd listen."

Winn thought Louie would have but he kept it to himself. Saying so would only hurt the boy.

Peter spoke again. "What you reckon he wanted more than Mr. Franklin's money?"

His ranch and his wife, was Winn's best guess. "Whatever it was, do you think Dempsey killed Franklin to get it?"

"Always wondered," Peter said.

Winn wasn't sure it was the time to ask, but he had to know. "Peter, how did your father die?"

Peter was silent for a long time. "Don't know," he said finally. "Wasn't home."

"But you have an idea," Winn prompted.

"Pa said Franklin wanted to run us off our land. Franklin always sent Dempsey."

Winn thought about it for a moment and shook his head. "None of this is proof, Peter."

"Not yet." Winn felt, more than heard, the boy leave.

Cynthie had been glad for Mary's help. She bustled around the kitchen fixing their supper and baking muffins ahead for the next morning. Cynthie had told her she would understand if Jeremiah wanted to quit. The job was getting dangerous.

"That'll have to be Jeremiah's decision. I know he's always been proud to work for you," Mary had said. "We would like a place of our own sometime, but I don't know when we'll manage that."

Mary had offered to go to the bunkhouse and prepare the meal for the men and check on Louie. Cynthie had accepted eagerly. Greg had gone along, giving her a few minutes of quiet.

A few minutes was all she got. At five o'clock, Kyle rode into the yard. She stepped out on the porch as he tied his horse in front of the house. "Where is everyone?" he asked, looking around the yard.

"They're all in the bunkhouse, I suppose. Jeremiah's friend, Mary, is fixing them their dinner."

"I wanted to be sure you're protected here, Cynthie. Somebody's declared war on you." He hung his hat on a hook by the door as he entered the front room.

"There's coffee," she offered. He followed her into the kitchen and watched her take two cups from the cupboard.

"What's this?" he asked, coming forward. He pushed open the doors she had started to close and lifted the gun from the top shelf.

"That's Winn's," she said. She took the cups to the table and when she turned was surprised to see Kyle still holding the pistol. "He asked me to put it out of Greg's reach."

Kyle nodded. "What's a blind man need with a gun anyway, except to kill himself."

Cynthie crossed the room quickly. "That's terrible!" she said, taking the gun out of his hand and putting it back on the shelf.

Kyle moved to a chair by the table. "I didn't mean it like that, I just mean it could be tempting, you know, to end it all."

"Have you eaten?" she asked, wanting to change the subject.

"I could eat a little something," he said. "You holding up all right?"

"I'll get by," she answered. Even though she had dismissed it earlier, she couldn't help but think of what Winn had said. "What do you know about what happened?" she asked.

"Not much," he said. "Just that somebody shot your foreman." He stretched his legs under the table and watched her move about the kitchen. She was beautiful and she was almost his, she and the ranch and everything Franklin owed him.

He was just pulling a cigar from his pocket when there was a knock on the door. Cynthie excused herself and went to answer it.

Dempsey got up quickly and went to the cupboard. He could hear Cynthie talking quietly, and another woman's voice. Glancing toward the door, he reached up and retrieved the gun. He had started to check the chambers when he heard Cynthie say goodbye to the other woman. He stuck the pistol in his belt at his spine where it was covered by his jacket. He grabbed the saucer he often used to catch the ashes from his cigar and was carrying it to the table when Cynthie came back into the room.

"That was Mary, saying she was going back to town."

"You sound tired, honey. This is all too much for you." He tried to take her in his arms but she avoided him.

"It can't be helped," she stopped.

"But it can be stopped," he said, taking his seat again.

Cynthie turned to look at him and a flicker of suspicion crossed her mind. "I marry you and it all ends?" she suggested.

Dempsey grinned. "Well, that might help but that's not what I was thinking. I think I should round up some men and confront Ott. Has he ever explained how he got the money together to pay off the loan?" Cynthie shook her head cautiously.

Dempsey made a quick guess at what Sutton might have told her and added, "Ott's been spreading lies about me in town trying to throw the blame on someone else. In fact, he probably set up Sutton and your foreman. I heard he was shot out toward my place."

Cynthie didn't know what to think. There was still some of Mary's chicken soup on the stove and as she dipped up a bowlful she considered what Winn had started to tell her. Could Kyle be lying to her?

Kyle thanked her as she set the bowl in front of him. "As soon as I'm done," he said, "I'll round up some neighbors and we'll go see Ott."

"But Kyle, is that wise?" she protested. "I mean, shouldn't you talk to the sheriff?"

"I'm just going to let him know we won't take any more of it." He patted her shoulder, certain that he had taken care of any misgivings she might have. When it was over, she would be able to say why he had gone and it would confirm his story. Ott, when he discovered his neighbors were aware of his activities, had opened fire and been killed.

He smiled at the picture. Everyone that could cause him trouble would be dead. He would even think of a way to get rid of Sutton. He felt the pressure of Sutton's pistol against his back and a plan took root.

Of course, no more of the Franklin cattle could be allowed to disappear, but that wouldn't matter. When Cynthie believed what he had been telling her all along, that Ott had been stealing her cattle, she would see that he, Kyle Dempsey, had saved her ranch. Then he would have it all. Yes. He would only have to wait a short time now.

Winn knew the minute Dempsey left. He put the knife and the toy handle in his pocket and walked to the house. He knocked on the door. He didn't know how he would do it, but he would make her listen.

Cynthie heard the knock and thought Kyle had forgotten something. She had started to say his name as she opened the door.

"Sorry, it's just me," he said.

The bitterness in his voice was impossible to miss. "Oh, Winn, don't say that." She took his arm and pulled him inside. She wanted to throw herself into his arms, she wanted his comfort almost desperately. His manner seemed more distant than ever and she bit her lip, waiting for him to tell her why he had come.

"I know you don't want to hear this," he said. "But I don't trust that man."

"I know."

"Will you hear me out?"

"Not now," she began. Winn braced himself for a battle but she spoke quickly. "I think we better do something. Kyle says he's taking a group of neighbors out to Ott's place. Winn, I just don't know who's right but I don't think this is the way.''

Winn was out the door before she finished talking. He hurried toward the bunkhouse with Cynthie running behind. He was taking longer steps and she was afraid he would run into the building.

"Peter, saddle some horses," he called as he walked. "Jeremiah, get a couple of rifles."

"I'm going, too," Cynthie announced.

Winn turned to her. "No, you're not!"

"Winn." But she said it to his back; he didn't wait to argue.

Peter came out of the bunkhouse with Greg behind him. Peter and Winn hurried toward the corral and Cynthie ran to Greg, taking his hand.

When she caught up with Winn, he was talking to Peter. "I'll need something reliable. Preferably something I don't have to sing to."

"Saddle Obsidian," Cynthie instructed.

"You're not going!" Winn said again.

Cynthie placed a hand on his arm. "You take him," she said.

A few minutes later she stood with Greg at her side, watching the three of them ride out of the yard. She had sent them after Kyle and now she worried that she had put them into danger, whatever the truth of the situation may be.

When the riders were becoming hard to see in the dust and the evening light, Cynthie turned toward the bunkhouse. "We better go sit with Louie," she told her son.

* * *

Winn didn't feel confident on the back of the stallion but he couldn't think about that now. He rode between Peter and Jeremiah and trusted them to help him if he needed it.

They had to get to Ott before Dempsey did. If he was truly rounding up neighbors, that should give them some time. Winn was afraid Dempsey would be meeting his rustler friends to ride with him instead. They might have been left waiting near Ott's.

"Be sure to watch for any other riders," he reminded his companions. Winn remembered that Ott had told him he was Cynthie's nearest neighbor. He hoped his place wasn't far.

It was Jeremiah who answered. "Don't be worryin', sir. I ain't lettin' nobody surprise us."

Ott's yard was quiet when they rode in. Winn could smell wood smoke and knew Ott was home. Before they had pulled up in front of the house, Ott was out to meet them. "Howdy, boys. It's good to see you sittin' a horse, Sutton."

Winn didn't answer. "Peter," he ordered. "Which way's the barn?"

"Left," was Peter's reply.

"Take a rifle and hide the horses in the barn then stay there. Jeremiah, find a position on our right where you're protected. We may need you both."

"What in the hell's goin' on?" Ott asked.

"Dempsey's on his way," Winn said. "Let's get inside."

Ott put his hand on Winn's shoulder and directed him into his house. "Is Louie dead, like I hear?" he asked. "Why's Dempsey comin' here?"

"Louie's hurt bad but he's still holding on." Inside, Winn stood with his hand on the latch of the closed door. "Stay near a window," he said. "I need to know as soon as they ride up."

"I'll do it," Ott said. "Can you answer my questions now?"

Winn explained the situation while they waited. It was an hour before Ott alerted him. "There's quite a bunch," he said.

"Do you know any of them?" Winn asked. Everything might ride on his answer.

"It's gettin' damn dark out there." After a moment he added, "Yeah, I know a few. There's about six here, though, I don't think I've seen around."

"Let's go make them welcome," Winn said, opening the door. He stepped out on the porch and Ott came to stand beside him. He could hear the horses moving toward the house, still a short distance away. "Greet them by name," Winn whispered.

When the horses came to a stop, Winn spoke first. "Evening, Dempsey."

Winn wondered if Dempsey was surprised to see him. It didn't show in his voice but Winn noticed he took his time before he spoke. "We're here to talk to Ott," he said.

"I'm listenin'" Ott said. "Evenin', Bob, Harold. You got somethin' to say, Eli?"

It was Dempsey who answered. "We know you shot Mrs. Franklin's foreman. You've been stealing her cattle right along, too."

"Ask Dempsey about Merlin's death, Bob, and Franklin's," Winn said. "You, Harold, ask Dempsey about the guns Franklin had him running to the Indians. And ask him about the circle *P* brand, Eli."

There was a murmur in the crowd and Dempsey shouted. "He's in it with Ott. He's making things up to try to cover Ott's crimes."

"Can you be sure Dempsey isn't the one trying to cover something up?" Winn asked.

There were some muffled comments Winn could make out in the general murmur of conversation. "... not as easy as I thought." "Never heard nothin' about guns." "... isn't for us to handle."

"Don't listen to him!" Dempsey yelled.

Ott leaned close to Winn and said quietly. "The neighbors are leaving. Dempsey and six others are left."

Dempsey watched the men ride away. He felt hot with fury. He considered giving the order. Ott and Sutton would be dead. Whoever else had come with Sutton, his men would find and kill.

But he'd never get away with it that way. He had counted on Ott to panic and the neighbors to be respectable witnesses. It wouldn't work now. Those cowards would say Ott had been alive when they left.

He wanted Sutton dead so badly he could taste it. One bullet. It would be so easy and Sutton would never see it coming. He'd have to wait for another time. He motioned his men to leave but he turned for

one last look at the two men on the porch and promised himself that he wouldn't wait long.

Winn added the scrape of the knife on wood to the
other night sounds. He was sitting on the bench outside the bunkhouse. He hoped he wasn't making
enough noise to wake the others.

There had been another dream, the worst one yet.
He had been in a wagon pulled by a runaway horse.
There was a body slumped at his side and it was Cynthie's. He had never had any trouble forgetting the
other dreams but this one played again and again in his
mind.

Somehow, he felt he could protect her if he stayed
awake. It was silly. There was nothing he could do. He
had to think of a way to catch Dempsey, and the only
good witness might never wake up.

He thought he heard a sound and held the knife still
for a moment. He didn't have to wait long to hear the
sound again. Though it came from several yards away
he was sure he knew what it was.

Cynthie stared at the moonlight that fell on the wall
of her room. She and Greg had stayed at the bunkhouse until Winn and the others had returned. By then
Greg had fallen asleep on Peter's bunk, and Peter had
suggested she leave him. He told her he planned to sit
up with Louie all night.

The house felt so empty with both Winn and Greg
gone. Finally she got up and walked to the window.
Outside the yard was bathed in moonlight. She could
make out a figure beside the bunkhouse and instantly

recognized Winn. He looked as if he were keeping guard.

She still found it hard to believe all the things he said about Kyle. It did make a certain amount of sense, but she had thought she knew Kyle so well. Winn had talked to her briefly after they returned from Ott's but she didn't have a clear idea of what had happened.

All evening, as she had sat beside Louie, she had prayed for him. Her ranch wasn't worth anyone's life. The old man had been such a good friend that she couldn't imagine the ranch without him. She knew she was missing Louie already and told herself that she shouldn't give up hope.

She watched Winn's hands working with something that was too far away to see. She should take him to Boston to the school. She and Greg could move there to be with him. She would miss the ranch but it wasn't worth the cost.

She saw Winn's head come up suddenly and his hands go still. She stiffened. Had he heard something? She looked out the window as far as she could in both directions. When she looked back at the bunkhouse, Winn was gone.

She stood a moment longer, looking for him. Something was going on. Perhaps he had heard Peter. Perhaps Louie had died! She turned quickly into her room and grabbed a robe. She ran down the stairs and stopped at her front door. Some sixth sense told her to be cautious. She stood a moment before quietly opening the door and stepping outside.

* * *

Winn had moved to the side of the bunkhouse away from the sound. He walked carefully along, one hand on the rough siding of the building. He was on the east side, the door was on the west. The sound he had heard came from the north, away from the rest of the yard.

When he reached the corner, he froze, listening for the sound again. There it was, a faint jingling. He placed it near the northwest corner of the bunkhouse. There might be a moon tonight and he couldn't risk being seen. He waited until the intruder moved to the far side of the building. When he was sure, he rounded the corner and moved after him, as quickly as he could without making noise. As he went, he tried to think of what he could use as a weapon. The little pocketknife was all he carried. He searched his memory for an ax or hoe left beside the bunkhouse, but knew there was nothing.

Kyle Dempsey moved stealthily toward the door of the bunkhouse. His horse was hidden in the trees by the creek. He had been careful to keep the building between himself and Cynthie's house. Those in the bunkhouse would be easy to handle. It was probably only the Merlin boy and the blind man. And, of course, old Louie. If he was lucky, the nigger would be out watching the herd. If not, he would kill him, too.

They would each die from a bullet from Sutton's gun. Everyone would think the blind man had snapped, killed the others, then killed himself.

Poor Cynthie would find them. She would have to handle it alone. She would have to go for the sheriff herself. But he would be along later to comfort her. There wouldn't be much left of her independence then. There wouldn't be much of anything left for her but Kyle Dempsey.

He smiled to himself and slowly opened the door a crack. Moonlight through a window revealed three occupied beds and one figure slumped in a chair. They were all together. His biggest threat, he knew, was the nigger. He'd take him first, then the half-grown boy. Sutton would go next. He would have to hurry once he started because Cynthie would hear the shots and she wasn't the type to cower in her room. He'd have to get it done and get away.

He eased the door open a little farther. As he moved to cross the threshold, he felt the point of a gun in his back. How could this be?

"I wouldn't move at all, if I were you." It was that damn blind man's voice! He looked again at the beds. One was occupied by Cynthie's little boy!

Sutton wasn't a threat. This could still work. "How will you know if I do?" he sneered.

"I'll know," Winn said confidently. "And at this range, I can't miss." He nudged him in the back again, pushing him inside.

Winn heard a sigh and a muffled curse and knew they had awakened the others. He had to get Peter or Jeremiah armed before Dempsey realized it wasn't a gun in his back. Sooner or later, he'd notice that the wood wasn't cold enough to be the steel barrel of a gun.

"Peter. Jeremiah. Better light a light." He smelled the sulfur flare almost immediately.

He heard running steps behind him and knew it was Cynthie. He tried not to think of the danger she might put herself in. He poked Dempsey again. "One of you better take his gun."

"Peter'll get 'em," he heard Jeremiah say. "I got my rifle on the son of a bitch."

Dempsey had watched his plans fall apart as the others awakened and Jeremiah grabbed a rifle. He glared at that rifle as he let Peter take the two pistols. Once he had decided there was no way to regain the upper hand, he started thinking of a story. It had to be something that Cynthie would believe. They were framing him, had gone to his house and brought him here. Anger was making it hard for him to think clearly but he knew he would think of something.

Sutton had backed off a step and Dempsey turned toward him. "How did you . . ." He stopped when he saw what the man was holding. A silly little wooden stick!

"I guess I won't be needing this anymore," Winn said and shoved it into his pocket as if he were holstering a gun.

"Why, you—" Dempsey started.

"Stop." It was Peter's voice. He had tossed one pistol on a nearby bunk but still held the other.

"Better tie his hands, Peter," Winn said.

"Did you kill my pa?"

Winn wasn't sure what Peter was doing but he knew he had made no move to tie Dempsey. He also knew Peter was the one who had taken Dempsey's gun and might decide to take matters into his own hands. "Peter," he warned.

Dempsey watched the boy as he turned a pistol slowly, studying it, and wanted to laugh. Merlin's brat wouldn't have the nerve to shoot him, no matter what he knew. His only worry here was Jeremiah. If he could get the little fool between himself and that rifle there might still be a chance. "It's kinda late now to be trying to prove it," he sneered.

Dempsey edged away from Winn as he spoke. Peter didn't move but continued to look over the pistol as if he had never seen one before.

"Maybe," Peter said.

"Peter." It was Cynthie's voice.

Dempsey turned to see her step inside and place a hand on Sutton's arm. He couldn't believe his bad luck. Until she arrived there had still been a chance of carrying out his original plan. He spoke quickly to Cynthie, "They've brought me here to kill me!"

"Forget it, Dempsey," Winn said.

Jeremiah spoke up, clearly nervous about the situation. "Get his hands tied, Peter."

Cynthie had just started to relax and now she felt all her fear return. She watched Peter as he handled the gun, oblivious to anyone but Dempsey. She wanted to step forward, to try to bring him out of his trance, but she would be between Betts and Kyle if she did. The boy slowly leveled the pistol at Dempsey. "Peter," she warned again.

"Did you kill my pa?" Peter's voice was soft.

Kyle went cold with fear. "The boy's gone crazy."

Peter sighted down the barrel of the gun. "W. M.," he said almost casually.

Kyle was afraid to move. He spread his arms out at his sides. "Cynthie, you've got to stop him."

"You ever notice those initials when you cleaned this gun?" Peter asked, slowly lowering the gun to his side.

Cynthie sighed with relief when Peter tossed the gun onto a bunk and turned to get a length of rope. Betts stepped forward to remind Dempsey that he and the rifle were still there.

"Initials, Peter?" Winn asked.

Peter nodded toward the pistol on the bunk. "Pa's," he said.

Dempsey was quiet as Peter tied his hands together.

Winn asked, "Jeremiah, can you deliver our friend, here, to the sheriff?"

"Yes, sir!" he answered.

"Where's your horse?" Peter asked Dempsey as he took his arm and directed him toward the door.

Dempsey stared at him in stony silence.

"We'll find it in the morning," Jeremiah said.

Peter left the bunkhouse to saddle two horses. Dempsey cast Winn a loathing glare as Jeremiah urged him to follow.

Chapter Fifteen

The bunkhouse seemed quiet. Cynthie watched Winn and knew he listened carefully to every sound she made, watching her in his own way.

"What made you come out here?" Winn asked her. "We weren't making enough noise for you to hear us at the house."

"I was watching you," she said a little hesitantly. She wanted to scold Winn for putting himself in such danger. At the same time, she wanted to slip into his arms and stay there until her knees quit shaking and her racing heart returned to its normal pace. With a rueful smile, she realized that that wouldn't happen in Winn's arms.

She felt a need to move around, break the tension she was feeling. Winn might not have forgiven her for doubting his warning about Kyle. She wasn't sure at all that she was welcome in his arms.

She crossed the room to the bunk where her son slept. As she tucked the blanket more tightly around his shoulders, she wondered how he had slept through all the excitement.

It was Winn who broke the silence. "I think you'll find that Dempsey was the cattle thief. You should be able to ranch in peace now, I hope."

Cynthie watched him a moment. She loved him so much and wanted to tell him but she wasn't sure he would believe her. Not after the way she had yelled at him when Louie was shot. "I'm sorry I didn't listen to you," she whispered.

Winn shook his head. "You were right, though. I had no business asking Louie to take me to Dempsey's."

Cynthie accepted that as hope that he would forgive her, but how could she convince him that what she felt was love and not pity, as he suspected?

She took a step toward him. How could she express something she didn't understand? How could she make him believe something that still surprised her? Could she tell him she loved him for the way he played with Greg, for the way he treated everyone, in fact? Would he believe her if she told him she loved him for who he was and that had nothing to do with sight?

"Winn," she whispered, moving closer.

"Will you two do your makin' up somewheres else and let an old man sleep?"

Cynthie turned quickly to Louie's bedside. "Why, you old fake. How long have you been awake?"

"The first words I recollect was someone tellin' me not to move and I took his advice. When I figured out

what was happenin' I decided it wouldn't be wise to go
distractin' nobody."

Winn followed Cynthie's footsteps to his bunk.
"You were hurt pretty bad, there, friend," he said. "I
sure didn't mean for this to happen."

"You've had us worried sick," Cynthie added.

"Would'a been worried myself, if I'd known it,"
Louie said.

Cynthie sat down beside the bunk. "Can I get you
anything?"

"Yeah. A shot of whiskey would be nice, then you
can go away and let me sleep."

Peter stepped through the door, hearing the old
man's words. "Water," he corrected.

"Whiskey, son. You know where we keep it." He
turned to Cynthie and added, "Medicinal purposes,
you understand. If this ain't a medical emergency,
there ain't never gonna be one."

Winn could hear Peter in the little kitchen setting a
cup on the table by the stove. He felt Louie's gnarled
hand close around his wrist.

"Mrs. Franklin," he said, "I think you need to be
lookin' for someone a little younger to run this place
for you. I'll be laid up a while and I got to admit I was
slowin' up a mite even before this bullet caught me."
He dropped Winn's arm as Peter brought him the cup.

Cynthie stood and moved to Winn's side as the boy
raised Louie's head and helped him take a sip. Louie's
reaction was immediate.

"Doc said water," Peter said quietly.

"Well, I said whiskey, boy!"

Peter was unperturbed. "You'll wake Greg."

Louie grumbled. "The whole damn world's tellin' me what to do. I quit. That's it. I just flat quit."

Winn chuckled and Cynthie struggled to keep from doing the same. "I'll leave you in Peter's hands," she said. She didn't want to leave Winn, however. "Can I talk to you?" she asked, placing a hand on his arm.

He nodded and walked with her across the room and out the door.

Once she had Winn outside, Cynthie wasn't sure how to say what she wanted to tell him. She kept him walking toward the house, wishing he would forget that he lived in the bunkhouse now. At the bottom of the porch steps, Winn stopped, and she had the distinct impression that he had just walked her home.

Deciding suddenly that she wouldn't settle for that, she turned and slipped her arms around his waist. She had expected a gentle embrace but he pulled her fiercely into his arms. She sighed as the warmth of his embrace kindled her desire.

"I don't like living so far from you," he murmured into her hair. The dream that had awakened him earlier came back to him along with all the anxiety it had produced. "What if I hadn't been awake and you had been the one to come up behind Dempsey?"

Cynthie was fairly certain that Dempsey wouldn't have hurt her, at least not that way. She had begun to suspect that he had different plans for her. But she didn't want to argue with Winn. Pulling away slightly, she asked, "Do you think you've earned the right to love me yet?"

There was more temptation in the sweet angel voice than Winn could resist. He chuckled but he knew his voice shook with more than mirth. "Well now, ma'am, what do you think?"

Cynthie moved against him seductively. She lifted her face toward his, wishing he would kiss her. "I think," she whispered, "that it's late and we should be in bed."

There was no mistaking the invitation in her words. Winn loosened his embrace enough for them to walk up the steps onto the porch. At the door he turned her into his arms again for a kiss. "Invite me in for coffee?" he whispered.

"Coffee?" Cynthie's lips sought his again. She didn't want coffee and she didn't want to talk. They could talk in the morning.

Winn kissed her quickly on the lips twice before pulling away to open the door. "Why, thanks, ma'am. A cup of coffee would be nice."

Cynthie let him lead her into the house and close the door behind them. "I'm not making coffee in the middle of the night and you know that's not what I invited you in for."

Winn chuckled. "I know. Go light a lamp in the kitchen."

Winn's purpose finally dawned on Cynthie and she protested, "Winn, I don't care what..."

"I do. Go light a lamp."

Cynthie reluctantly moved out of Winn's arms. It felt cold and lonely just walking away from him, though the night was warm and he was only a few feet away.

She hurried into the kitchen and found her hands trembled as she tried to strike a match. Winn wouldn't know if she lit the fool lamp or not, she decided, tossing the match on the table and heading back to him.

He was waiting where she had left him. Almost as soon as she was through the kitchen door he spoke to her. "Go back and light the lamp, Cynthie. I don't want people talking about you."

"How did you know?"

"I would be able to smell the lamp if you had lit it," he said. When he heard her steps retreating again, he added, "Or at least I think I would."

She joined him in a moment. "In other words, it was a good guess?"

"Well, I had my suspicions. I've got to protect you in more ways than one."

Cynthie slid her arms around his waist and laid her head against his chest. "Don't carry your protection too far. I don't want to be protected from what I feel for you."

Winn clutched her against him again. "Sweet, sweet woman, I still can't believe you love me."

"I can prove it, Winn," she whispered.

He groaned, leading her into the bedroom and to the bed they had shared once before. He held her in his arms again, not wanting to let her go even long enough to remove the clothes that had become a barrier between them. "I kept telling myself I had no right to hold you," he murmured.

Cynthie laughed. "I'm glad you didn't listen." Her fingers made short work of the buttons on his shirt and in a few minutes they stood amid a pile of discarded clothes. Cynthie came back into his warm embrace and thrilled at the feel of his skin against hers. She took his bearded face in her hands and raised herself on her toes to bring their lips together. She had promised to prove she loved him and she intended to do just that.

Winn molded her body against his and stroked her silken hair. After a slow, deep kiss he scooped her into his arms and laid her on the bed, tumbling in after her when she refused to loosen her arms from around his neck. He chuckled softly and drew her against him, seeking her lips with his own.

Cynthie knew this was how it was meant to be. The joy she felt at the sight of Winn always turned to desire at his touch. And now, when they came together, passion erupted inside her, filling her body and her mind and finally, it seemed, her soul. In the end she knew she belonged to Winn forever and he to her. The knowledge was almost unbearably sweet.

Winn awoke from a peaceful sleep to hear the clock strike four times. He should get up and return to the bunkhouse, or at least the bench in front of it, before the other men began their day. But Cynthie's soft body snuggled against him and her silky hair lying across his chest made it hard to leave. He wanted to lie here forever.

He was conscious of how much she meant to him, more than his sight, evidently, or he wouldn't be thinking of himself as the luckiest man in the world. He had been lost and almost desperate the last time Cynthie had come to this room with him. Now he felt as if, after years of wandering, he had found his home.

This generous, loving woman deserved to be happy. He may have had his doubts earlier but now he was prepared to avow that he was the man she needed.

When the clock chimed again, he knew he had procrastinated long enough. He tried to slip his arm from beneath her but she stirred. "Go back to sleep," he whispered.

Cynthie frowned when a cool sheet replaced the warm body. She came fully awake when she felt Winn leave the bed. "Where are you going?" She rubbed her eyes as she sat up. "It's still dark."

"I have to go back," he said softly. He found the pile of clothes and began separating his from Cynthie's.

"Wait, I want to talk to you." Cynthie threw off the sheet and joined him. She slipped on her gown and robe quickly and stopped him as he started to put on his shirt.

"Cynthie," he pleaded, knowing how easy it would be to crawl back into the bed with her.

Cynthie giggled. "I should let you wear it and give us away." She took it from his hand and added, "It's inside out."

Winn laughed. "The seams, of course. I was trying to hurry."

"Maybe you were distracted," Cynthie suggested, running her fingers down his chest before placing the shirt in his outstretched hand.

"You know I was distracted. Now let me get out of here."

"Winn, I do need to talk to you," Cynthie pleaded, trying to think fast. "About what Louie said." She saw him hesitate and plunged on. "Can we sit on the swing and talk?"

Winn grinned. "Not with you dressed like that."

"They saw me dressed like this last night," she teased. "What's the difference?"

"I wasn't sitting beside you with a silly grin on my face."

Cynthie giggled. "All right, I'll get dressed. Wait for me on the porch?"

As Cynthie hurried away, Winn sighed. Peter or Jeremiah would come out of the bunkhouse early in the morning and find the two of them sitting together on the porch and she was going to pretend they had been there all night. Or that she had just that minute joined him. She didn't seem to appreciate his efforts to protect her reputation.

He was sitting on the porch swing, listening to the shells clatter in the wind, when Cynthie joined him, breathless from a run down the stairs. He wrapped an arm around her and she settled against him, reminding him of the way she had slept in his arms.

He cleared his throat. "You wanted to talk to me about Louie?"

Cynthie was momentarily startled before she remembered her excuse. "Yes. Louie. I think I know of someone who can run the ranch, at least until he's better."

Winn nodded. "I hope so." He put the swing in motion and felt Cynthie curl her legs up under herself and snuggle closer. He wondered if she was having any more luck concentrating on their conversation than he was.

"I'm not sure what Louie will want to do when he heals, but it is true that he's been giving both Jeremiah and Peter more responsibilities lately and he might want to cut back some more."

"Jeremiah could take charge," Winn suggested.

"I've thought of that, but he and Mary want to get married and I think he'd like to have his own place. I know Mary would."

Cynthie was quiet for a moment then continued. "No, I have someone else in mind. He's a good manager, great with figures. He hasn't been around here very long, but I think I know him well enough to trust him."

Winn felt a touch of jealousy that Cynthie would know of someone he hadn't met yet, someone she was planning to bring onto her ranch. "Does he know anything about cattle?" Winn hoped it sounded like professional interest.

"He's had quite a bit of experience, I understand." After a moment she added thoughtfully, "I'm not sure his judgment's quite so good where horses are concerned, but I have Peter for that."

Winn was still skeptical. To hear her talk, she'd found a miracle. He warned, "What about the men? Jeremiah and the others do what Louie says out of respect—"

She interrupted enthusiastically, "He's a born leader. I've seen him, Winn. He takes charge and people want to follow."

Winn didn't like to hear her sound so eager. It took a moment to get the nerve to ask, "Who is this man?"

"You."

Winn was speechless. He stopped the swing abruptly and Cynthie strained to see his face in the early, pale light.

"Cynthie." He shook his head. He couldn't think of what to say to reason with her.

She laughed, planting a kiss on his cheek. "Now don't tell me you've had a better offer."

"Cynthie," he repeated.

She laughed again and snuggled against him. In a moment he put the swing back in motion. When he spoke, he sounded serious. "I guess we better discuss my terms, then."

"Terms?"

"Well, I don't take a job unless I know what's expected of me. You need to know where I stand on certain things, too."

"But, Winn, I meant—"

He didn't let her finish. "My word goes unless you can convince me I'm wrong. You won't hire or fire anyone without discussing it with me."

"Winn . . ." She tried to interrupt.

"I want it understood, right now, that I'll run this ranch a little different. I don't want to hear all the time that Victor did this or Louie—"

Suddenly his lips were covered with hers. She gave up the kiss when he started laughing. "Will you shut up!" She sounded so exasperated, he almost felt sorry for her.

He tried to look innocent. "Ma'am, I'm sorry, but I thought you were trying to hire me."

"That wasn't exactly... Oh, never mind!" She was embarrassed to admit it but she had been asking him to marry her. She straightened and started out of the swing.

His arms tightened around her and held her there. They could hear the muffled sound of the clock inside as it chimed five times.

"It's nearly sunrise," he said, tugging her arm a little to try to coax her back to him. "I was almost done with my terms. There's only one more."

She turned toward him but kept a little distance, not ready to give in yet. "One last term and then I'll have to think about it. I'm not sure you're what I'm looking for, after all."

Her tone wasn't very convincing but Winn didn't smile. "My last term, and this one's the most important. You'll have to marry me."

Cynthie turned to face him. In a second she threw her arms around his neck, causing the swing to rock crazily. He pulled her to him and kissed her. "I love you, sweet woman," he whispered. "Would you wait here with me and tell me about the sunrise?"

"Yes, my love," she said through happy tears. In a moment, with her head on his chest and his arm around her shoulder, she was curled up in the swing beside him to wait for the sunrise.

* * * * *

Harlequin® Historical

WESTERN SKIES

This September, celebrate the coming of fall with four exciting Westerns from Harlequin Historicals!

BLESSING by Debbi Bedford—A rollicking tale set in the madcap mining town of Tin Cup, Colorado.

WINTER FIRE by Pat Tracy—The steamy story of a marshal determined to reclaim his father's land.

FLY AWAY HOME by Mary McBride—A half-Apache rancher rescues an Eastern woman fleeing from her past.

WAIT FOR THE SUNRISE by Cassandra Austin—Blinded by an accident, a cowboy learns the meaning of courage—and love.

Four terrific romances full of the excitement and promise of America's last frontier.

Look for them, wherever Harlequin Historicals are sold.

Harlequin® Historical

From *New York Times* bestselling author

Elizabeth Lowell

Reckless Love

The powerful story of two people as brave and free as
the elusive wild mustang which both had sworn to
capture.

A Harlequin Historicals Release
December 1993

HHRLOVE

Harlequin® Historical

HARLEQUIN HISTORICALS
ARE GETTING BIGGER!

This fall, Harlequin Historicals will bring you bigger books. Along with our traditional high-quality historicals, we will be including selected reissues of favorite titles, as well as longer originals.

Reissues from popular authors like Elizabeth Lowell, Veronica Sattler and Marianne Willman.

Originals like ACROSS TIME—an historical time-travel by Nina Beaumont, UNICORN BRIDE—a medieval tale by Claire Delacroix, and SUSPICION—a title by Judith McWilliams set during Regency times.

Leave it to Harlequin Historicals to deliver enduring love stories, larger-than-life characters, and history as you've never before experienced it.

And now, leave it to Harlequin Historicals, to deliver even more!

Look for *The Bargain* by Veronica Sattler in October, *Pieces of Sky* by Marianne Willman in November, and *Reckless Love* by Elizabeth Lowell in December.

HHEXP

Coming in October!

From

Harlequin® Historical

It was a misunderstanding that could cost a young
woman her virtue, and a notorious rake his heart.

Award-winning author of JESSIE'S LADY and
SABELLE

Available wherever Harlequin books are sold.

Harlequin® Historical

Nora O'Shea had fled to Arizona seeking freedom,
but could she ever find love as a mail-order bride?

MARIANNE WILLMAN

From the author of THE CYGNET and ROSE RED,
ROSE WHITE comes a haunting love story full of
passion and power, set against the backdrop of the
new frontier.

Coming in November 1993 from Harlequin

Don't miss it! Wherever Harlequin books are sold.

Calloway Corners

In September, Harlequin is proud to bring readers four involving, romantic stories about the Calloway sisters, set in Calloway Corners, Louisiana. Written by four of Harlequin's most popular and award-winning authors, you'll be enchanted by these sisters and the men they love!

MARIAH by Sandra Canfield
JO by Tracy Hughes
TESS by Katherine Burton
EDEN by Penny Richards

As an added bonus, you can enter a sweepstakes contest to win a trip to Calloway Corners, and meet all four authors. Watch for details in all Calloway Corners books in September.

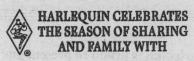

**HARLEQUIN CELEBRATES
THE SEASON OF SHARING
AND FAMILY WITH**

Friends, Families, Lovers

Harlequin introduces the latest member in its family of
seasonal collections. Following in the footsteps of the popular
My Valentine, Just Married and *Harlequin Historical Christmas
Stories*, we are proud to present FRIENDS, FAMILIES,
LOVERS. A collection of three new contemporary romance
stories about America at its best, about welcoming others into
the circle of love.... Stories to warm your heart...

By three leading romance authors:

> **KATHLEEN EAGLE
> SANDRA KITT
> RUTH JEAN DALE**

> Available in October, wherever
> Harlequin books are sold.

Harlequin is proud to present our best authors and their best books. Always the best for your reading pleasure!

Throughout 1993, Harlequin will bring you exciting books by some of the top names in contemporary romance!

In August,
look for
Heat Wave by BARBARA DELINSKY

A heat wave hangs over the city....

Caroline Cooper is hot. And after dealing with crises all day, she is frustrated. But throwing open her windows to catch the night breeze does little to solve her problems. Directly across the courtyard she catches sight of a man who inspires steamy and unsettling thoughts....

Driven onto his fire escape by the sweltering heat, lawyer Brendan Carr is weaving fantasies, too—around gorgeous Caroline. Fantasies that build as the days and nights go by.

Will Caroline and Brendan dare cross the dangerous line between fantasy and reality?

Find out in HEAT WAVE by Barbara Delinsky... wherever Harlequin books are sold.

BOB4